Boysie Blake solves problems. Yours. be rich or poor, famous or not, it doesn't matter. What does, is that you're straight with him. The last thing you want is to become the problem he has to solve.

~

Michael Santoro, Boysie's stepdad, was found floating face down in Sycamore Cove. Drowned while surfing, apparently. His long time friend, Detective Lawton, Santa Monica PD, tries to help, but he's got his own problems.

Marjorie Wallace, art dealer to Hollywood's powerful elite, has brokered a deal between two of its most formidable and dangerous players, for a previously unknown and never before seen Jackson Pollock. Problem is, the painting's a 3D printed fake, and now she's on the hook for a $150 million.

Boysie knows there will be blood. He has to make sure it's not his, or Marjorie's.

The buyer, her ex-husband, David Gandolfo, is connected to the Vatican and the US government; now he wants her dead.

The seller, Jack Valentine, more violent gangster than B movie producer, wants Boysie dead.

Valentine has a minder, Bruno, monster of a man. Gandolfo has a minder, Cardinale Christoforo, monster of a man. Violence can wield a gun or a chalice. The Hollywood rumor mill has it that in 2002, Gandolfo had tried to buy Dan Brown's manuscript, The Da Vinci Code. Boysie's stepdad had backed the wrong horse by loaning the agent that was brokering the deal, one million dollars so that he could buy the manuscript for himself. Brown smelled a rat and withdrew it. Gandolfo never forgave Michael or the agent. Now both are dead.

At 63, Marjorie is beautiful, very much alive and Boysie is unable to resist. However, she's twice his age and after their one night together, the guilt of it weighs on her, especially as she is also his mum's best friend. She breaks it off with him, much to his disappointment.

Boysie is summoned to meet Cardinale Christoforo in the one place he shouldn't – the Vatican. He returns to L.A. understanding that there is no justice, only the perception of it and if you can't find it one way, then find it another, because that's all you have.

Amanda,

Thanks for reading Boysie & hope you enjoy it!

Love & Peace.

May 30 15

BOYSIE BLAKE
PROBLEM SOLVER

MAX MYERS

U.S. INDIE BOOKS

Boysie Blake ~ Problem Solver
© 2014, Max Myers
www.usindiebooks.com
Library Of Congress Control Number: 2014941718

ABOUT MAX MYERS

Ex boxer, bouncer and former Vice President of a Brooklyn MC, Max is the embodiment of the American Dream; he completely turned his life around, and is now a multiple award winning writer & director.

Born in Iserlohn, West Germany, he is the son of an English Army soldier and a local German woman. He spent the first years of his life traveling with his family to a variety of postings including London, Germany, South Australia and Gibraltar.

At age 12, he landed on the mean streets of East London, where he joined a rock-n-roll-band, learned to play drums and a respectable blues harp, and did some serious amateur boxing. He left home and school when he was 15, eventually moving into tour management and sound mixing, working and playing for many famous European acts: Mungo Jerry, Manfred Mann, Wings, Berlin Rock Ensemble and Moonraker. Inevitably, he was drawn to the American shores, landing in Baltimore, MD, where he continued to work and play for now-forgotten bands, Face Dancer and Objects, amongst others.

In the early 90s, Max relocated to New York and started a music production company, but soon the collapse of Wall Street left him homeless and penniless. He drew upon his early days as an amateur boxer and informed by his experiences in the violent neighborhoods of East London, took on a succession of jobs as doorman and bouncer at some of New York's edgier nightclubs. It was in this era that he continued his street education, joining a biker gang and experiencing firsthand the lawlessness and corruption of society's underbelly.

By 1994, he recognized there was no future for him on the streets, so he took a job waiting tables and began his writing career. His first big break came in 1997 when he landed a development deal with Martin Scorsese's Cappa Productions, under the sage and gentle guidance of Barbara De Fina. Succumbing to the lure of Hollywood, Max moved west where he continues to write, direct and teach.

ACKNOWLEDGEMENTS

For Maria who supported me and lovingly kicked my arse.

To Philip Plough, whom I met in the bathroom of Writers and Artists in the Spring of 2003. He kindly washed his hands before shaking mine.

My friend and gifted artist, Swarez, who generously painted the Pollock inspired cover art. www.swarez.co.uk

Doctor Adrian Grimes, who edited Boysie over and over and over again; thanks, mate. Besides saving lives, he's also an amazing rocker.

Michelle Flevotomas, who read and reread Boysie, and set me back on the path more than once.

And my friend Katharine Ross, who always encouraged me to pursue my dreams.

My heartfelt thanks to my friends who appear as themselves in my novel, listed in order of appearance.

Matt Sugarman, Gianni Capaldi, Amanda Fitz, Philip Plough, Jim Amos, Sam Sokolow, Shannon Makhanian, Swarez, J.D. Fortune, Eddie Perez and Levi Kreis.

CHAPTERS

1 ~ BLOOD

VIOLENCE CRACKLED IN THE SMOKE filled pub, igniting the atmosphere as it danced gleefully from person to person. The Butcher's Arms, nicotine yellow over everything, stank as cheap and menacing as a whore's offering.

Teddy Blake, legendary amongst London's gangster elite, sipped his glass of Bushmills, eyeballing his firm dotted around the room. Shifting looks exchanged in anticipation of the bloody carnage that everyone knew was going to take place.

Boysie, although only twelve, was as familiar with the vibe of premeditated violence as he was with the sweet-sour smell of a pub. He'd heard talk around the manor that his dad and Charlie Thompson, the boss of another firm, were now at odds. He loved his dad more than anything and although he had never shown fear, there was something different about tonight. Boysie knew his dad wouldn't let him stay, but he thought he'd try it on anyway.

"Can I have another cider, please, Dad?"

Teddy smiled lovingly at his son and handed him twenty quid. "It's almost time, and I don't want you here for this one."

Worry suddenly edged his young face. "But--"

"--Take a cab home and I'll see you in the mornin'. Alright, boy?"

He locked eyes with his dad and wanted to say more, but knew it was a waste of time. He nodded and left.

The pub door closed behind Boysie and he stood on the sidewalk, immune to the bitter London cold. He scanned the street; yellow smudges from occasional streetlamps tried to push back the dark. Here, Victorian warehouses, angry in their desolation, stood like decaying monoliths, specters from a bygone age. A lot of England was like that back in the early nineties; an era that had refused to go quietly into the night. But change is inevitable and corporate gangsters were fast moving in. For now, this was neutral ground for both firms and few, including the Ol' Bill, braved the waterfront or this pub, particularly at night. Two sets of headlights turned onto the deserted street. Boysie watched the Rolls Royce Silver Spurs pull up; black, shiny and new. Seven hard bastards cautiously got out, scanning the area. These were not your hoodie brigade, garden variety of thug. These were the real deal. Dressed to the nines. Bulges under their coats. They blocked the sidewalk as their boss emerged from the second Roller; Charlie Thompson, a nasty piece of work. His impeccable Savile Row, all midnight blue and grey chalk stripes, framed by the fawn cashmere overcoat that was draped across his heavy shoulders. Old Spice drifted on the night air.

Charlie looked at Boysie. His aging creased forehead gaining another red, grooved furrow, "Aren't you Teddy Blake's boy?"

"Yeah," he smirked, locking eyes with him.

"Do you who I am?"

"You're a Charlie Ronce, aren't you?"

"Oy, ya little sod!" snapped one of Charlie's thugs, taking a menacing step toward him.

Charlie Thompson waved him away. "Is that what your dad said, I'm a ponce?"

"Ask him yourself."

Charlie nodded, contemplating him. "You've got balls, son. I'll say that for you."

Boysie held his stare.

Charlie moved toward the red pub door. One of his soldiers opened it; inside, everything came to an abrupt halt. They entered and the door banged shut.

Boysie sprinted down the alley to the back of the pub and tried to peer in, but the condensation was too thick on the unwashed window. Didn't matter because a moment later the back door burst open, pouring out angry, cursing soldiers from both firms, hostile in their intent. Hiding behind a stack of old tea chests marked with the familiar East India Tea Company logo, he caught his breath as tempers flared. Teddy jabbed a hard finger into Charlie's chest, accusing him of a double cross on some bank job or other. The latter just smirked, not resisting, not denying, not afraid. That confused Boysie. Everyone around the manor was scared of his dad. Confusion became clarity when Charlie's soldiers melted into the darkness and Teddy's own pulled out their shooters, aiming at his back; double cross. Fear slows time and with snickering complicity, trapped Boysie's voice for a moment that would always seem like an eternity.

Some of Teddy Blake's men were frozen with stupid, fixed grins. Most with faces set hard. The only thing that penetrated the back alley stink of betrayal, was the taunting chuckle of his mortal enemy, Charlie Thompson.

"Dad, behind you!"

Teddy Blake spun around and locked eyes with Boysie. In that one fateful moment, that final embrace, they both understood it was over. He knew his dad would go out fighting and, quicker than anyone expected, Teddy pulled out a gun, managing to squeeze one off into Charlie's fat torso. A second muzzle flash seared the darkness and for a split second, Teddy Blake wavered at the entrance to eternity. He turned and looked into the smirking eyes of his trusted lieutenant, Chalky White. His five white knuckles gripped the .45 as a thin wisp of smoke drifted carelessly out of the barrel. The smell of it taunted Boysie's senses and reminded him of Guy Fawkes Night; betrayal on no grander a scale. Chalky fired again. So did Teddy's men. Boysie could only watch helplessly as his dad danced the Spandau ballet; pumped full of death. Gunshots echoing off into history. The acrid choke of cordite mixed with the metallic smell of blood, as unmistakable as the stench from a slaughterhouse. Teddy Blake lay in his own piss and blood as his traitorous soldiers, except for one, ran away.

"Dad! Dad!" Boysie collapsed in a miserable heap onto his father's body.

Chalky White knew there was no coming back from this, so he took aim.

Charlie Thompson opened his suit coat, revealing the bulletproof jacket and shook his head. "Leave it."

"But he's seen us. He knows who I am," hissed Chalky White.

Boysie, his father's blood all over him, screamed at him in despair, "You bastard!"

Chalky smirked and moved the gun as if to shoot him. BANG! Surprise bulged his eyes. Blood seeped out of the hole just above his heart. His knees buckled and he sank to the cold, hard, concrete. It was his dying time but instead of fear, he felt a compulsion to laugh. The blood that was forcing its way up his throat killed that, too.

"I don't top kids. No matter who they are," growled Charlie, slipping the gun back into his shoulder holster.

Chalky White shivered a coupled of times, his eyes glazed over and death claimed its prize.

Boysie looked up at Charlie Thompson, his massive frame in silhouette. For the second time that night, they locked eyes. "I'm gonna kill you!" he spat venomously.

"Whenever you're ready, Boysie, come see me."

2 ~ A BEAUTIFUL DAY

BOYSIE DROPPED DOWN FROM 4TH TO 3rd and hit the gas. Celeste, his 1972 E-Type Jag, took the curve on Mulholland Drive, like a shark effortlessly doubling back on its helpless prey. He smiled as the bright California sun reflected off the new British Racing Green paint. His crew of expert restorers had just completed the frame off restoration of the 2+2 convertible coupe and the powerful V-12 hummed contentedly.

"Time for a pint," he said, stroking her new, supple, tan, leather interior. She continued to purr as he guided her down off Coldwater Canyon, making a quick right onto Beverly Glenn. At Sunset Boulevard, the light smiled green and he made the right, driving past the warm pink of the Beverly Hills Hotel.

Boysie left the twists and turns of Sunset, drifted down onto the Pacific Coast Highway and cruised the last few miles to Ocean Avenue, turning into the parking lot opposite the Royal Arms.

After the murder of his dad, he had started to follow in his criminal footsteps. For the next three years he went on a spree of stealing, fighting and general mayhem, leaving school when he was fifteen. It was then that his mum, a devout Catholic, and a long time family friend, Father Murphy, intervened. The priest convinced him to start boxing and learn a trade. He did the first but declined the latter and within 3 years, ended up an Amateur Boxing Association champion.

He and Father Murphy had grown very close, so when the priest was given the parish of Santa Monica, Boysie, then eighteen, decided to also relocate to Los Angeles for a fresh start. His dad had left a fortune, with the lion's share of it going to him. The rest was split between his mum and older brother, Harry. With some of the money, Boysie purchased the pub, an exact replica of a London Tudor. Now, fifteen years later, it brings in a very healthy profit. The interior is exactly as one might find in the UK; dark brown wood, hardwood floors, pictures of the Royal family, British beer, dartboard and a pool table.

The Sex Pistols, "Anarchy In The UK," rocked the jukebox as Boysie made his way to the bar, nodding at the regulars greeting him. His mum, Toni, her face now clearly showing signs of her sixty years, along with Summer and Autumn, twenty-two year old identical twins, were serving pints to the punters.

They said in unison, "Hi, Boysie."

"Ladies. Mum."

Toni placed the ice-cold pint of Newcastle Brown Ale on the dark wooden bar. He took a sip; the bitter, nutty flavor washing across his tongue.

"The new Jag running alright?" she asked, her New York accent strong as ever.

"Celeste and yes, she's running like a charm."

"You look tired."

"Bit knackered. Had another bad dream."

She nodded slowly, but offered no words of comfort. Harry, as usual, was propping up the bar, sipping on a glass of white wine.

Boysie's iPhone buzzed. "Yeah?"

"Are you coming in?" asked Jose, his foreman.

"Hadn't planned on it. Why?"

"That dude didn't pick up his car."

"Did you call him?"

"Sí. Left him three messages."

"No worries. I'll give him a bell later."

"Okay, Boss." Boysie hung up and took another sip.

Crystal Sorensen, Harry's sometime girlfriend, put down her pint and opened the middle buttons on her dress, exposing her belly-button ring on which dangled a little, golden heart. She turned to Boysie. "Look, I've got a new, cute, little heart."

"It'll make up for the one you don't have," he replied.

Those in earshot giggled.

"I guess you read my article, then?"

"Yeah, right before I flushed it."

"That's not nice."

"I don't think he agrees with you," grinned Boysie.

"Who, him?" frowned Crystal, indicating Harry.

"No, him."

He pointed to the front door through which a red faced, snarling and very pissed off Father Murphy was entering.

Crystal choked out, "Oh no."

Father Murphy roared, "Crystal!"

She ignored him and entered the relative sanctuary of the Loo.

"That woman should be burned at the stake."

"She's allowed to voice her opinion," offered Boysie.

"Not when it jeopardizes the Innocents."

"No one's innocent."

"Ah, away wi'cha," replied the priest and focused on the waiting pint of Guinness.

As was his habit, he stared at it for a long time. No one ever asked him why. Didn't seem important. Boysie smiled as he waited for the familiar, gravely, Irish lilt to sing forth. Nothing. Not even a murmur. Only the continual sound of the priest breathing out of his bulbous nose that had as much hair growing on it, as out of it, evidenced by the upside-down forest that continually glistened in his nostrils. He blessed the pint, picked it up and drank it down in one, wiping the creamy white froth from his beard and smearing it on his frock coat. He turned his piercing blue, watery eyes on Boysie and said, "I need to have a word."

"Can it wait?"

Father Murphy looked at Toni. "Glass of ancestral mist, if ya please?"

She poured the priest two fingers of his favorite, Bushmills, sixteen year malt.

Boysie finished his pint. "What, exactly, beside the article, did Crys--"

"—Sshh. Ya cannot say her name in me presence."

"In any event, what else did she do?"

"Consorted with the enemy."

"She became a Protestant?"

"You're a blasphemous bastard, Boysie Blake."

Boysie headed across Ocean Avenue and onto the grassy area that runs along the top of the eroded cliffs. They, in turn, overlook the beach that's framed by the ubiquitous traffic on Pacific Coast Highway and the tumble of white caps, forever reaching out from the glisten of Pacific blue. On this particular October afternoon, the wind was cutting in from the sea, filled with the cold promise of an evening fog. He walked briskly along and ladies, dressed in their weekend best and fully armored with all their hooks, lures and snares, smiled at him. Always the polite East Ender, he smiled back but never removed his coal black Pradas, thus avoiding the much sought after eye contact. Boysie's dad had always been well dressed and he definitely followed in his footsteps. His love of hip, casual two-piece suits, hand-made Italian shoes, coupled with his chiseled good looks, fair hair and blue eyes made him a target for the lonely, and the not so.

Boysie crossed over the pedestrian walkway to the Georgian Hotel, a beautiful art deco building constructed in 1933, and was about to sprint up the steps, when he heard a faint 'meow' coming from the alleyway that ran down the side of the hotel. About half way

in, he found a tiny kitten hidden behind the dumpster, shivering and crying. He smiled and gently picked it up, cupping his hands around it to give it some warmth. From the other end of the alley, its mother, a large tabby that looked the worse for wear, anxiously appeared and bounded toward them. She was obviously the kitten's mum, one of several feral cats that Jimmy, the Concierge, had been regularly feeding with kitchen scraps.

She stopped several feet in front of him and meowed nervously, her eyes darting from him to her kitten and back again.

"Sorry," said Boysie and gently placed the kitten on the ground, taking several steps back. Cautiously, she edged a little closer. He added, "I'll leave you to it then."

Quickly, the cat gently gripped the kitten in her mouth and trotted off, casting a wary glance back at him.

"That's her momma," said Jimmy, the Concierge as he emerged from the side door, a cigarette in hand.

"How many cats are there?"

"Five or six."

"And how many kittens?"

"About the same."

"Before this gets outta hand and we become a pettin' zoo, I'd like you to call the vet and have them all checked out, and spayed and neutered."

"Okay."

"I also want them given shots and medication. The mum looked kind'a ragged out. Flea bitten."

"They wild, Boysie."

"Yeah, but as we feed 'em, or rather you do, we're sort'a obligated to look after 'em a bit better. Don't you think?"

Jimmy shrugged. "Sure."

Boysie handed him one of his credit cards. "Use this and please make sure it's done today."

"Okay," replied Jimmy and took the card.

Inside the hotel lobby, Boysie stepped into the elevator and pressed the access code for the Penthouse. The heavy brass doors closed silently and a moment later, he stepped out into his loft that took up the entire top floor. He had moved in after buying the hotel four years earlier at the height of the Great Recession. Polished hardwood floors framed Persian rugs on which sat antique furniture. Paintings in gilt frames, intermingled with Warhols and taking up almost an entire wall, one of his favorites from his friend and famed British artist, Swarez. On the wall above his iMac, a framed black and white movie poster of his personal hero, Michael Caine, in 'Get Carter.'

Boysie took a long, hot shower and settled down on his balcony that looked out to sea. A sip of Beaulieu bourbon mixed perfectly with the flavor of his Cuban cigar. He relaxed as Jussi Bjorling's, "Au fond du temple saint," quietly drifted out of the stereo. Boysie loved this time of day; the sun beginning its evening romance with the horizon, turning the sky glorious amber with smudges of red, tinting the gathering clouds pink. The tranquility was interrupted by the incessant vibrating of his iPhone, prompting him to look at the received text from Father Murphy, 'Pier.'

The priest was staring out to sea when Boysie joined him. For a long moment, neither spoke. Eventually, Father Murphy said quietly out the corner of his mouth, "Michael fell out with Bergman an' Martinez. He told me that Bergman threatened him."

Boysie looked at him. "And why am I only hearing of this now?"

"'Cause it only happened yesterday and when they find out he sold me that land for a dollar, it's going to get a little anxious."

"Who for?"

"Them, of course."

"I see. A dollar?" The priest shrugged and peered at him out of the corner of his eyes. "So what do you want from me?" asked Boysie.

"Nuttin'. I'm just telling ya what's going on, is all."

"Is he still their partner?"

"In principle, aye."

"I know I'm gonna regret this but I do have to ask, why would he sell you land for a buck that's worth at least seven million times more?"

A smile crept over Father Murphy's wrinkled face. "You'll have to ask him."

"And what do you plan to do with it?"

"I'm not sure. But I'll think'a something."

"Wouldn't have anything to do with a rehab unit, would it?" asked Boysie nonchalantly.

"Aye, it might."

"Now I'm beginning to see."

"What are they going to do, huh? The Homeless have a right to lay their heads on clean sheets as much as anyone."

Two women ambled past them, the breeze flowing their hair back off their faces, flushing their cheeks. Smiling, they glanced at Boysie.

"Ladies."

One of them opened her mouth to reply, but Father Murphy activated his first. "Pay attention."

"You can't put a shelter and rehab unit in between two five star hotels. It's not on."

The priest glared at Boysie. "And why the hell not?"

"Isn't it obvious?"

"Just because those people can afford to stay there, doesn't make 'em any better than a person that can't."

"I didn't say that. But those people, are the ones that help fund your food program."

"Ah! Blood money."

"All money has blood on it."

"That's 'cause those people are all guilty of doing something, somewhere."

Boysie shook his head in disbelief. "Does the word 'hypocrite' mean anything to you?"

"Exactly. You're right. That's exactly what they are. Fuckin' hypocrites."

A passing couple looked incredulously at the priest.

Boysie asked, "Do you want me to talk to Bergman?"

"No. I'm just making conversation 'cause I have nuttin' better to do."

"Humor. Not one of your strong points."

"Ah, away wi'cha. I'll see yous later at the pub."

"Can't wait."

Father Murphy strolled off, muttering to himself. The wind pushed his black frock coat and mop of tangled white hair out behind him, giving him the appearance of Dracula. Boysie watched as his friend crossed Ocean

Avenue, but the 1963 Chevy Impala low-rider and its occupants, three shaved head, tattooed, gang-bangers, caught his attention. He watched them as they watched Father Murphy. Suddenly the driver pulled a U-turn, gassing the Chevy past Boysie who pretended to be looking at the screaming gulls, surfing the wind. He punched the license plate into his iPhone and headed back to the Georgian. He walked in, slipped off his black, handmade, Michael Toschis and put the kettle on. While he waited for it to boil, he got on the Internet and using License Plate Search, entered the number. In a few seconds he had the Boyle Heights address and printed it out.

The piercing whistle called him to the kitchen. He poured the hot water over an Earl Grey tea bag; Twinings, of course, adding a splash of organic low-fat milk. While he waited for the tea to steep, he called Chris Bergman at his luxury hotel, the Bergman, situated just off Ocean Avenue.

"Mr. Bergman's office," offered his evidently very young secretary.

"What a stereotype Bergman is," he thought to himself. "May I please speak to Chris?"

"Who's calling?"

"Boysie."

"No, not where you're from. Who are you?"

"My name's Boysie and he knows who I am."

"I'm sorry, Mr. Boysie, I can't put you through unless you give me more information," came her chilly response.

"You're new, right?"

"Yes, but--"

"--What's your name?"

"Janis."

"Okay, Janis. You can either put me through, or force me to come down there. It's your choice."

She breathed hard as annoyance flushed through her. "Just a moment please."

Bergman barked down the line, "Boysie. How are you, buddy?"

"Michael sold the land to Father Murphy."

Silence. Louder and more telling than any conversation. Bergman finally sucked in some air. "When?"

"Doesn't really matter, does it?"

"How much?"

"Not for sale."

"Why the hell not?"

"Because it isn't," confirmed Boysie, again.

"Michael was having mental problems. We'll contest the sale."

"Chris, I understand that you're upset but--"

"--I want that land."

"We all want a lot of things. However, that particular piece of dirt is not--"

"--I knew this was gonna happen. I did. I knew he'd do something vengeful like this. You better tell that crazy priest to--"

"--What?" Bergman stopped the verbal diarrhea. Boysie added, "I have the address of your East L.A. friends."

"What're you talking about?"

"You're testing my patience. Don't."

"Listen--"

"--You and your partners need to stop, before you force my hand. Know what I mean?"

"I'll pass on your advice."

"You do that."

Boysie hung up.

Outside the world continued its madness. In the relative serenity of the Georgian, he was soothed by the aria. He sipped his tea and nibbled on a McVitie's chocolate biscuit.

Boysie steered Celeste off Third, her headlights illuminating Larchmont Boulevard. He loved this area. The Fichus tree lined main street with its head-in parking, reminded him of small town America. Cool boutiques, great little restaurants and Larchmont Village Wine & Cheese, a particular favorite. The entire neighborhood, known as Windsor Square, included

Hancock Park and had been designed for strolling in quiet safety. Nosing the E-Type into a parking spot, he grabbed the bottle of 2005 Nadeau Petite Syrah, activated the alarm and headed for the intimate Girasole.

Sophie Devaru was sitting on the little bench outside of the Italian restaurant. Her long, dark hair tumbled over her shoulders as she crossed her legs, right foot flicking in the way that some women do when displaying irritation. This action always reminded him of a cat giving off its unmistakable warning – "I'm pissed and you better tread lightly." He had met her at a party in the Hollywood Hills and although attracted to her, he was more intrigued by the haunting familiarity of her ice-blue eyes.

He smiled down at her, "'Allo darlin'." She glared her response. He felt the flush of annoyance tingle his skin, but kept himself in check, and sat next to her. "Are you alright?"

She gave him the kind of look that should have glaciated the blood in his veins. "Why did you bring me here?"

"What?"

"Here, to this place. Why?"

"I thought you'd like it."

"You mean you like it?"

"Yeah, I do but--"

"--How long have we been seeing each other?"

"Three weeks."

"And you're already bringing me to a dump like this?"

He gritted his teeth, eyes narrowing. "A dump like this?"

"Why not Ago, Cellar Door or Asia De Cuba or somewhere where there's life? Something happening. Going on. Christ, this area's boring."

"Is that where you'd like to go?"

"Is that supposed to be funny?"

He smiled and stood up. "Then might I suggest you take yourself to whichever one tickles your fancy."

"What?"

"Have a good night."

He walked into Girasole and took a table, deliberately sitting with his back to the window. Sophie sat there, too humiliated to move. To self-entitled to fully comprehend that he had just dumped her. She was, after all, a fast rising and well-known movie star. Normally he didn't date actresses. Most were too deeply shallow and playing second fiddle to their ego didn't fit well with him. She glared at his back and stomped off to her black BMW. Boysie ordered the insalata caprese and washed it down with a couple of glasses of wine, leaving the rest for the waiters.

It was late when he walked back down the deserted boulevard. A chilling breeze blew small pieces of trash in little whirly gigs across the sidewalk. Remnants of sautéed garlic drifted out of a closed Greek restaurant. Randomly, he thought about an old black and white photo he had once seen of Larchmont, depicting the Keystone Cops filming another of their crazy movies. He laughed to himself and didn't hear the soft purr of the cherry bomb mufflers until the 1963 Chevy was almost on him. Boysie darted around the corner and the Chevy roared to life; tires squealing in protest, headlights blasting away the dark. He ran into the alley drawing a parallel line to the boulevard, and slid behind a dumpster that was leaking putrid fluid. He slowed his breathing and waited. Three rats eyed him curiously and went about their business. Three more rumbled into the alley and didn't. High beams cutting the night for all to see. They slinked out, black gang tattoos, plaid shirts, Dickies and guns; a stereotypes wet dream.

The leader spat hostility. "Find that fool!"

The other two edged along the alley, while he waited by the idling Chevy.

Boysie didn't carry a gun, but he did a knife. In fact, two, and always clipped onto the inside of his pants. He reached down, took one out, opening it quietly and wrapped a battle-hardened fist around the handle, blade pointed down, cutting edge forward. Slipping off his shoes, he padded slowly up behind the leader who didn't hear him, but did feel the blade press against the side of his neck, just under his jaw.

"Easy," hissed Boysie with deadly intent and grabbed his gun away from him. The gang-banger froze. "Tell your Homies to put their guns down."

"Mira!" The other two, now halfway down the alley, turned and looked, squinting in the high beam glare. "This fool got me cold. Put your heaters down."

They glanced at the silhouette standing directly behind their boss and laid down their guns.

"Kick 'em away," Boysie growled. They didn't. He pressed the blade harder onto the gang-banger's neck, splitting skin, drawing blood.

"Do like this fool sez."

They kicked away their guns into the dark.

Boysie searched the leader's pockets and pulled out his wallet. He flipped it open and looked at the California driver's license, reading out loud, "Jose Coronel. 23709 Whittier Boulevard. East LA. There's a surprise."

"So what, cabrón?"

"So I'm only gonna ask you once. If you don't tell me, I'm gonna cut you to the bone. Nod if you understand."

He nodded.

"Who sent you?"

"No one, esse. We was gonna--"

Boysie drew the razor sharp edge across Jose's cheek. Skin split to bone. Blood burst out. Jose screamed. One of the other gang-bangers whipped out a blade lunging at Boysie who sidestepped and slammed his knee into his gut. The gang-banger doubled over, gasping for air, holding his stomach. The third was a much more experienced street fighter and dropped down, sweeping out one of Boysie's legs. He hit the black top hard and the gang-banger jumped on top of him, launching into an MMA style barrage. Boysie covered up, avoiding most of the blows and ended the fight by kneeing him up into his balls. Jose reached under the driver's seat, pulled out another gat and unleashed a hail of gunfire where he thought his target to be. Only he wasn't. He was right next to him. He screamed as Boysie snapped his arm like a dry twig and slammed his face onto the car. He let him go and turned, expecting the first two gang-bangers to be on him again, only they lay in pools of their own slowly spreading death; victims of friendly fire. In a matter of moments, LAPD would come roaring into the alley. Guns drawn. Fingers twitchy.

3 ~ MICHAEL

IT WAS FIVE AM WHEN Boysie was released from the Wilshire Division Precinct. Matt Sugarman, his attorney, knew the Captain, Mike Samuels. The cops kept the knives as evidence, telling him that the DA would want to interview his client after reviewing the facts.

Celeste ate the 10 Freeway ravenously, passing the occasional vehicle as if they were late for the banquet. Soft fingers of turquoise and light pink behind grey, wispy, night clouds, began to herald the dawn in that California way. His iPhone buzzed and he looked at the ID: Mum.

"'Allo--" is all he got out before she burst into tears.

"--Michael's dead!"

"What?"

"He drowned, surfing."

"When?"

"Yesterday."

"I'll be there as soon as I can."

"Please, hurry."

"Is Harry with you?"

"Yeah."

Boysie walked into the pub and his teary eyed mum burst into hysterical tears, throwing her arms around him.

"Oh, Boysie, it's terrible. How could this've happened?"

"Come on," he said gently, "sit down."

Toni sat meekly and blew her nose into a wad of tissue. "I don't understand." She blew her nose again.

"Did the police say how?"

"An accident."

"No specifics?"

"Only that he was surfing alone at Sycamore Cove and was found by some other surfers."

Harry said, "I called Father Murphy. He's on his way over."

Boysie looked at him. "How did you find out?"

"Charlie called from the station house. Do you want a cup of tea? I just made it."

"No, thanks." He turned to his mum, "Will you be okay if I leave for a while?" She nodded and tried to smile. "Alright. I'll call you later."

Boysie parked Celeste out front of the Santa Monica Precinct on Olympic. The Duty Sergeant rang Detective Charles Lawton. The cop lumbered his massive frame, with some effort, down the hallway. He wore his outlook on life in the way that some men wore a pair of dirty, beaten sneakers - begrudgingly. He had seen way too much and the burden of it had cut deep grooves across his forehead.

"Boysie," he growled in his base-baritone voice, offering his massive hand, clothes more Mickey Spillane than GQ.

"'Allo, Charlie."

They shook hands and went into the detective's office. "How's she doing?" he asked.

"Not good. What happened?"

"The Ventura Sheriff's Department has logged it an accidental drowning."

"You know the primary?"

"There isn't one. Not when the Medical Examiner's ruled it that way."

"We both know he was a very experienced surfer."

"Yeah, but he was seventy-one."

"So what? He was tough as nails."

"No one's tough as nails against the ocean. Maybe there was a bad undertow, or he slipped and hit his head. Who knows?" shrugged the detective.

"Injuries?"

"Yeah, but consistent with being battered by high surf."

"And that's as far as you're gonna take it?"

"Come on, Boysie, I know he was your dad--"

"--Stepdad."

"But it was a tragic accident. Nothing more."

"You don't know that for sure."

"No, but this is California and surfers die all the time. It happens."

Detective Lawton extracted the silver pen that he always kept in his jacket breast pocket and began tapping it on his fingers.

"You're probably right, but it's my mum and you know how she gets."

"Yeah, I do. But it doesn't change the fact that I don't have time, or jurisdiction to investigate a non-crime, as ruled by the Coroner." He stared evenly at the detective, causing him to shift uneasily in his chair. "It's not that I don't want to, Boysie, but there's too much legitimate crime to deal with. I don't have the man power."

"Isn't that an oxy-moron, legitimate crime?"

"I'm sorry, man, I really am, but it's just another tragic accident. Nothing more."

Boysie fell silent.

The detective cleared his throat. "I got a call from Captain Samuels, about last night."

"And?"

"You okay?"

"It's outta your jurisdiction. Don't concern yourself."

"How did you manage to pop two of 'em?"

"I didn't."

Lawton smirked his disbelief. "Right. Anyway, the survivor won't make bail."

"Must be 'cause it's legitimate crime."

The cop's smirk faded into uneasy silence.

"You coming over the pub later?" asked Boysie.

"Yeah. I wanna give her my condolences."

"She'll appreciate that." He stood up and shook the detectives hand, "Who found him?"

"A couple of kids."

"You have their info?"

"No and I've got no pull with the Ventura Sheriff's Department."

"No worries."

It was too early to see Bergman and fatigue was beginning to catch up with him. On his way back to the Georgian, he called Harry. "She okay?"

"I gave her an Ambien and she went to bed."

"Have you looked in on her?"

"She is my mum too, you know," he replied.

"Sorry."

Back in his sanctuary, Boysie showered, shaved, had a glass of water with Emergen-C and went to bed, falling straight to sleep.

4 ~ LIES, LIES, LIES, YEAAAH!

HARRY WAS EATING AN OVERSIZED English breakfast, heart attack on a plate, when Boysie walked in.

"She in the office?"

Harry mumbled something and nodded. Boysie opened the door and climbed the stairs to find his mum lying on the sofa; eyes, red and watery. She smiled weakly as he sat next to her.

"How're you doing?"

"Did you talk to Charles?" she asked anxiously.

"I did. It's been ruled accidental by the Coroner."

Anger flashed in her eyes and she shifted herself into a semi-sitting position, forcing him off the sofa. "An accident?" she hissed.

"Mum, look, in all probability it was. It sucks, I know but--"

"—Bullshit. It was no accident. What about Bergman?"

"Come on, he's a slimy bastard, for sure, but murderer?"

She stood up, went over to her desk and rummaged through some papers. She found what she was looking for and thrust it at him. "That is your card, right? Problem solver."

Boysie sighed. He hated it when she got like this. "Anything else, Mum?"

"Should I pay you to find my husbands killer?"

Bergman pulled into the underground garage of his hotel and parked the Mercedes. He got out, chirped the alarm and turned to find Boysie smiling at him. For a moment, Bergman considered screaming, but knew that it was a waste of time. Instead, he tried to smile, but his lips struggled against that, like a fly caught in a web. He wiped away the rapidly forming sweat from around his mouth and said, "Bit dramatic isn't it, buddy?"

Boysie put a Fisherman's Friend in his mouth, savoring the extra strong menthol. To Bergman, it seemed like an eternity while he waited for him to reply. When he did, it was icily calm, filled with East End menace. "I know this might be rhetorical, but I'll ask anyway. What 'appened, mate?"

Bergman stammered, "I'm sorry?"

"Chris, I've got the agroes so please, don't bullshit me."

"But I don't know what you're referring to."

Boysie griped the dissolving lozenge between his teeth. "Michael's murder."

"Murder?"

"You Mutt-an'-Jeff?"

"What?"

"Deaf."

"No, wait, what're you talking about? I spoke with him Friday."

"He was found yesterday," he replied bluntly. Bergman waited while he crunched the last of the Fisherman's and Boysie added, "What do you know about it?"

"Me? Nothing," protested Bergman innocently.

Boysie studied him for any sign of guilt, but all he saw was fear. He picked a piece of lint off Bergman's lapel, causing him to flinch. "Why're you so nervous?"

"Because you scare me."

"But that's silly. Unless you're guilty, of course." Bergman swallowed hard. "Are you, guilty?"

"Of what?"

"Don't play silly buggers with me."

"I've heard enough," he exclaimed and tried to walk past Boysie, who remained where he was, blocking his exit.

"Last night, your three Muppets from East L.A. tried to snuff me." Bergman, his face glistening with sweat, was beginning to shake. He drew a nervous hand across his mouth. Boysie continued, "I told you yesterday to back off."

"But--"

"--Don't." Bergman closed his quivering lips. "They'll think twice before they try that again. Correction, the one that survived will."

This last piece of news was all he could take. "I swear I had nothing to do with that."

Boysie smiled.

"Can I go, please?" asked Bergman.

He stared at him for a long, tense moment, then stepped to one side.

The singing kettle called Boysie. He turned it off and ground the Five Country, organic coffee beans he had purchased from Trader Joe's and dropped them into the stainless steel French press. One egg, over medium and an organic sourdough roll. He spread on the unsalted butter and on one half, added black currant jam that he had made a couple of weeks before. He plunged and poured the coffee and went out onto his balcony. He was about to eat when his iPhone buzzed.

"Yeah?"

"Are you coming over?" asked Harry.

"How is she?"

"You know mum, hard as nails but marshmallow on the inside."

"She's pulling pints, isn't she?"

"Yeah."

"Probably the best thing for her. Keep her mind off it."

"You playing soccer today?"

"It's called football."

"When in Rome."

"No, I better not. You?" Boysie replied and stared longingly at his fast congealing egg.

"I'm gonna look after mum."

"Alright. See you in a few."

Harry hesitated, gathered his strength and said, "If you need me to help, you know, look into what happened, I mean, I know I'm a fat fuck and useless at most things, but if you need me, let me know."

Boysie replied softly, "Harry, you're not useless and I appreciate the offer."

There was a sudden silence as Harry fought to choke back the rising emotion in his throat. He lost and abruptly hung up.

Boysie felt sorry for his brother. Many times he had managed to get him to stop drinking and train with him. But, he would always fall off the wagon and sink even deeper into self-loathing. He finished his breakfast, washed the dishes and headed for the pub.

Boysie walked in to find his mum serving beer to the capacity Sunday crowd.

"What're you doing?"

She glanced at him. "I'm fine."

"Why don't you go upstairs and rest?"

"No, but there is something you can do for me."

"Which is?"

"Go and see Marjorie."

"Why?"

She smirked nasty. "She has a problem that needs solving."

Boysie ignored that and replied, "Do I have to see her today?"

"It's not like you have anything better to do, is it?"

"I'll give her a bell."

"No need. She's expecting you."

"All worked out then, mum, yeah?"

She glared at him, slapped on a smile and turned to the punter waiting for a pint.

Twenty minutes later he pulled up to the entrance of Marjorie Wallace's multi-million dollar home. He smiled into the security camera and the next moment, the heavy wrought iron gate rattled open. Celeste reverently crunched the gravel on the palm-lined driveway, surrounded by manicured lawn, permanently locked in a heated argument with the ever-encroaching California foliage. The housekeeper, a pretty Mexican woman, Carla, opened the front door for him. She smiled broadly as he brushed his eyes across her lithe, toned, olive-skinned body, wrapped in the tan uniform. He could never figure out if Marjorie was enjoying a private joke, having her dress that way. Or, if she was simply unaware of the stereotype she was perpetuating.

"¿Cómo estás, Señor Boysie?"

"Bien, gracias. Y tú?"

"Toda bien. I'm so sorry to hear about your father."

"Stepfather, but appreciated, thank you."

Carla nodded and stepped to one side. "The señora is on the terrace."

"Thanks."

He made his way into the enormous living room, furnished with beautiful antiques and, as always, stared at the incredible artwork hanging proudly on the walls.

Marjorie called out from outside, "Boysie?"

Tearing himself away, he went through the open French doors. She was lying on a chaise longue at the other end of the lattice-covered terrace that was almost as big as Wembley Stadium. She smiled. Sixty-three. All woman. Well preserved in a natural way without the help of surgery and very proud of it. Her skin held the luminous elasticity of a woman half her age. She was draped in a vaguely transparent, hand printed, Japanese silk housecoat. He bent down and kissed her cheeks.

"'Allo, Marjorie."

"Thanks for coming," she drawled in her smooth, Savannah, accent. Sexuality oozing from her as freely as the martinis she loved to drink.

Had she not been his mum's best friend, he would most certainly liked to have dated her. *"Ah,"* he thought to himself, *"the love of an experienced woman."*

Marjorie smiled knowingly as she teased the edge of her martini glass with her tongue. Boysie realized he was staring and reluctantly, flicked his eyes away toward the view, hoping he hadn't been drooling.

"Martini?"

"No, thanks." He sat down opposite her.

"Are you okay, my dear?"

"Yeah, I'm fine. Why?"

"I'm sorry. I didn't mean to appear insensitive about Michael's death."

"No worries. It's all good."

"Your mother's very upset."

"Yeah. So what's going on?"

Marjorie finished her martini and rang the little brass bell on the table next to her. "Last week I brokered a deal for a Jackson Pollock."

"Expensive."

"Very and unfortunately the buyer is now claiming it's a fake."

A huge and apparently pissed-off crow, screamed overhead. Boysie watched as it sailed down toward the reservoir, over a thousand feet below. "Is that possible?"

"No, of course not."

"Then what are they basing it on?"

"The buyer brought in their own authenticator who declared it as such."

"And they did this post-sale?"

"Yes."

Boysie shuffled his feet for no particular reason and asked with a bemused smile, "Seems a little odd, doesn't it?"

"It does, yes, especially as they had fully accepted our verification."

"So then their claim's invalid."

"Normally I would agree, but this is a very powerful client."

"Okay, then for the sake of redundancy, I'll ask anyway; it is in the Pollock-Krasner catalogue, right?"

She finished her martini and tried to smile. It didn't work. "No."

"No?" The unease in his gut snickered and started gnawing at him. Reason tried a brave defense. It lost.

Marjorie said, "It's from a private collector."

"What about provenance?"

"It's never been out of the collection."

"But there has to be some type of proof. A magazine article? Photo with Pollock standing in front of the work? Something." She smiled thinly and took another sip. "At least tell me it's signed."

"Yes, of course it is."

"Who was the collector?"

"Valentine won't--"

"--Wait, Jack Valentine, the sleazy B-movie producer is the collector?"

"No, he's the seller."

"I'm afraid to ask; who's the original owner?"

"Valentine wouldn't disclose that."

"Who the authenticator?"

"Stanford Mills."

"Of Beverly Hills?" Boysie asked incredulously.

"He is one of the worlds leading authorities on Jackson Pollock."

"He's a Muppet."

"He is well regarded by art historians and dealers everywhere."

"The ones he's paid by, you mean."

Although she could hold her liquor as well as anyone, in fact better than most, she was clearly overflowing with it. This really troubled him because as long as he had known her, she had always maintained an air of cool composure. The enticing scent of jasmine drifted across on the warm afternoon air. He stood up and poured himself a Glenlivet from the mobile bar.

"Who else verified it?" he asked.

"No one."

"Oh dear, oh dear. Was it at least carbon dated?"

"Not accurate enough."

"That's convenient." He took a sip of the Glen. "How much?"

She smiled, which came off more as a grimace. "A hundred and fifty million dollars."

"Jesus Christ, Marjorie."

"And I have no desire to get crucified."

"Let me get this straight; you brokered a deal for an unknown, unproven, supposed Jackson Pollock original that the buyer, sorry, idiot, paid for without one iota, not one shred of evidence to support the claim of authenticity?"

"As I said, an expert authenticated it, that the buyer pre-approved, along with a scientific fractal analysis of his style."

"But that expert does not include the only one whose opinion counts, Pollock-Krasner."

"They are not the only ones," she stammered defensively.

"If you don't mind my saying so, Marjorie, this sounds like complete bollox."

"Is that your considered opinion?"

"You want my advice? This is the seller's problem. Have the buyer call Johnnie Law. They take a real dim view of fraud. Alleged or otherwise."

"No, absolutely not!"

"But Marj--"

"--I can't. I've built my reputation on discretion and guaranteeing any sale, without question."

"A hundred and fifty mill's a lotta weight to carry, darlin'."

"And so is losing everything I have if the accusation turns out to be true."

Carla drifted past him with a new martini and placed it on the table for Marjorie, who smiled graciously. He waited for her to leave.

"But you told me that's impossible."

"There are no absolutes. You know that."

"And more and more, this sounds like a set up. Who's the buyer?"

Marjorie took a sip and replied quietly, "David Gandolfo."

Boysie almost choked on his drink. "Are you mad? I mean have you totally taken leave of your senses?"

"Apparently."

"What I'm failing to grasp here, is why would you not call me before dealing with that snake, Valentine?"

"This is not the first deal I've ever done." Her ice-blues glared defensively. He let that go. Marjorie sipped her martini and gazing out over the reservoir, asked in an almost child-like voice, "Can you help me?"

"Of course."

Tears filled her eyes. "What's your usual fee?"

"This one's on the house."

"No, this is business. Please, what's your usual fee?"

"It varies."

"Mine was ten percent of the sale; fifteen million. I'll split it with you."

"Seven million, five hundred thousand. Are you sure?"

"Yes," she replied and handed him a glossy, full color catalogue raisonné.

He flipped it open to the center spread. Staring up at him was the painting. Primary colors of black, red and gold, dripped and swirled across a massive canvas. The gold, in fact, looked like two dragons locked in a lovers embrace.

"At least I'll know what it looks like." She was traumatized. Boysie knelt down next to her, held her hand and said quietly, "Marjorie, I promise you, I'll take care of this." She smiled and the tears tumbled down her cheeks. He added, "But I need you to do something for me."

"Name it," she replied, slightly slurring.

"Easy with the libation, darlin'. Please?" She nodded. He kissed her forehead and left, carrying the curious mixture of gin, Eau de Violet and sweat on his lips.

Alphonso Martinez was waiting in the lobby of the Georgian and caught Boysie's eye as he walked in. The older man wiped the sweat from his face with a white cotton hanky and stepped forward, trying his best to smile.

"Excuse me, Señor Blake?" Boysie looked at him. "May I converse with you, in private?"

"About?"

"Michael." Boysie nodded and motioned toward the bar. "It is a little crowded, no?"

"We can sit in one of the private booths."

A smiling waitress appeared. "Drinks?"

He looked at Martinez, who shook his head. "I'd like a glass of organic raw milk, please."

"Anything to eat with that, Boysie?"

"No, we're fine, thank you."

"Be right back."

He locked eyes with the scared man sitting opposite him. Martinez gathered himself. "I am Alphonso Martinez and--"

"--I know who you are."

This caught Martinez by surprise. He let out his breath and said, "I had nothing to do with Michael's death. It was an accident. I wasn't even there."

"And I suppose you have no idea who the three Homies are that tried to snuff me last night, either?"

"No Señor, I do not."

Boysie let that hang in the air like a blanket of fog.

"Please, you must believe me." Señor Martinez tried to swallow, but his mouth was too dry. "My partners, they can be very insistent."

"So can a five year old."

"They tried to get him to sell the land, but he would only laugh."

"And who might they be?"

"Bergman, but you know this."

"That would be partner, not partners and if I'm not mistaken, which I believe I'm not, you said partners, plural." The waitress returned with his glass of ice-cold milk. "Thank you." He took a sip and watched Martinez shift uneasily.

"I liked Michael, Señor."

"So did my mum."

He fell silent and rubbed his hands together in the way that older men do. "Please, offer her my condolences."

"Keep 'em."

"Please, Señor Blake--"

"--Agnes, my German granny, survived two World Wars. Hard as nails and wise as Solomon. She would always say, "The fish stinks from the head down." He took another sip of milk. "You, Bergman and whomever your partners are, are hiding something. I can smell it and I promise you that I'm going to find out what it is. So my advice to you, is run back to your cohorts and tell 'em that I don't take kindly to murder, especially when it's a family member or, someone trying to off me. Know what I mean?"

Martinez hastily slid out of the booth. "What do you intend to do?"

"I'm not sure yet, but when I am, you lot will be the first to know. I promise you." By now, Martinez was so scared, that his hands shook badly. Boysie felt sorry for him. "Look me in the eyes, Señor Martinez and tell me the truth. Did you have anything to do with Michael's death?"

"No."

"Do you know who killed him?"

"No. I swear on the soul of my grandson."

Boysie contemplated him and finally he said, "I believe you."

Martinez looked so relieved that Boysie thought he was in danger of the older man trying to kiss him. Instead, he asked, "May I also rely on your discretion? I do not need Bergman knowing I came to see you." He nodded his agreement. Clearly Alphonso wanted to say more, but changed his mind and left.

Boysie got out of the elevator and locked it off. Secure in his kingdom, he undressed, hung up his suit and lay down on the oversized brown sofa with a glass of Lagavulin 16 year. With night rapidly closing in, he turned on the TV. Unfortunately, even the fine Islay single malt couldn't quell the growing restlessness. Bergman, Martinez, Michael, Father Murphy and his mum kept rolling through his mind. A bad land deal, that resulted in the death of his stepfather. Although it had been ruled an accident, he knew that something wasn't quite kosher. Nothing for it but to make a cup of tea. He put the kettle on and, looking out of the French windows that led to the balcony, finished the single malt. The black Pacific, dotted with lights from passing ships, rolled endlessly under a canopy of stars. He sat on the balcony, nibbling on a McVitie's milk chocolate biscuit as the night air cooled his tea. He put it down, dialed the pub and his mum picked up.

"Yeah?"

"How're you doing?"

"I'm okay," she replied tersely.

"I'm gonna help Marjorie."

"I know."

"She's insisting on paying me."

"So?"

"It makes me feel weird."

His mum shrieked, "No, no, no. If you didn't help, she'd be bankrupt."

"Yeah, I s'ppose."

"Are you coming over?"

"No, I'm knackered. Long day."

"Did you see Bergman?"

"I did."

"And?"

"And I'm working on it."

She hung up.

He finished his tea, went back to the sofa and channel surfed, but it was no use. He turned off the idiot box and sitting at his iMac, searched out Jack Valentine's home address and programmed it into his iPhone. A call came in from his friend, the actor and producer, Gianni Capaldi.

"'Allo, G."

"You coming over the pub?"

"Can't, mate. Little busy."

"Is it true that you've got a beef with Valentine?" he asked. His Scottish brogue softened by living in L.A.

"Didn't you two produce a couple of films together a few years ago?"

"Is that what it says now on IMDB?"

"No idea."

"If it does, I'll have it taken down, which is what I should've had done to him."

"Good friend of yours then?"

"Aye, you could say that," he growled. "Is this about the Jackson Pollock?"

"More precisely, Marjorie Wallace."

"I heard."

"Then why the redundant question?"

"Can't believe everything you hear. Especially in this town," he replied, matter-of-factly.

"And who did you hear it from?"

"I was having a late lunch at the Ivy and Gandolfo stopped by to say, 'Hello.'"

"Interesting how six degrees has become one."

"Facebook and Twitter. No more secrets, mate."

Boysie nodded. "But why bubble in your ear?"

"I dunno. Maybe it's because I have history with Valentine and Gandolfo knows that you and I are friends."

"Smart. He tells you knowing that you'll tell me." Boysie ambled over to the balcony. "Anything else I should know about Valentine?"

"He has a minder, Bruno. Monster of a man. Samoan."

"Yeah?"

"Be careful. They both carry shooters."

"Is that right?"

"Want me to watch your back?"

"No, but appreciated."

"Alright. Laters."

Boysie massaged Celeste through the quiet streets of Beverly Hills and pulled up at Jack Valentine's hilltop home. Obviously, he had more money than taste, exemplified, in glorious detail, by the faux pillars holding up the massive porch overhang; a gaudy facsimile of a Southern Plantation Mansion. He pressed the buzzer and waited but no one answered. He pressed it again, this time a little longer and still no answer. He was about to back out of the driveway, when he sensed someone watching him from the shadows just beyond the gate. He turned off the motor and got out, looking directly toward whoever it was that was spying on him.

"Tell Jack that Boysie wants to see him."

The man stepped out of the darkness, glaring at him. Judging by his size, this had to be Bruno; six-three, three-hundred and thirty pounds, none of it fat, wrapped in a casual two-piece suit. His head was the size of a melon and his brown eyes looked angry. They would always look angry.

"You need an appointment," he replied in his thick, Samoan accent.

"Give him my card."

He handed Bruno a business card. He looked at it, smirked and dissolved back into shadow. Boysie slid back into Celeste and waited several more minutes. Finally, the gate slid open. He fired up the V12, drove in, parked and headed for the front door. Bruno pulled it open and blocking his way, raised a massive paw.

He barked, "Assume the position."

"And what's your favorite, exactly?"

"Just put your hands on the damn wall."

"I don't carry a shooter."

"We'll see."

Boysie shrugged and placed his hands on the wall. He hadn't yet replaced the two knives from his confrontation with the gang-bangers. The big man expertly searched him and finding nothing, grabbed his shoulder and yanked him around hard.

"Oy!" Boysie called out angrily as he tried to rub the feeling back into it.

"Thought you were a tough guy?" grinned Bruno.

"Only on Wednesdays."

Bruno glared at him. "Inside."

Cheesy, full-length B movie posters of films that Valentine had "produced," lined the walls. Above the slate fireplace, a large, guilt framed portrait of him stared down with meaningless authority. Bruno led Boysie to the back of the house and into the office. Jack Valentine was sitting behind his walnut desk, clipping the end off a cigar. Hanging on the wall behind him, was the real Jackson Pollock. Or maybe it was another fake. He couldn't tell. He flicked his eyes at it and then at Valentine; salt and pepper hair neatly coiffed away from his face. Jeans and a casual shirt opened three buttons down; two too many. Around his well-oiled neck, a gold medallion and lastly, too much spiced cologne. Valentine gave him the once over, slid open a desk drawer that Boysie suspected might contain a gun and pulled out a lighter. Slowly and very deliberately, he lit the cigar, blowing the smoke toward him.

Boysie waited patiently.

Valentine snapped the lighter shut, picked up his card and read it out loud, "Boysie Blake. Problem Solver." He smirked and handed the card to Bruno. "So what can I do for you, Mr. Problem Solver?"

"It's more like that which I can do for you, ol' son."

"Yeah? What's that?"

"Help you return the money."

Valentine chuckled, "I'm sorry?"

Boysie nodded toward the painting, "You seem to have the market cornered on never before seen Pollocks. It's amazing."

"Yeah, huh?"

"How many of those do you have?"

"Three."

Boysie couldn't hide his surprise. "You have three un-catalogued Jackson Pollock originals, authenticated by the Pollock-Krasner Foundation?"

"Who?"

Boysie grinned. "How did you come by them?"

"Why are you here?"

"I already told you."

Valentine puffed on his cigar, staring coldly at him. "Then I guess we're done here, Mr. Problem Solver."

"Or give Gandolfo the real Pollock." He pointed up at the one hanging on the wall. "Is that it, or another forgery?"

Valentine exchanged a smirk with Bruno. "Should I return the money?"

Bruno chuckled and replied, "No, Boss, but I'd love to know why this clown thinks you should."

Boysie locked eyes with Valentine. "I implore you, please, don't become the problem I have to solve."

"Is that a threat?"

"As the cobra said to the mongoose."

Bruno stepped forward. Valentine stopped him with a curt wave. "But he has the painting."

"Correction. He has the fake, or maybe it's a copy of a fake. I dunno and don't care, but it is going to get sorted. Know what I mean?"

"Go to the police."

"That's what I said," exclaimed Boysie enthusiastically.

"Give me one good reason why I should listen to anything else you have to say?"

"I could give you one hundred and fifty million of 'em. But I'll give you just one; Marjorie Wallace."

"Hey, this is business," he shrugged indifferently.

Beginning to tire of this, Boysie sighed his annoyance. He placed a Fisherman's Friend in his mouth. "Not when it comes to friends and family and defo not when I've been hired to do a job. Are you listening?"

"How much is she paying you?"

"None of your bees-wax."

"Huh?"

Bruno explained, "He means business."

"I don't get that," replied Valentine.

"Bees-wax means business," offered the big man again.

"Can't you speak English?"

Boysie looked at Bruno, shrugged, turned back to Valentine and offered, "In other words, what she's paying me, is none of your business; bees-wax."

"Then we're done here."

"I know. You produce films, right?" grinned Boysie.

"You gonna pitch me?"

"Yeah."

Valentine smirked and leaned back. The cigar clenched between his teeth.

Boysie continued, "A woman, two men and a multi-million dollar painting. One of them either ends up dead or goes to jail and she lives happily ever after. What do you think?"

"Get out!"

"I forgot the part about the arbitrator she brought in. I'd like to play that role."

"Bruno, show this asshole the sidewalk!"

The big man's eyes lit up at the prospect of doing something he obviously liked – hurting people. He took two steps forward, raising his massive paws. Boysie sidestepped as if he were taking a penalty and kicked Bruno's kneecap so hard, that it split away with a sickening crack! He screamed and collapsed to the floor, writhing in agony. Boysie and Valentine watched as the big man tried to hold back pain-propelled tears. He lost.

"I don't think ice is gonna help, mate."

Valentine lunged for the desk drawer and got his gun halfway out just as he was introduced to Boysie's fist. His head snapped back, eyes rolled up and he spat blood, dropping the gun. Boysie picked it up and slowly spun the chamber, emptying the bullets onto the rug, one at a time. Valentine watched; blood and ego leaking from his mouth.

"I hate guns almost as much as I hate shit-heads like you, Jack."

Bruno was squeezing his thigh in an attempt to numb out the pain. It didn't help.

"Now pay attention," continued Boysie, "I want you to give Gandolfo his money back. Don't and the five percent vig on the sale, that you now owe me, will increase one percent every day. I'll give you twenty-four hours to make good before it starts. Now be a smart villain, Valentine and take care of it. Don't make it that I have to come back. Know what I mean?"

Boysie handed him a bunch of tissues from the box on his desk. Valentine snatched them, wiped the blood away and nodded. Boysie smiled, placed the empty gun on the desk and before he left, using his iPhone, took a photo of the painting.

The hot shower cascaded over him, washing away the slimy encounter with Valentine. He dried off and pulled on a pair of black, soft cotton house pants. Making a cup of tea and toast with homemade jam, he sat on the sofa, chewing over the day's events. On the surface, there were two distinct problems; Bergman and Martinez on the one hand. Valentine and Gandolfo on the other. With he and Marjorie, right in the middle. Floating over the top of it all, the death of Michael and one hundred and fifty million dollars. Growing in the pit of his stomach, was this niggling feeling that, somehow, it was all connected. He called his mum.

"Yeah?" she spat into the phone.

"You alright?"

"The funeral is Tuesday at eleven."

"Where?"

"Hollywood Forever."

He frowned at the short answers. "Are you pissed at me about something?"

"I am a little surprised that you haven't been to see me."

"I've been busy. This Marjorie thing is much more complicated than I first thought."

"Gianni told me that you spoke to him about Valentine."

"So?"

"You should have just asked me. I know Jack. Met him at Marjorie's."

"And you were planning to tell me this when?"

"I didn't think it was important. Sorry."

"Anything else I should know before I hit meself in the head?"

"Stop being so melodramatic." She hung up.

He finished his tea, brushed his teeth, lit a stick of incense and went to bed.

Three a.m. Boysie opened his eyes and lay in the dark, his heart doing its best to pound its way out of his chest. Beads of hot prickly sweat clung the sheets to him as if he had been sleeping in the middle of a Floridian summer with 100% humidity and no AC. Frankincense, always mysterious, embalmed him in the thick, turgid and oppressive darkness. He had difficulty breathing. Once again he felt something watching him, hiding behind the slightly open closet door. He hated open doors and closed them all every night before he went to bed. So why was that one cracked open? Slowly, he sat up, wiped the film of confusion from his eyes and the soaking wetness from his face. He took a breath, swung his legs off the bed and was suddenly aware of a terrible thirst. His mouth, covered in the thick, pasty film of sleep and fear. A few faltering steps toward the living room and he passed the open closet, warily keeping an eye on it. He stepped into the vastness of his loft, making his way over to the refrigerator.

He tried to control the dread that was sliding up his throat like an unwanted acid reflux attack; no good. In his peripheral, he saw the bedroom closet door move. He didn't want to look in case something materialized that he never, ever, wanted to see again.

Grabbing a bottle of water from the fridge, the weak interior light tumbled out, only to be eaten by the dark. He watched the shadows watching him and tried desperately to act nonchalant, as if that would make them go away. Spinning the cap, he put the ice-cold bottle to his lips and was grateful as the water brought relief, to his mouth, at least. He closed the fridge, drew in a breath and held it, turning reluctantly toward the bedroom. Bam, the closet door banged shut with a vengeance. He wanted to scream, but all he could do was stand and stare as it once again popped open, slowly creaking ever wider and wider. From out of the dark, the hulking silhouette of Charlie Thompson moved toward him. Boysie took a step back as his eyelids fluttered like terrified butterflies. The last thing he felt was the cold, hard smack of grey slate as his body slammed onto the kitchen floor. Then merciful darkness.

5 ~ HOLLOW POINT

BOYSIE ENTERED THE PUB, TIRED and drawn. Summer and Autumn, serving pints to the punters, looked over at him.

"Pint, Boysie?" asked, Autumn.

"Coffee, please."

"Okay," she replied and busied herself making it.

Father Murphy blustered in and sat next to him, smelling more of whisky than frankincense. Sneaking a glance out of the corner of his eyes, he growled, "What?"

Boysie, in no mood for his shenanigans, ignored him.

"What can I get'cha, Father?" asked Summer.

"A large glass of ancestral mist, if ya please." He ran a dry-skinned hand across his tired, craggy face.

Summer poured him a healthy three fingers and slid the almost full glass of Bushmills across the oak bar. She glanced at Boysie to make sure it wasn't too much. He nodded, almost imperceptibly, but enough for her to understand. She smiled at the old priest but he was already lost in the mist. Replacing the empty glass, he was about to ask for another, when Boysie pointedly put a Guinness coaster on top of it. The priest's normally red face grew a darker shade of angry. It was, no doubt, fueled, in part at least, by the triple shot of Bushmills now flowing through his veins. Not to mention whatever he had consumed at the rectory. He turned to Boysie and his mouth curled into an ugly sneer.

"And what the hell is your problem?"

"It's not even noon and you're already slinging it down your neck like it's the Last Supper."

"Spare me your pious blasphemy. I'll drink what I want, when I want and with who I want!"

"Whom," replied Boysie, sipping his coffee.

"Ah, to hell wit'cha."

"Have something to eat."

"I had me porridge this morning."

"Oatmeal's not enough to sustain you. Have some Shepherd's Pie."

Boysie looked at Summer who nodded and ordered the food. He turned back to the priest.

"Now, why don't you tell me what's going on?"

Father Murphy pulled something small out of his worn, black suit jacket and stood it up on the bar; a shiny, nine millimeter, hollow point bullet. Boysie looked down at it, but refrained from picking it up. "This was in the collection plate from this morning's mass."

"Any ideas?" asked Boysie.

"None. Well, a few maybe, but none that live in Santa Monica."

Boysie placed its twin next to it, obscuring them from prying eyes with a cupped hand. "Somebody's defo sending us a message."

Father Murphy nodded. "Where was yours?"

"I found it on the front seat of my motor this morning."

"Did you check the security cams?"

"I did, but there's people walking past it all the time. Obviously it was just a casual drop in. No way to tell who it was."

"Shite."

Boysie put the bullets into his pocket. "I bet you a pound to a penny it's something to do with Michael's death."

"Work that out all by yaself, did ya?"

Boysie stood up and looked at Autumn. "If he's a good boy and eats all his lunch, give him a pint and another glass of mist. But that's all and put it on my tab."

"Okay," she smiled.

"Thank you," said the priest with his trademark lopsided grin.

"No worries, you sarcastic prick."

Boysie drove into the affluent neighborhood of Beverly Hills, busy with Monday morning locals and gawkers, parking in one of the numerous city-owned, free garages. He strode over to Rodeo Drive and entered the gleaming, glass fronted, Stanford Mills Gallery. Jackie, twenty something, ultra hip and too cool for herself, peered at him from behind her smoked glasses. She pushed her chair away from her desk and drifted over. Unfortunately, her perfume got there before she did.

"Hi," she hissed, giving him the instantaneous body scan.

Boysie continued to look at some of the artwork. She, however, wasn't used to being ignored. Her smile evaporated.

"How may I help you?" she asked icily.

"Is Stan in?"

"Stanford."

"Is he?"

"Do you have an appointment?"

"No."

"Then no, he's not," she smirked.

"You handle all the sales?"

"No. I'm just an added bonus."

"Really?" Her green eyes flashed hard. Face turned to stone. She spun away. He grinned and asked, "Was it something I said?"

Her eyes glistened, with cat like ferocity, at her unbelievable luck with being presented an opportunity to cut him down to size. "We cater to a very discerning and exclusive clientele. Perhaps the generic artwork in Woolworth is more suited to your taste and wallet."

"Perhaps, but in the meantime, go tell Stan it's about Gandolfo's Pollock." She froze on the spot and her cheeks flushed pink. He watched curiously as she tried to gather herself, carefully formulating a response. He handed her his card. "Go on."

Stanford Mills drifted out of his back office. Forty-five, hair gelled into an overly relaxed style. Beige, crumpled linen suit hanging from his sprayed-on-tan body. He gave Boysie the once over and held out his hand; all friendly smile wrapped in peppermint breath. "Mr. Blake?" Boysie nodded reassuringly that he was, and shook the offered hand. "How may I help you?" smarmed Stanford in his affected Beverly Hills voice.

"Marjorie told me that you authenticated the Jackson Pollock for David Gandolfo."

"You're here on Mr. Gandolfo's behalf?"

"I'm here on everyone's behalf."

"I'm sorry, but that's confidential."

"I'll give her a bell."

"Excuse me?"

Boysie took out his iPhone, pressed the speed dial to Marjorie and placed it on speaker. "Hello, Boysie."

"I'm here with Stan. Can you please authorize him to answer my questions?"

"Can you hear me, Stanford?"

His mouth puckered as if he'd been sucking on lemons. "Yes, Marjorie."

"Please accommodate Boysie with full disclosure."

"Certainly." Stanford pressed his lips into a tight smile.

Boysie asked, "I presume you're aware that Gandolfo is claiming the painting's fake?"

The art dealer nodded. "I received a call from his attorney." Stanford was beginning to look very nervous and swallowed, adding, "I've been in business for twenty seven years and never made a mistake, at least not of this magnitude. The Jackson Pollock that I authenticated was authentic. I'd stake my reputation on it."

"You already have."

Stanford's eyes welled up. Boysie felt sorry for him.

"I don't know what to do. I can lose everything, Mr. Boysie."

"Just, Boysie."

"I have a family. Three kids. Since it happened, the gallery's been a ghost town. If this doesn't get resolved, I'm finished. Then what? What do I do? How do I tell my wife? My kids? How do I support them?"

"I can't answer that, Stan, but I can sort this mess out." Embarrassed, Stanford nodded and wiped the tears away. Boysie asked, "Where did you do the examination?"

"At Jack Valentine's house."

"Alone?"

"No. He and his bodyguard was there."

"Were there."

"What?"

"Never mind," replied Boysie. "Was the bodyguards name, Bruno?"

"I don't know."

"Big guy. Six three. Samoan?"

"No, this guy was American."

The back of Boysie's neck was beginning to tingle. Stanford continued, "And he had three other guys with him."

"From the security company that were transporting the painting?" Stanford nodded and sat down, rubbing a weary hand across his head. Boysie looked over at Jackie, who was sitting behind her desk texting. "Jackie," he called out. She looked up. "Can you get us some bottled water, please?"

Her mouth expressed displeasure at being told what to do, especially by him. "Mr. Mills?" she asked.

"Please."

She stomped over to the office and Boysie waited until the door closed. "What was the name of the company?"

"I don't know. It was a black SUV and as soon as I was done, I watched as they loaded it in."

"You went with it?"

"Absolutely. Otherwise my authentication's invalid."

Jackie returned with two bottles of water and handed them one each.

"Thanks," said Boysie. She ignored him and went back to her desk. He spun the cap and took a sip. "You appraised a never before seen Jackson Pollock, at a hundred and fifty mill?"

"No, no way. That's not the value I placed on it. That was the seller, Jack Valentine."

"But you authenticated the painting so in essence, you agreed to its value."

"I was employed to give my expert opinion on its authenticity, which I did. Maybe Mr. Gandolfo got cold feet. You know, buyer's remorse? I don't know, but that painting is a Jackson Pollock original."

"So then you validated a fake."

"Just a minute!"

"I'm not accusing you, Stan."

"You're not?"

"No. A hundred and fifty million dollar art theft is very specialized and with all due respect, mate, it's not a suit I'd fit you out for."

"But I know what I saw. It was a real Pollock. I mean you just don't see one of those every day."

"Exactly."

Jackie was busily texting again, pretending not to listen to their conversation.

Stanford looked even more confused. "I don't understand."

"Neither do I, but I will. You have my number. If you think of anything, no matter how insignificant or unrelated, please give me a bell."

"Okay," he agreed, his fearful eyes threatening to leak again at any moment.

Heading for the parking structure, Boysie decided to have a quick double espresso at the Brighton Coffee Shop. He sat at an outside table and the friendly waitress delivered it with a smile. Twisting the lemon peel, across the street he noticed Jackie striding toward a waiting black SUV. He dropped the peel into his coffee and watched as she dropped into the passenger seat. He had an idea who might be driving. Quickly, he punched the camera icon on his iPhone and snapped a photo of the back of the SUV as it pulled into traffic, heading toward Wilshire Boulevard. Bringing up the pic, he expanded it, trying to see the license plate, but all he could make out was what appeared to be M and 9. He sipped his coffee and watched the arrogantly insecure, flutter and twitter around on Brighton Way.

6 ~ STUPID SOD

BOYSIE WALKED INTO THE PUB and sat at his private booth. Liz, green eyes and pretty smile, shimmied up to his booth. "Hi."

He looked up at and cracked his lopsided grin. "'Allo."

"You're Boysie, aren't you?"

"I am, yes."

"I just started, today. Sorry, Liz." She held out her hand.

He shook it and replied, "Welcome, Liz."

"What can I get'cha?"

"Vegetable curry and chips, please."

"Sure and a pint?"

"Please. Newkey."

"Newkey?"

"Newcastle Brown Ale."

She laughed. "You Brits and your terms. I'll get used to 'em, I guess." Bemused, he nodded slowly, ignoring the passing flash of irritation. "Anything else?" she smiled, eyes full of promise.

He considered her for a moment that was as long as her legs. "Nothing that comes to mind right now. Thank you anyway."

Liz pouted, not very much, but enough for him to notice. She wiggled off toward the bar; her curvy bum, wrapped in her black uniform, moved like the plump cheeks of a girl chewing bubblegum.

His iPhone rang, "'Allo?"

"Sorry to hear about Michael," offered Tommy.

"Thanks."

"How's your mum?"

"Resilient."

"I'm gonna drop by and see her later."

"And what's going on with you?"

"I got the bubble about this sixty-six E-Type that's for sale."

"How much?"

"Ninety-eight-five. But it's been restoed by the owner."

"Any good?"

"Yeah, as it 'appens."

"Will he come down?"

"She," corrected Tommy.

"Whatever."

"No."

Liz returned with his pint of Newkey. He smiled his thanks and said to Tommy, "Pass."

"You might wanna take a look. Beautiful lines. Very polished," he insinuated.

"Her or the motor?"

"Both and she's friends with Gandolfo."

"Is that right?" asked Boysie curiously.

"Yeah."

"Who in L.A. doesn't know what's going on, bedside me, that is?"

"Harry told me. Why?"

"And who did you tell?"

"Gianni, but he already knew."

Boysie took a sip of beer and looked at the curry and chips that Liz was placing down in front of him. "Where are you?"

"In the doorway."

Boysie looked to his left. Heading toward him, phone jammed in his ear, was Tommy Gonzalez. He was the best mechanic he had ever met. In fact, his work was as close to artistry as you could get. Grinning, he sat down.

"I heard you paid Valentine a visit," he said as they shook hands.

"I did," replied Boysie matter-of-factly and took a mouthful of hot food.

"Bruno had to have emergency surgery on his knee last night."

"That's a shame."

"You know Valentine's connected to the Chinks, right?" Tommy said without prejudice.

"Yeah, so?"

"Be careful. You may have muzzled his dog, but he still has some bite."

"What can I get you?" asked Liz.

Tommy looked up at her. "Pint a'diesel, please."

"I'm sorry," she replied, embarrassment overtaking confusion.

Tommy smiled at her reddening face. "Sorry. Guinness."

"Got that. Anything to eat?"

"Yeah, same as him, please."

"Okay," she replied and left.

Harry drifted over and watched the shapely waitress as she glided toward the bar.

Boysie washed the curry down with a mouthful of beer and looked at him. "You might wanna pick the gravel out of your tongue before you roll it back in."

"She is lovely," Harry replied wistfully.

Tommy asked him with a sly grin, "How's Crystal?"

"At the vets, getting de-clawed," he replied and disappeared into the kitchen.

Boysie grinned. "How's business?"

"Paying the bills," shrugged Tommy.

"Lot more than a lotta people are doing right now."

"Yeah, it's tough out there."

Boysie put down his pint. "Why don't you change your mind and run my shop for me?"

"Not that again."

"I'll pay you sixty-five large a year plus twenty-five percent of the profits."

"No."

"But--"

"--No."

"Bastard."

The head waitress, Amanda, 28, blond, pretty, placed Tommy's Guinness on the table. "Here you go."

"Thanks," he said and took a sip.

Boysie asked, "Who's training the new girl?"

"I was, but she just quit," replied Amanda.

"Why?"

"Something about not being able to grasp British terminology."

Tommy chimed in. "My American Misses never has a problem grasping my--"

"--Don't," warned Boysie.

Tommy clamped his mouth shut and focused on his beer.

"Thanks, Amanda."

Clearly uncomfortable, she looked at Boysie, "Sure," and went back into the bar.

"I know you were only having a giggle, Tommy, but she's a Christian, mate. You can't do that."

"So what? I wasn't trying to be offensive."

"I know but leave it out, please?"

"Sorry, I was only--"

"--Yeah, okay, mate."

Gianni came in and sat down, shaking hands with Tommy and Boysie. "Alright, lads?"

Tommy grinned. "Good. You?"

"Aye. No worries."

"I watched you on Netflix last night."

"Was it the porno?"

Tommy choked on his Guinness and grinned. "No, thankfully. Blood of Redemption. It was pretty good."

"Thanks."

"Didn't know you were such a good actor."

Boysie interjected, "He's also producing now. Coming up in the world."

Tommy nodded. "Nice. Always fancied meself a bit of an actor too, you know?" Gianni and Boysie stared at him in silence.

Tommy pretended to be hurt, then burst out laughing. "I'm just having a giggle."

"That's a relief," offered Gianni, looking genuinely so.

Boysie said, "G, when Gandolfo bubbled in your ear, exactly what did he say?"

"He told me about Valentine and the painting and sort of laughed."

"Laughed?" frowned Boysie.

"Aye. Not the, 'I find this funny,' laugh. More the, 'I was a stupid sod not to realize what was going on,' laugh."

"That's very odd."

"Why?"

"Marjorie never divulges client info. It's too dodgy. Causes too much conflict."

"So you're saying Gandolfo knew?" asked Tommy.

Boysie nodded, "Yeah, I dunno if he knew he was gonna get stitched up. But, it would seem that if he did know who the seller was, how could he not be suspicious and on top of that, how did he find out?"

Gianni shook his head. "You can't keep secrets in this town, everybody knows that and anyway, what does it matter?"

Boysie replied, "Because given their history, why would he not also have the painting appraised by his own independent expert; not just the ones supplied by Valentine, before agreeing to let the Escrow funds drop?"

"I dunno. He trusts Marjorie, I suppose."

"What exactly happened between them?"

Amanda delivered Tommy's curry and chips and looked at Gianni, "Pint?"

"Yeah, please." She left and he continued with, "Rumor has it that about fifteen years ago, Valentine and Gandolfo had been partners in a new start-up. Gandolfo already had some success and a slate of films in various stages of development. Some with A-list attached. Valentine uses that portfolio to go to this hedge fund and pulls in a hundred mill. The first twenty-five gets dropped into their business account. Only it's no longer in both their names. In fact, it's a new account and only he controls it. He then tells Gandolfo to 'pitch' him his projects, cheeky bastard. As you can imagine, the shit hit the fan and they've been mortal enemies ever since."

Boysie asked, "How come Valentine never got pinched?"

"No idea."

"So he gets the wedge and Gandolfo gets the shaft?"

Gianni nodded. "Aye. That about covers it."

"Knowing Gandolfo, I'm very surprised that he didn't have him buried. Know what I mean?"

Tommy said, "The dodgy goings on of Hollywood. If only people knew it's not all glitz and glam, hey?"

"Fame and fortune hides a lotta sins," concurred Gianni.

Tommy said to Boysie, "You sure you wanna pass on that motor?"

"Let me think about it." He stood up, motioning Amanda to come over.

"You off?" she smiled.

"Yeah and please put everything on my tab."

"Sure," she confirmed and went over to another table.

"Thanks," said Tommy.

"And leave her a nice tip and not a photo of your bell end."

Gianni laughed, "God Bless you too."

Tommy swallowed and called out to Boysie as he headed for the exit, "What time you wanna see her?"

"I'll let you know."

"Alright."

He got to the exit as Benny 'The Fixer' Blanco, a hard looking man in his forties, entered and stopped, blocking his way. "Orale, vato."

"Benny."

They shook hands. "Can I talk to you, holmes?"

"I'm in a bit of a hurry, mate. Is it important?"

"Sí."

He led Benny to the private dining room at the back of the pub and locked the door. He glanced cautiously around and frowned his question. Boysie reassured him, "I had it swept yesterday. No bugs. No one's listening. Better turn off your cell phone." They turned them off and Boysie laid them on a table at the other end of the room, well out of earshot.

Benny relaxed and pulled a small velvet pouch out of his pocket. "I got something really good for you, man." He opened it and spilled the contents onto the red cotton tablecloth; twenty-three diamonds.

Boysie made no move to touch them. "And what am I supposed to do with them?"

Benny looked puzzled. "Take a look, man. They fucking good. The real deal."

"Yes, very nice. And?"

"I got these and the same amount again."

"Go on."

"These ain't no manmade shits. They straight outta Amsterdam."

"And where'd you get 'em?"

"Come on, man, you know I can't tell you that."

"Are they bloody?"

"You mean like that DiCaprio movie?"

"No, I don't mean like that DiCaprio movie. I mean like was anyone topped for you to get your grubby little mitts on 'em?"

"No, man. A couple people got fucked up, but no one got smoked."

Boysie nodded and studied him intently. "Don't give me that, Benny."

Irritated, he started putting them back in the pouch. "You don't want 'em? Okay, no problemo. I go somewhere else."

"Relax yourself." He relaxed. Boysie continued, "What kind'a paper you looking for?"

"Sixty cents on the dollar."

"No thanks. Anything else?"

"I got about a hundred cases of booze. All top shelf."

"How much?"

"For you, esse, let me see--." Benny started doing his mental calculations. Boysie started tapping his irritation on the tablecloth. Benny, very familiar with this signal, stopped his mental gymnastics and smiled. "Forty cents on the dollar."

This meant that if a case of top shelf vodka, say, Grey Goose, normally sold for around twenty six dollars a bottle, retail, then Benny would pass it on to him for ten dollars, forty. Boysie's mirthless grin was a clear warning of his growing annoyance. Benny, who had done regular business with him over the years, knew this.

"Okay. For you, esse, thirty cents. Ninety-three sixty, a case."

"You're basing that on a single unit price of twenty-six dollars?"

"Sí."

"No. I'll give you twenty-five cents on the dollar."

"Come on, man, how can I make any monies? I still gotta pay the dudes I get it from."

Boysie leaned in and said in a quiet, menacing tone, "Don't give me your sob story, Benny. I know you all too well, mate and we both know that you get it straight off the docks at Long Beach."

"Me?" he exclaimed innocently.

"Your boy, Raoul, still a Longshoreman, right?"

"Sí," he replied, scratching the back of his head.

"Like I said, twenty-five cents and if you aggravate me anymore, you'll be giving me sixteen cents a bottle to take 'em off your hands."

"Okay, okay, man, relax. It's a deal."

Boysie sat back in his chair. "Marvelous."

"You still pissed at me for that thing, huh, holmes?"

"Yes, I'm still pissed at you for that thing."

"I'm still sorry, man."

"I know," said Boysie and softened his face. "Tell me about these stones and don't lie."

"Okay. They came to one of my people in Little Tijuana. You know, downtown?"

"I know where it is."

"Semone. Anyway, he got it from some dudes in Chinatown."

"He paid cash money for 'em? He nicked em? They begged him to take 'em? Or, he paid 'em in lead? Which is it?" Benny shrugged his answer. "Jesus, Benny, that's not business you want."

"It's okay, I fixed it. He gone back to Guatemala for a very long vacation."

"How long?"

He grinned. "Permanent."

Boysie knew exactly what that meant. "I'll pass."

"Come on, man. They untraceable."

"Really?"

"Sí. Look for yourself. They clean."

Benny handed him a jeweler's loupe. Boysie examined one and found that there was no laser ID cut into the stone. He replaced it on the table, checked several more and handed Benny back the loupe. "How much?"

"I already told you, man, sixty cent."

"No."

"Fifty?"

Boysie picked one up, rolled it between finger and thumb and replaced it with its cousins. "Sixteen."

"You crazy, man!" Benny hustled the diamonds back into the pouch. "What's with all the sixteens today, man? Is your lucky number?"

"You wanna pint?"

Benny dropped the pouch in front of him. "When can you give me the money?"

"Bring the other pouch around six."

"Here?"

"No. The Hollywood sign. I'll get TV coverage."

Benny stood up. "You one crazy gringo."

They shook hands and he left, grinning and muttering to himself.

7 ~ THE WIZARD'S LAIR

BOYSIE HIT THE GAS AND Celeste shivered down the Lincoln Boulevard on-ramp to the 10 Freeway, gliding into the number three cruising lane. He glanced in the rear view and saw the 1963 Chevy Impala low-rider cutting through traffic in an effort to keep the tail pinned on him. At this time of day, the traffic was fairly light. He down shifted and punched the gas. The V 12 screamed in delight as he shifted back up to fourth and within seconds, he was hurtling along at over a hundred and forty miles an hour. The Chevy had no chance and disappeared into the haze. He eased up and took the Overland exit, dropping him down onto Washington Boulevard. Pulling over, he dialed his long time friend, Philip Plough.

"Boysie," stated the polished and very educated voice.

"Mr. Plough. How are you?"

"I am well, old boy and you?"

"Getting by."

"And to what do I owe the pleasure?"

"David Gandolfo."

"And the case of the errant Jackson Pollock."

"You've been keeping your ear close to the ground."

"Stating the obvious are we, Boysie?"

"Marjorie's on the hook for the hundred and fifty mill. Not good."

"Be very careful of Gandolfo. Dangerous territory, even for a Boysie."

"So I've been hearing. What's the scoop?"

"He has his ten digits in as many pies and not all of them will come out clean."

"This I already know."

"Yes, but he has ties to organizations in several countries. You don't want to show up on their radar. Believe me."

"You doing business with him?"

"No. Way too muddy of a playing field."

An ambulance, lights flashing and siren blaring, screamed past Boysie. He waited for it to pass and said, "How's your new gig?"

"PharmaJet and 3D printing."

"Interesting technology."

"Yes and is going to alter society in dramatic ways."

"Philip, would it be possible, I mean I know this might be far fetched, but given how hard it'd be to forge a Pollock accurately, could you 3D print one?"

"Certainly."

"Really?"

"Scientists are printing body parts, from live tissue."

"Yeah, I saw that on 60 Minutes. Rapidly changing world."

"Take construction, for instance. That particular industry will undergo a radical upheaval as houses are 3D printed."

"Blimey. That's remarkable, but there's gonna be a lotta unemployed people."

"Destruction of the Middle Class."

"Yeah, no shit."

Philip coughed several times, cleared his throat and continued, "There's a Dutch company, FormArt, that's been perfecting a printer to do just that. Recently they replicated a Van Gough. It's quite something."

"You okay?"

"Oh yeah, that's nothing. Just allergies."

Boysie said, "But an art expert could spot the forgery, right?"

"Probably, but not necessarily. That's how good they are."

"So a layperson looking at it on a wall, couldn't?"

"They'd be hard pressed."

"Amazing."

"Indeed. Anyway, you remember Jim Amos?"

"Yeah, the guy who wrote The Memorial."

"Yeah."

"Great novel."

"We're thinking about launching organic, Memphis barbeque in Europe. The real deal and potentially very lucrative. You interested?"

"Southern barbeque in Europe? Hmm. Let's have dinner and bounce that around."

"You know, you should speak to Sam Sokolow. Gandolfo had asked him to partner on a reality show."

"Can you conference him in?"

"Yeah, hold on."

The ambulance that had earlier screamed past him, now screamed back the other way, escorted by a police cruiser, whose own lights and siren were angrily warning motorists to get out of the way.

"Boysie?"

"Yeah."

"I've got Sam with us."

"Hey, mate."

"Philip brought me up to speed on David," Sam said.

"Great, so?"

"So he had wanted me to do a show on the Vatican, when the molestation scandal started, but after my initial meeting with him, he suddenly went cold on the idea."

"Do you know why?"

"No. He never deemed to let me know, but I heard it was something about a problem that had arisen in Mexico."

Boysie said, "I know David, not well and even less about his business dealings."

"Keep it that way."

"Would that I could, mate."

"As you Brits like to say, he's a very dodgy geezer."

"Thanks, Sam."

"Sure."

"I watched your Mike Tyson documentary last week."

"Aw, man, that's years old."

"Yeah, but it's good. Love the title, Fallen Champ."

Philip interjected, "We're doing a new show together, United We Brand."

"What's that?" asked Boysie.

"Putting returning Vets back to work by giving them a shot at owning an American franchise."

"That's great. So needed, mate."

"Indeed," agreed Philip.

"Okay. Thanks for the info Sam, Philip."

"Sure," they replied in unison.

"Laters," he said and hung up.

Boysie nosed Celeste up to the gate of the studio lot and glanced over at the small, modest, brass plaque; The David Gandolfo Company. Two armed guards approached. The one holding a steel pole, at the end of which was a small mirror, slipped it under Celeste and began checking.

The other guard, his jaw tightly clenched, looked at Boysie and barked, "License." Irritation coursed through him as he slid it out of his wallet and offered it to the guard. He snatched it and staring at the picture, snapped, "State your business, Blake."

"There's a Mister in front of my name and you don't know me well enough not to use it, 'ol son."

The guard, now pissed off, motioned to the other. He sauntered over, took the ID and asked in his best tough guy voice, "Is there a problem, sir?"

"You should have a drive on for me."

The guard checked his list. "Yeah, it's here."

"Marvelous." Boysie held out his hand.

The guard, smirking stupidly, motioned as if to flick the license at him. "I asked if there's a problem?"

"Only if you make one," Boysie replied, hardening his eyes as he glared at him.

Clearly, the guard wanted to say more, but instead handed it back along with the security pass. He drove slowly through the gates and headed for visitor parking at the back of the lot.

Boysie walked into reception, and over to the very pretty twenty something sitting behind her desk. She watched his every move and smiled as something played across her soft, brown eyes.

He said, "I'm--"

"--Mr. Blake. Yes, I know. Mr. Gandolfo's expecting you." She stood up and he followed her toward a large, ornate, brass and mahogany door at the end of the hallway. Grabbing the handle, firmly, she smiled and held his gaze. "Can I get you something to drink?"

"Do you have espresso?"

"Sure."

"May I please have a double and if you would be so kind, pre-heat the cup."

"Certainly. Anything else?"

"A twist of lemon?"

"And a biscotti?"

"No, thanks."

"Consider it done, Mr. Blake," she said and tapped lightly on Gandolfo's door.

"Boysie."

She liked that. He could tell. She teased her lip and stood to one side.

"Come in," came the friendly voice. David Gandolfo, late fifties, handsome, easy smile, grey hair, impeccably dressed, walked toward him across the office that was as confined as the Grand Canyon. "Hey, man, good to see you again," he said and hugged Boysie.

"You look good, David."

"How's your mom doing?"

"Okay, considering."

"Yeah, I read it in the Times. Tragic accident." Boysie sank into the massive leather sofa. Gandolfo sat opposite. "Give her my best."

"I will."

Boysie looked up at the apparently fake Pollock hanging behind Gandolfo, above his desk. He glanced over his shoulder, shrugged and refolded his hands. "Marjorie called me last night and told me that you're gonna try and take care of this."

"Have you spoken to Valentine?"

"No."

Boysie smiled. "And why, pray tell, not?"

"What's he gonna say, "I screwed you out of a hundred and fifty mill?"

"It's a start."

"Yeah, we all know he did, but how do we resolve it. Right? That's the real issue. Conflict resolution."

"David, I'm confused and would really love some clarity."

"I'll do my best," he smiled. Two rows of perfect pearly whites, about a hundred grand's worth.

"No matter how much wedge someone has and I know you have a lot, a hundred and fifty million dollars is still a hundred and fifty million dollars and presumably, well worth the price of a call."

"Life's about choices."

"Very philosophical. Did you contact the FBI?"

"No, good Lord and anyway, I have attorneys to do that."

Boysie nodded, letting out a little sigh of exasperation. "Okay. The good news is that he either has to return the money or give you the real painting."

"Assuming he has it."

"I don't know if it's the real one or not, but," Boysie pointed a hard finger toward the painting and continued, "I did see the twin to that one last night at his house."

David looked impressed. "Wow! You don't waste any time. Is it genuine?"

"I'm no expert but as far as I could tell it was, is, I mean, assuming it's not a 3D printed copy."

Gandolfo smiled thinly and crossed his legs. His foot twitched. Not a lot, but enough for Boysie to know that he had just touched a nerve. "Things they can do these days," he observed.

Boysie grinned, "Yeah but that's not the point, is it?"

David leaned back and smiled. "No."

"Because Valentine can claim that as it was verified and delivered by an armed security company, either they switched it, or you did."

"Correct."

"And as you're in the middle of negotiating a merger with Blackstone, any hint of impropriety on your part, true or false, could put the kibosh on it."

"Correct again."

"I read on the BBC that their offer was over two billion."

David took a deep breath, held it for a moment and let it out, propelling his response, "Two point seven."

"Plus you'll retain a percentage of the catalogue, and whatever else you and they might produce in the future?"

"Yes."

"So what you paid for the painting, you would be willing to sacrifice. Right?" smiled Boysie.

"As you so rightly pointed out, I can't afford the publicity."

The door opened and his secretary brought in the espresso on a small tray. She offered it to Boysie, who smiled and took it. She looked at Gandolfo who shook his head, "no." She left.

Boysie sipped the coffee. "You never answered the question."

"No, I'm not willing to sacrifice a hundred and fifty million dollars."

"Even though, logically speaking, it's a small price to pay for immunity against screwing up the deal."

"Yes."

Boysie finished his espresso. "Now we're getting somewhere."

"Can you take care of this off the radar?"

"Maybe."

David nodded. "And what will it cost?"

"You? Nothing. Marjorie's taking care of me."

"I'd like to add something to sweeten the pot."

"That would be a conflict, wouldn't it?" he grinned.

The slightest trace of annoyance flashed across Gandolfo's eyes. "How?"

Boysie put his empty espresso cup on the table next to him and picked some lint off his trousers before replying. "Because you're one of two players involved in the deal. If anything gets nasty, which it probably will, it could be seen as partiality. Yeah?"

"I understand."

The intercom sounded, "David, your lunch date is here."

"Thank you," he called out over his shoulder and turned back, fixing his gaze on Boysie.

"Gianni delivered your message."

"Sorry?"

"You heard me."

"I don't quite understand."

"No, neither do I," he grinned. "But, I suppose it'll all come out in the wash. Know what I mean?" They looked at each other across the silent void. Boysie squinted, not a lot, but enough to make his point. "David, is there anything you want to tell me before I go?"

Gandolfo frowned his surprise at the subtext and hesitated, ramping up the tension. "No."

Boysie stood up. "Okay."

"Would you like to meet my friend and casting agent, Shannon Makhanian?"

"Not an actor."

"With your looks, you could be, and she's very pretty and available." Boysie smirked and shook his head almost imperceptibly, but it was just enough for David to notice. Irritated at the mild put down, he motioned toward the door, "Shall we?"

Boysie took out his iPhone. "Do you mind if I snap a couple of photos?"

"I don't think she would like that. Privacy. You know?"

"I'm talking about the painting." David didn't know what to say or do as his face reddened. "I'll take that as a yes."

As they walked into reception, Shannon stopped texting and stood up. "Boysie!"

They hugged and kissed. "'Allo, darlin'. How are ya?"

"Fabulous."

"Indeed."

David, bemused, said, "I didn't know you guys knew each other?"

"Old friends," smiled Shannon.

"Very," confirmed Boysie.

"Are you joining?" she asked.

"Next time."

Shannon almost, but not quite, pouted, then laughed teasingly as she hugged him. "I'm in need of a beer and fish and chips."

"Mum would love to see you." He turned to David, "I'll call you."

"You do that," he said testily.

Jose was buried in the engine of a silver, nineteen sixty-eight E-Type Roadster as Celeste rumbled onto the lot. He stood up, sweating and as he always did, smiled at Boysie. "Hey, Boss."

"Any problems?"

"No, but that dude never came in and he's called like a million times."

"Right, sorry. I forgot to call him. I'll do it now."

"Semone."

Boysie walked into his restoration facility, and bounced up the stairs to the office that overlooked Arizona Avenue. Carmella, Jose's wife, was working on her computer and grinned up at him. "Buenos dias, Boysie."

"Hola!"

"Bien?"

"Sí, gracias. Y tú?"

"Todo bien."

Boysie sat down at his desk. "Can you get that guy, Steve, on the line please?"

She dialed the number. "It's ringing."

"Thanks." He picked up his extension.

"Who's this?" snapped the angry voice.

"Boysie."

"About damn time."

"You were supposed to come in on Saturday."

Steve paused, cleared his throat and said, "I've changed my mind."

"Why?"

"I want my deposit back."

"It's non refundable. You know that," offered Boysie calmly.

"Look, don't give me that crap. I want my damn money back."

"Calm down, mate."

"Don't fucking tell me what to do."

"Why don't you tell me what's really going on?"

"I don't have to tell you shit."

"No, of course not but it might help me to decide on your deposit."

"You damn arrogant Brits, you're all the fucking same."

"I'd prefer if you didn't use that language."

"Fuck you."

"As the Bishop said to the actress."

"I want my twenty-five grand and I want it today."

Boysie sighed and pinched the bridge of his nose. "I'm at a bit of a loss. You seemed so in love with the motor."

"Don't try to soft sell me."

"I'm just trying to get a clear picture of why you don't want it, especially after I dropped the price fifteen grand for you."

"It's not your concern."

"Au contraire," Boysie chuckled. "It--"

"--Are you gonna gimme my money back or not?"

He put the phone on speaker. "In spite of your rudeness, yes, I am leaning that way, Steve."

"That's a smart move," he hissed, the threat edging his voice.

Annoyance flushed through Boysie. He gritted his teeth. "Then again, you gave me twenty five after I'd dropped the price fifteen, so maybe I'll just give you the diff, ten grand."

"You better give it all back."

Boysie paused and realized that he had been holding his breath. He let it out, hard and fast. "Things come up, mate. I understand."

"I ain't your mate, mate."

"Money's tight. I understand that too. But rudeness, is something I'll never understand nor tolerate."

"Last time, fucko."

Boysie tried not to laugh, but it was only a half-hearted attempt. "Sorry."

Steve snarled, "I'll be right there."

"Probably not the best idea you've had today. Know what I mean?"

"Fuck you!" he spat and hung up.

Carmella asked apprehensively, "Should I call the police?"

"No, it'll be fine. Can you please make out a check for his deposit?" he asked as he stood up.

"Sure."

Boysie, Jose, Ramon and Pedro were leaning against Steve's E-Type, having a lunch-time beer, when the latter skidded to a halt in his brand new Mercedes. Sweating and puffing, his face contorted with rage, Steve heaved his two hundred eighty pound frame out of the driver's seat. They all watched him as he pounded the concrete in their direction, every angry footstep vibrating the ground like a charging bull elephant. Boysie put down his beer and moved to a more open area. Steve halted about two feet from him. Boysie could smell the booze on his fetid breath.

"Give me my fucking money back, you fucking asshole."

"Relax yaself, mate. There's no need for this."

Steve balled up his fists, warily eyeing Jose, Pedro and Ramon. "That's your back up?"

"No."

Steve swayed a little uncertainly as he tried to refocus on Boysie. "Then let's go around back and handle this."

"You're a big bloke, but you're outta shape. If I was you, I'd take this check and a cab home." He held it up for him to see.

Steve snatched it out of his hand, trying to focus on the amount. He gave up. "And don't stop payment, either."

"I won't."

"Better not," he grunted and turned to get into his car. Boysie came around him and grabbed the keys out of the ignition. "Give 'em to me!" Steve yelled angrily.

"One of my guys'll drive you home."

Steve wiped the sweat off his big, red face. It would always be big and red. As clear a sign of an alcoholic as a Belisha Beacon. He took a step toward Boysie and swung a loping left hook. He stepped back out of range and giggled. "Now stop that."

"Fuck you!" Steve took another swing and missed, again. His face contorted with a mixture of rage and humiliation. He tried to close in on Boysie, swinging a wild series of lefts and rights, which he avoided with ease. Out of breath, he slumped against his Mercedes.

"You done?"

Steve nodded and put his hands on his knees as he tried to force air back into his burning lungs.

Ramon stepped forward. "You want me to drive him, Boss?"

"Yeah and have Pedro follow you in this."

Ramon grinned. "The one he was gonna buy?"

"That would be the one."

"Semone," he replied and signaled Pedro.

Boysie turned to Steve, who now had no fight left in him at all.

"Be nice on the way home. Don't do anything stupid because if you do, they're gonna hurt you. Okay, mate?"

He nodded and quietly got into the back of his Mercedes. Ramon took the keys, got in and drove north on Arizona, followed by Pedro in the E-type. Carmella came out of the warehouse looking anxious.

She said, "I'm sorry Boysie, but I called the police."

"No worries."

"He is a pendejo," said Jose.

"No, just desperate."

Jose nodded. "It's good you didn't hurt him."

"What shall I tell La Jura?" asked Carmella.

"Tell 'em to call me if it's a problem."

"Okay," she replied and went back up to the office.

Boysie pulled up to a meter on Rodeo Drive and chirped Celeste's alarm. Casually, he entered the very expensive and hallowed jewelry store, Le Parie. Gordon, looking every part the gay Parisian with his pencil thin moustache, beautifully tailored suit and diamond-encrusted rings, smiled at him.

"Ah, Boysieee!" he exclaimed excitedly, hugging him, kissing both cheeks in that very French way.

Boysie followed him into the private and secure back office. "You're looking great, Gordon."

"I am in love."

"Who's the lucky fella?"

"Carl. We meet at your birthday party. Do you not remember?"

"The waiter that works for me?"

"Yes."

"I didn't know he was gay."

"Neither did he," he declared mischievously.

"Fair enough."

"So may I see them?" he asked with an exaggerated coolness that belied his anxiety to get his nimble digits on the stones.

This surprised Boysie, because he was normally a very cool customer who never broke a sweat on any deal. He handed Gordon the pouch and he poured out the stones onto a black velvet cloth on the desk. Using long, silver tweezers, he picked one up and examined it with an ornate, illuminated jewelers loupe. Gordon pursed his lips, nodded appreciatively and replaced the diamond, carefully placing the tweezer next to it. Crossing his legs, he folded his hands on his lap and stared at them. His foot twitched intermittently, not enough to cause alarm, but enough for Boysie to notice.

He narrowed his eyes. "What?"

Gordon looked at him for a long moment before responding. "These are very high quality. Flawless."

"That's good then, isn't it?" he replied flatly.

"Depends."

"On?"

"On how you came to possess them." Boysie started to feel the flush of irritation and drummed his fingers once on the tablecloth. Gordon flicked his eyes down to them and then locked eyes with him. "These stones were cut in Amsterdam."

"Correct."

"Yesterday a Chinese courier was robbed and killed downtown," he said with insinuation.

"Yeah?"

"Boysie, these are not just warm, they are hot enough for a sauna."

"Do you want 'em or not?"

Gordon stood up, went over to the bar and poured two glasses of Cordon Blue. He gave one to Boysie and sat back down. They tipped their glasses to each other and took a sip. "Oui, but only for a fraction of their true worth because I will have to sit on them and when I do dispose of them, I will have to be very, very careful."

"So?"

"So I can give you twenty eight cents on the dollar."

"And what's that a carat?"

Gordon wrote that on a piece of paper and slid it across the desk to him. He glanced at it, nodded, folded it methodically and placed it in his breast pocket. He finished the cognac, stood up, leaving the diamonds on the velvet and held out his hand. Gordon smiled and they shook on the deal.

"Were you involved in how they were acquired from the unfortunate courier?"

"Why?"

"I only inquire because he was gutted." He shivered with disgust. "That does not seem like your style, Boysie."

"We've been close friends for a long time."

"Oui."

"And you're a gay French Jew."

"What does this have to do with anything?"

"If anyone knows anything about persecution based on misconception, you do." Gordon shrugged and blew air from pursed lips in the way the French do when they feel exasperated. Boysie added, "Have I ever asked you anything about your business dealings?"

"No."

"Then why are you asking me about mine?" Gordon kept his mouth shut. "Have the cash delivered to me at the pub in the usual way, please."

"Certainement."

"And it's 33 cents on the dollar. Not 28."

Again Gordon pursed his lips, thought better of it, smiled thinly and nodded his acquiescence.

Benny stopped chewing his nails when Boysie entered and quickly followed him into the back room. Boysie locked the door and they sat down at the same table covered with the same red tablecloth. Benny's face twitched as he wiped the beaded sweat from his face.

"You bring my monies?"

"You bring my merch?" asked Boysie.

Benny pulled out the second pouch and handed it to him, flicking nervous eyes from him to the diamonds and back again. "My monies?"

"Why're you sweating?"

Benny shrugged. "I just had some tacos that did not agree with me. Too much jalapeno, man." He put a hand to his mouth and faked a burp.

Boysie rolled his bottom lip between his teeth and locked eyes with him. Leaning forward, he motioned with a finger for him to the do the same and whispered, "You're a lying bastard, Benny."

Benny leaned back, opened his mouth to say something, changed his mind and clamped it shut again. A moment passed, he sagged and replied, "He was just supposed to knock him out but the pendejo cut him like a fish, holmes."

"Who knows that you came to see me?"

"No one."

"No one?" glared Boysie.

"Semone. On my jefa's soul, man."

"I hope for your mother's sake you're right because if this ever comes back on me, don't let me find you."

Benny nodded and licked his dry lips. Boysie went over to the bar, opened the freezer and took out three large, manila envelopes, placing them down in front of him. "Count it."

He opened the first one, sliding out the twenty-five bundles that were each held firmly by a $10,000 band. His eyes lit up and he nodded with satisfaction. "Told you they was good stones."

"Are."

"Wha'?"

"Never mind." Benny placed the quarter of a million dollars back into the manila envelope and found the same amount in the second and third. "I gave you eighteen cents on the dollar and that should be more than enough to cover the booze too."

"Sí, gracias."

"It's time you took a vacation. At least until the Chinese have eased up on looking for you."

"But they don't have no way to make the connection to me."

"You have family in Guadalajara, right?"

"Sí."

"Leave. Tonight."

"You hear something?" he asked thickly, his saliva turning gooey from fear.

"I hear a lotta things. Leave."

"But what about my family?"

"Take 'em with you. In fact, take your bloody pigeons too for all I care but leave you will and if, by chance, through some miracle, you've gotten away with this, I'll let you know."

"Fucking Chinese, man, they crazy."

"And thorough."

"Semone."

"Was he alone?"

"The Chinaman?"

"Your guy." Benny made an apologetic face that indicated he had not been. "Jesus. No loose ends, you said. Who is he?"

"My son. He was the lookout."

Boysie shook his head in dismay. "What the hell were you thinking?" Benny looked down at his hands and shrugged. "And there was just one of 'em?"

"No, tres."

"If you don't level with me, Benny, the deal's off."

"The Guatemalan and my son, they took 'em as they came out a restaurant. You know how big he is. He knocked two out but this other pendejo, he just cut the dude. The one holdin'."

Boysie sighed his weariness. "Then he should've cut all three."

"Semone."

"Call me when you get there."

"If I could give the fucking stones back, I would, but they don't forgive too much and I love my son."

"You didn't have anything to do with this?"

"No."

Boysie nodded. "Okay. You better go and make sure your boy leaves too."

"Thank you, my friend."

They hugged and Benny left. Boysie went into the bar where his mum and Father Murphy were locked in conversation.

"Pint?" asked Summer.

"Yeah, please."

Peter came over and said quietly, "We received one hundred and eleven cases of mixed top shelf today."

"Good."

"But there's no invoice."

"No? Have a pint."

Peter grinned. "Is this another test?"

He turned to Summer. "Give him a pint."

"Sure," she replied, smiling at Peter.

"I'll have a Bass, please."

Summer pulled the pint and Boysie looked over at his mum, who was still not making eye contact with him. He said quietly, "We need to talk."

"We have nothing to talk about."

"Let's go to the office, please."

"I'm busy."

He snarled, "Get un-busy! Now!"

She eyed him, saw the anger building and stomped toward the office. He looked at Peter and shook his head. He nodded and sipped his pint.

His mum heard Boysie climbing the stairs and hissed at him like an angry cat when he entered, "What is it you want?"

"I know that you're impatient about Michael, but you have to trust that I'll get it done."

"I find it amazing that you can solve everyone else's problems, but not your father's murder."

"For the last fucking time, he's not my father."

They glared at each other. "He treated you like a son."

"And I treated him with respect. Anything else?"

"No," she huffed.

"Don't air our business in public again. You understand?" She continued to glare at him, but said nothing. "Good night." He didn't bother waiting for the reply that would never come.

Cold air wrapped penetrating fingers around Boysie as he sipped his Earl Grey on the balcony. Stretched out before him, the black Pacific met the blackness of night. Together, they melded into one impenetrable mass, on which tiny lights of distant ships moved as slow as molasses in January. Dawn was fast approaching as he finished his tea. After stretching for fifteen minutes and with first light pushing back the night, he laced up his Nikes and headed out.

Pounding the concrete runners path that ran along the roadside edge of the beach, he kept up a steady pace as he headed toward Malibu. Others were also working their limbs along with walkers and cyclists. The early morning breeze kept everything to around forty-three degrees; the cold air sharp and clean in his lungs. Passing Topanga Canyon, he eventually arrived at Las Flores, turned around and ran back home, completing his seventeen-mile run. After stretching, he enjoyed the sauna and a long, hot shower.

Swarez had always kept himself isolated, living and working from an old textile mill buried deep in the heart of rural Gloucestershire. Boysie had never bothered to inquire how his friend had acquired the moniker that everyone knew him by. It didn't seem to matter. What did, was that he's also a Jackson Pollock aficionado.

Boysie went over to his iMac and Skyped him. The bearded, smiling face of Swarez appeared on screen. "Boysie, ol' chap. How are you?"

"I am well, my son and you?" he asked, sipping his Earl Grey and sitting down.

He took a drink of bottled water and replied, "Perplexed."

"With life, your girlfriend, the dog next door or Jackson Pollock?"

"All of the above," he replied with a grin, "but yes, in particular, the painting. Very interesting."

"Is it real?"

"Difficult to tell from a digital photo. But, and I don't wanna stake my reputation on it without a hands on examination, but, yeah, it does bare a lotta Pollock characteristics."

"I didn't wanna muddy the water, so what I didn't tell you was that the images, are actually of two of 'em."

"What?" Swarez exclaimed, staring intensely into his webcam. "Two paintings? But they look identical."

"Yeah, it's uh, it's puzzling."

"This is incredible. I've never seen or even heard about that original, let alone a forgery of it. Who has 'em?"

"This movie producer, Valentine, here in L.A. He'd purchased the original from a private collector. It's never been shown and nobody knew anything about it, 'til now."

"He admitted to having the original and the forgery?" he asked, surprised.

"Who?"

"Either of 'em."

"I don't know because I never spoke to the original owner, and Valentine and I aren't exactly buddy-buddy, so I've no way of knowing who he, or she, was."

"You can find out through tax records."

"Not until it's declared, which isn't 'til next April."

Swarez nodded and dragged a hand across his beard. "So you think this producer might've had a copy made?"

"I dunno, mate. That's where it gets murky."

"Sounds like it."

"So what's your opinion now?"

"The same, but with serious reservations."

"What do you know about 3D printing?" Boysie asked, and finished the last of his tea.

"Something I'm looking into. It'll eventually replace prints, as the cost comes down."

Boysie gave a half knowing smile into the webcam. Swarez grinned and shook his head. "Bloody 'ell, Boysie, you think that's how they made the forgery?"

"I do, yeah."

"You do know that once this hits the net, the art world will explode?"

"I'm trying to get it all sorted before that 'appens."

"What wicked company you keep."

"As the spider said to the fly."

Swarez grinned and took another sip of water.

Boysie asked, "What're you working on?"

"Interestingly enough, a new work in honor of the great master himself."

"There are no coincidences."

"You sound like my ex."

Boysie laughed and replied, "Thanks for the help. When's your new exhibition?"

"Jan 28th."

"Pollock's birthday. I'll come over for it."

"Nice."

"Laters."

It was around noon when Boysie finished the Newcastle, washing down the last mouthful of Shepherd's Pie. Toni walked in, sipping a glass of Orangina. She stood in front of his booth, but didn't sit down.

"Have you made any progress?"

Boysie swallowed. "With what?"

"With Marjorie's problem, of course!"

"Some."

"And with Michael?"

"Since last night?" She took another sip and glared. Irritation was beginning to gnaw at him. "Are you going to sit or not?" She considered this for a moment and sat opposite him. It was then, in noticing her glassy stare, that he picked up her drink and tasted it. "Little early for vodka, isn't it?"

Her eyes hardened. "You, do not lecture me!"

"Rarely have I seen you drink. A good red, perhaps, but not hard liquor and not at lunch time."

"Tomorrow I bury my second husband," she snapped, her New York hardness, slightly slurred. "How would you like me to feel?"

"You're right. I'm sorry." He leaned across the table and tried to kiss her on the forehead. She pulled back. He let the insult go and pressed himself back into his seat.

"You are just like your father." Her venom-laced words propelled the intense anger in her eyes.

"Not now."

"Yes, now!" she snapped.

"I told you last night not to--"

"--He thought I didn't know about the other women."

Boysie squinted and glared at her. "Careful."

"Of what?"

"Of some memories that are better left forgotten."

"I have no idea what you're talking about."

"No? Okay. Remember when I was seven and caught you swapping spit with the house painter?"

The blood drained out of her face. "You're a liar!"

He grinned, savagely. "Then I must've also imagined you giving me that five quid to keep schtum."

"You're disgusting."

"And you're a hypocrite." He watched her suck down the remains of her vodka and Orangina. Trying hard to quell the anger now coursing through him, he said, "Gandolfo asked me to convey his respects."

"He's a good man." She picked up a paper napkin and blew her nose. "If it was his father that had been murdered, he'd have the FBI investigating."

"I suppose I'll just have to do." Boysie finished his pint and stood up.

"Will you be here for dinner?" she asked, feigning innocence at the animosity now between them.

He locked eyes with her and chewing his bottom lip in a desperate attempt not to explode, left the pub.

Celeste nosed up Ocean, drifted left down California Incline and on to the Pacific Coast Highway. Sycamore Cove would be a pleasant thirty or so mile drive north along one of the most famous roads in the world. Passing through the exclusivity of Malibu, he always enjoyed the beautiful villas and mansions perched on the Santa Monica Mountains. The Pacific Ocean, glistening as if freshly varnished, continued its love affair with the rugged, famous, coastline.

Boysie steered off PCH onto the little, almost hidden cove. Dotting the beach, gnarled, ancient Sycamore trees stood like old men, bent by time, unwilling to give up the burden of life. Wooden picnic benches, bleached and weather beaten, sat patiently next to well-used concrete barbeque pits, waiting for the next human invasion.

His foreman, Jose and his wife, Carmella, often came here with their kids. Many Hispanic families, primarily on the weekends, summer and winter, would stay the entire day. Their own little bit of paradise. Boysie liked it there too. Sometimes he would bring a wild caught salmon steak, a half bottle of red and some mesquite charcoal. He'd sit under the shade of the trees, staring at the ocean for hours. He loved to do this, particularly in winter when he knew it would be completely deserted and the sea most active. He pulled up at the ticket booth and the friendly Park Ranger smiled at him.

"Beautiful car, sir."

"Thanks," said Boysie.

"Seventy-two Coupe, right?"

"Yeah, as a matter of fact. You have one?"

"Naw, I wish. Been saving for an E-Type for years, ever since I saw one in that old drag racing movie, Two Lane Blacktop."

"That's a minute ago."

"Yeah, but you know how it is; wife, kids, mortgage, college," he shrugged and added, "but that's okay; my kids are straight A students and my wife loves me."

"Sounds like you're ahead of the game, mate."

"Yeah, I think so," he smiled again; the lines on his face etched deeply by the California sun and the responsibilities of married life. "Australian?"

"American by way of London."

"Sorry. You just sound like Crocodile Dundee."

"Great movie. At least the first one was."

"Yeah, but why is it that most sequels suck so badly?"

"Can't leave a good thing alone, I suppose. Gravy train."

The Ranger nodded. "You in the movie business?"

"Only by way of injection." The Ranger looked a little puzzled, then got the joke and burst out laughing. Boysie asked, "How long do I have before you close?"

"A couple of hours."

He gave the Ranger a ten spot and he handed him a pass. "Make sure you display it in the window, otherwise they'll give you a ticket."

"Okay, thanks."

He pulled Celeste into one of the many vacant slots, chirped the alarm and went back over to the Ranger. "Were you on duty last Saturday?"

"No, why?"

"My stepfather drowned here, surfing."

"Oh, I heard about that. Sorry, man. That's a tough break."

"Yeah, thanks. He was found by a couple of surfers. Kids, I think."

"Surfers?"

"Yeah, why?"

"Not allowed."

"Surfers?"

"No boards. Only body surfing and besides, none of the hardcore kids would surf here anyway. The waves are no good. See?" The Ranger looked out at the surf rolling toward the beach. "It breaks too far out. Nothing to ride in."

Boysie watched as the whitecaps broke a fair distance from the beach. "Yeah, I see."

"Sometimes there's good surf, but not often."

"You ride the waves?"

"Yeah, every now-and-again. You?"

"I have, but let me ask you, how deserted is it here, early in the mornings?"

"During the week, very. You get the occasional loner or transient sleeping here. Apart from that, it's dead." He grimaced. "Sorry."

"It's cool," smiled Boysie and added, "thanks for the heads up."

"You bet," he replied and shook his hand firmly. Boysie tickled Celeste to life, turned around and stopped at the Ranger Station. "Let me give you a refund."

"Naw, that's okay."

"You sure?"

"Yeah. What's your name?"

"Bruce Willis."

"Moonlighting?"

The Ranger grinned. "Yeah, incognito except for none of his money or good looks."

Boysie chuckled and punched the gas. Driving southbound, everything was bathed in the golden-yellow, last light of day. As it dissolved into sunset, numerous windows in hillside homes reflected the sun in a fiery, copper-red display. Although gorgeous, it had proven deadly for careless motorists, blinded on the long, gentle curves.

Mulling over the revelation from Ranger Willis, he rolled his bottom lip between his teeth, negotiating the increasing traffic. Michael had chosen to surf on a beach where boards were banned and no self-respecting surfer would go. "Why? Why would he do that, Celeste?" he said out loud. "It just doesn't make sense, does it?" A woman with more money than taste, evidenced by the neon yellow, late model Ferrari she was driving, smiled as she watched him talking to himself. He looked at her from behind his Ray-Ban Aviators and accelerated away. She must have thought this was a challenge and raced past him in a cloud of screaming retaliation. He turned into Neptune's Net and parked.

Boysie ordered a lobster tail and some shrimp. He grabbed a Negro Modelo and sat at the long, wooden tables under the awning, sipping his beer. The sun kissed the world goodnight and disappeared into the shimmering ocean. He felt a brief moment of calm.

A metallic woman's voice called his number over the loudspeaker and he ambled to the counter and collected his food. As he headed back to his table, he saw the female driver sitting there. She was, he concluded, as fast as her Ferrari. Sighing his annoyance, he sat back down. She looked at him as a smile played on her collagen lips. He ignored her and tucked into his lobster tail, dipping it into the melted butter.

She said, "Aren't you just the least bit curious?"

"Not right now. Maybe after I finish eating. Come back then."

Anger flashed across her eyes and turned the playful smile into a sneer. She looked much older, worn and tired as if keeping up the arrogance-laced pretense, was far more than her body wanted to do. She stood up and hissed through clenched teeth, "Asshole."

"I'll live with that."

Climbing back into her Ferrari, she throttled it out of the gravel parking lot, swerving across PCH in a wild, anger fueled fishtail, narrowly missing several cars. Boysie stared out over the ocean and felt a sudden wave of sadness. He used to think that it was just L.A. that attracted and perpetuated so many lost souls, behaving badly in a desperate attempt to feel something beneath the veneer. He had come to realize that it's everywhere now. So many not just influenced by the Cult Of Celebrity, but actually wanting to be one. Famous just for being famous. No talent. No integrity. Nothing to offer the world other than vanity, and the emptiness of it all. His appetite took a sudden vacation. He washed his hands and headed home.

8 ~ MURPHY'S FOLLY

FATHER MURPHY PRESIDED OVER THE simple ceremony as Michael was laid to rest. Boysie's mum deliberately kept the guest list to around a hundred mourners and surprisingly, Gandolfo, with Shannon on his arm, was amongst them. She left him alone and went over to talk to Boysie's mum, who was being consoled by Marjorie. Gandolfo turned and catching his eye, slid over to him.

"Any progress, Boysie?"

Bemused but not surprised by the crass timing, he replied, "Yeah."

"Sorry, I know this is inappropriate, I'm just a little anxious."

"Didn't seem to be the other day."

Gandolfo's face began to harden. "So what's the deal?"

"I said there was progress. I didn't say that I have anything to tell you, yet."

Clearly not used to being spoken to that way, he gritted his teeth. "When might I expect you to condescend to give me an update?"

"When I have something concrete, you'll be the first to know. Okay, mate?"

Gandolfo tried to hide his contempt, but failed and ended up with a lopsided smirk that was more revealing than any dialogue.

Boysie looked steadily at him. "I do have one question." Gandolfo's jaw muscles flexed annoyance. "Why didn't you have your own independent expert authenticate the painting, prior to the sale?"

"I trusted Marjorie. How was I to know that she'd screw it up."

"Wait." Boysie chuckled his astonishment. He didn't mean to. He just couldn't help himself. "You're blaming her for this?"

"She did broker the deal."

"And you approved Stanford Mills."

"Then they must be in league." Boysie smirked. Irritated, Gandolfo demanded, "What?"

"If you really believe that, David, might I suggest you call the Ol' Bill?"

He glared angrily at Boysie, his jaw muscles twitching rapidly. "I'll take that under advisement."

"You do that."

"Anything else, Blake?" he sneered contemptuously.

"No, that'll do for today. Off you go."

Gandolfo's sparkling blues turned a nasty shade of rage, as his pupils retracted at the shock of being so curtly dismissed. For a long moment he just stood there like an errant schoolboy, not knowing whether to laugh or cry as his face reddened.

Boysie hardened his eyes. "Go on."

Gandolfo spun on his heel, slapped on a big, plastic smile and made a beeline for Toni, Shannon and Marjorie. Boysie watched as he was warmly greeted by the ladies; Marjorie casting a sly glance in his direction. He was about to join them when his iPhone buzzed. He looked at the screen and smiled.

"Jason. How are you, mate?"

"Sorry to hear about your stepdad."

"Thanks. Where're you calling from?"

"New York."

"How's it going?"

"Great. About to do another seven songs in seven days."

"I love the tracks from the first one you did here in L.A."

"Thanks, bro."

"When you back in town?"

"Tonight."

"You staying at my gaff?"

"Only if you ask nicely."

"You need me to pick you up?" asked Boysie with a chuckle.

"No. I bought a car."

"What?"

"You'll see."

"Okay. Laters." Boysie hung up and felt good. His close friend was coming for a visit and would have lots of funny stories to tell over bottles of great wine. He ambled over to his mum, as Gandolfo and Shannon moved away to mingle with some of the other mourners. "What did David have to say?"

Toni took a deep breath, "He offered his condolences."

"That's nice, Mum."

"It was awkward though," added Marjorie.

Toni said, "Yeah and I'm surprised to see him here. I mean it's not that I'm ungrateful, he's a very important man, but he hardly knew Michael."

"Yeah. I was thinking that myself," stated Boysie.

Annoyance flicked across his mum's eyes. "What does that mean?"

"Nothing. Nothing at all."

Boysie slipped in between her and Marjorie, put his arms around them and escorted them back over to the waiting limo.

Marjorie smiled. "Glad that chivalry is not lost."

9 ~ NUTS

THE WAIT STAFF BUSIED THEMSELVES serving the mourners who were busy entombing their sorrow in voluminous amounts of alcohol and pub food. Toni, much to Boysie's approval, was the center of attention. This, he observed, seemed to help in healing her. She was smiling and simultaneously shedding the occasional tear as she sipped on a vodka and Orangina. Summer and Autumn were behind the bar pulling pints as fast as they were being snatched up. Harry was drifting amongst the gathered throng, also soaking up some of the over abundant sympathy. Much to Marjorie's obvious relief, Gandolfo was nowhere to be seen.

Boysie slipped quietly out the back door and into the crisp fall sunshine. Father Murphy was sitting at one of the patio tables, staring forlornly into a full glass of Bushmills. He looked up at him, quickly wiping away the evidence from his watery eyes.

"Are ya spyin' on me, Boysie?"

"It was a great eulogy."

"He was a good man."

"Have you heard anymore from Bergman?"

"No, b'Jeasus and I don't want to."

"Call me if you do."

Father Murphy nodded and resumed staring into his whisky. Boysie wished he could've made his friend feel better, but knew that some burdens must be born alone.

Celeste purred north up PCH, cruising at a steady 50. The occasional Harley thundered past him, its rider enjoying the cool sea breeze. Boysie owned a fully restored, cobalt blue and pearl white, pin-striped, 1977 Harley Davidson FLH. He, too, had many times ridden Highway One. Of late, however, he'd been too busy to even kick her over. He was pulled out of his thoughts as he rounded the sweeping curve beside the massive rock that signaled the beginning of Sycamore Cove; now forever tainted by Michael's murder. He could never enjoy the solitude of that beach again.

Twenty minutes later, Boysie pulled up at 3291 Loma Vista Road, in the city of Ventura, the County Coroner's Office. He chirped Celeste's alarm, entered the building and walked up to the receptionist. She was in her thirties and smiled warmly as her eyes evaluated him in a blink thereof.

"'Allo, Miss," he smiled.

"How may I help you?"

"I'd like to see the Medical Examiner."

"Do you have an appointment?"

"No."

"Then I'm sorry."

"My stepfather was murdered last Friday. They found his body at Sycamore Cove and I have some unanswered questions that I'd like to have answered."

She nodded, sighed and looked at him sympathetically. "I'm sorry for your loss. Can you tell me who the investigating officer is?"

"There isn't one. It was ruled accidental."

Her face lost some of its sympathy. "Then I can't help you."

"But the Coroner can."

"You're not hearing me. Once the case is closed, it's closed."

"I'd like to make an appointment, please."

"On what grounds?"

"Is that a joke?"

"Sir, the stress of losing a loved one is tremendous. I understand but--"

"--Please give me an appointment."

"I'm sorry."

Boysie put a Fisherman's Friend into his mouth and looked steadily at her.

"Is there anything else?" she asked. Abruptly, he turned and walked past her toward the door leading to the morgue. "Sir! Sir, please!"

Boysie pushed it open and strode down the corridor looking at the nameplates on each door. He found the one he wanted, D. Kantor. MD. PhD. County Medical Examiner, and knocked.

"Come in."

He opened it just as the secretary burst into the corridor, followed by two very pissed off looking Sheriffs. He closed the door and smiled at the forty something woman, dressed in a crisp, neat, two-piece, grey wool suit. Her neat hands were folded neatly in front of her on the neat and tidy desk.

"I'm assuming you don't have an appointment?" she asked rhetorically.

Boysie smiled and sat in the chair opposite as the door burst open and the two Sheriffs rushed in, guns aimed at him.

"FREEZE!" screamed the first Sheriff.

Boysie froze.

"GET ON THE GROUND, ASSHOLE!"

Boysie looked at the Coroner who sighed and said, "Guys, please, relax."

This did not go down well with the Sheriffs. "Ma'am, he's under arrest!"

The Coroner ran a hand across her tired face. "Yes, yes, all in due course. For now, I want to know why he felt the urgent need to see me. If that's okay with you?"

"We can establish that after he's been secured and processed," offered the Sheriff hopefully.

Realizing that they were in imminent danger of losing their would-be prisoner, the other Sheriff snarled through gritted teeth, "Ma'am, he could be a terrorist."

The receptionist did a double take. Boysie giggled.

The Coroner grinned and looked at him. "Are you a terrorist?"

"Not lately."

"There you have it, gentlemen. Close the door on the way out please."

The really pissed off Sheriff decided to stand his ground. "I need to see some ID."

The Coroner looked at Boysie who nodded his agreement. With his left hand, he opened his suit jacket and took out his wallet. Flipping it open, he handed it to the officer, who snapped a hairy paw around it. Boysie could tell that he was reading the license, because his lips moved. He grunted and showed it to his fellow officer, who also grunted and handed it back to Boysie.

"Next time, make a damn appointment," snarled the Sheriff.

Boysie saluted casually. "Yes, sir."

The Sheriffs glared violently at him and left, followed by the now red-faced receptionist. The Coroner leaned back in her chair, crossed her legs and leveled her gaze at Boysie.

"So, to what do I owe the pleasure, uh--"

"--Boysie Blake," he replied, handing her one of his business cards.

Dr. Kantor read it and squinted. "Your father was Michael Santoro?"

"Stepfather."

"I know who you are and why you're here," the sudden chilliness in the Coroner's voice unmistakable, emphasized by the irritated flicking of her foot. Boysie didn't respond. It wasn't necessary or required. "Mr. Santoro drowned. A tragic accident, but an accident nonetheless."

"Who did the autopsy?"

"Irrelevant."

"I was beginning to like you," said Boysie.

"Are you threatening me?"

"My stepfather was murdered and his widow, my mum, is beside herself with grief. She wants answers and I promised I'd get 'em."

"Mr. Blake, there is nothing out of the norm. He was surfing. He drowned. It happens. A lot, unfortunately."

"He was a life long surfer who would have known that no one would bother to surf there, even if they were allowed."

"Maybe he was drunk."

"That's reasonable. Was there alcohol in his blood?"

Dr. Kantor barred her teeth for a moment, then swiveled her chair to the computer and punched in some letters. A moment later the autopsy report flashed onto the screen. She found what she was looking for and read it out to him, ".003%"

Boysie nodded. "Nothing. Not even one beer."

"No," she agreed.

"Narcotics?"

"No."

"So drugs and alcohol are evidently not a factor in his death. Right?"

"No, but seawater is," she smarmed.

"And someone who's ridden the waves at every beach in California, over his entire life, is found accidentally drowned, at a beach that no self-respecting surfer, especially one with his vast experience, would go to." The good doctor shifted uncomfortably in her seat. Boysie added, "That doesn't bother you?"

"No."

"Were there bruises on the body?"

"Yes, but consistent with being battered by high surf, rocks, maybe even his board."

"Still doesn't answer the question of why he was there."

"Other than surfing? I have no idea."

"And no desire to find out," he asked pointedly.

"The case is closed."

"Then reopen it."

"We have issued our official position."

Boysie felt the nervous energy, generated by his growing anger, begin to course through his veins. Dr. Kantor must have sensed it too; her right eyelid twitched nervously. He stood up, towering over her.

"Thanks for your time."

They looked at each other across the void of deceit. He bit the cough lozenge in half with a hard crack and jabbed his left index at her. "Doctor, you appear to be caught in the middle of a swirling mass of bullshit. I hope for your sake, you're not involved."

"Get out."

"In the words of our ex-governor, "I'll be back."

"Make an appointment."

Before leaving, Boysie, his jaw flexing angrily, stared for a long, silent moment at the Coroner. Passing the secretary and the still hovering Sheriffs, he ignored them and stepped out into the late afternoon sunshine.

On the drive back, Boysie kept going over the meeting with the Coroner. He knew that he hadn't seen the last of her. Sycamore Cove was just ahead and he decided to pull over. As he guided Celeste past the closed Ranger's booth and into the deserted parking lot, he felt a growing unease in the pit of his stomach. Oma, his German grandmother on his mother's side, had been one of the kindest and most intuitive women he had ever known. She had always told him to trust his gut instinct and up to now, it had never let him down. He climbed out of the E-Type and ambled over to the beach, sitting down on one of the sand-sprayed picnic tables. The grease-spattered, concrete barbeque pit still bore the long dead, white charcoal ash of someone's feast. He poked his finger absently into it, smelling the faint hint of steak and onions, rubbing the ash between finger and thumb. The cold wind blew in off the surging ocean, bringing with it the unmistakable rank odor of seaweed. Above, seagulls squawked their arguments as they circled and hovered.

Boysie heard the slow crunch of gravel behind him and turned to see the black Escalade with black tinted windows pull up behind Celeste, blocking her in. His first thought was how so many gangsters, or at least those that believed they were, stuck to the stereotype. Three thugs, dressed in black paramilitary outfits, emerged from the vehicle, resplendent in coal black sunglasses and short-cropped hair. They fanned out and headed toward him. Boysie eyed the guns strapped to their sides, but made no attempt to run. It was an exercise in futility and he would need to conserve his energy. The first thug stopped about six feet in front of him; a nasty looking chap, about twenty eight, blond hair, earrings and cold, blue eyes. His cohorts stood on either side of him.

Blondie smirked at Boysie, skimmed his eyes to the Pacific and back to him. "You like the ocean?"

"That depends."

"On?"

"If I'm in it voluntarily."

"You've been asking a lot of questions about someone else who also liked the ocean."

"You know that first hand?" asked Boysie.

"What?"

"That Michael liked the ocean."

Blondie's eyes hardened. "We've been asked to express a different point a view."

"That's original."

"Our client would very much like you to focus your attention somewhere else."

"And where would that be, exactly?"

"Wherever you choose. Just so long as you choose not to continue troubling yourself about this unfortunate accident."

For the second time that day, Boysie giggled. He didn't mean to. He just did. Blondie glanced at the meathead standing to his left. He had the appearance of being sentient, but none of the signs. Meathead grunted and stepped forward, balling up his fists that looked like blocks of concrete. He was in mid stride when Boysie quickly stepped to one side and throat punched him. Meathead sank to his knees in the cold sand, grabbing his neck, desperately trying to force air back into his lungs. Blondie, blocked by

Meathead, tried to come around him and swung a wild left. Boysie blocked it and came over the top with a hard right, cracking him squarely on the side of the jaw. He didn't see the third guy, but felt the gun butt as it smashed into the back of his skull. White light exploded through his brain. Then darkness.

Boysie's wet clothes clung to him as he floated through space, miles above Sycamore Cove. Crimson fingers spread out around him, cloudy, swirling, like blood in water. He pushed a hand through them, watching with fascination as they dissolved into nothing. Suddenly, he was aware of his pounding heart and the smell of bacon and eggs. The unmistakable aroma forced its way up his nose, but all it did was make him vomit. After heaving several times, nothing else came up. Instantly, he was plummeting at incredible speed toward the ocean and slammed into it, hard, sinking like a stone to the sandy bottom. He sat on the ocean floor and something big, black and ominous appeared in the distance. It moved bizarrely, one massive leg at a time and, when it was almost upon him, he realized what it was, Charlie Thompson; as big as a killer whale and just as intimidating. Boysie screamed and thousands of air bubbles burst from his mouth. Seawater poured into his lungs and with one, final, Herculean effort, he kicked for the surface. It took a moment to realize that he was awake and floating out to sea. He felt the death-tug of the current as salt water forced its way up his nose and down his throat. He vomited again, coughed out his lungs and with pain searing through his head, swam back to the beach. He hauled himself out and, completely exhausted, rolled onto his back. The moonlight bathed everything in eerie blue-grey light, making the white caps look like ghosts dancing on the waves. He shivered and slowly, painfully, crawled on all fours over to one of the picnic tables and, holding on for balance, hauled himself up and sat down. He touched the back of his head and looked at his blood-covered fingers. A second wave of nausea hit him, but nothing came up. His head felt like it was going to burst and his ribs ached from the evident kicking that Blondie and his crew had given him. Taking slow, deep breaths, something caught his eye in the sand. A moment later, the iPhone screen lit up. Fighting back the nausea, he slid to his knees and crawled over to it. It was another email, which he ignored and instead, dialed Jason with a shaking hand.

"I'm starving. Where are you?"

Boysie replied before he passed out, "Help me. Sycamore Cove."

10 ~ WATCH YOUR BACK, JACK

THE EARLY MORNING GREY SEEPED through the bedroom window. Boysie woke up with a splitting headache, and squinted at the glass of water and some Advil on the nightstand. He popped two, washed them down and swung his legs off the bed. Shuffling slowly toward the open door, every step brought new heights of pain. Jason was asleep on the sofa in the living room and woke up, peering at him.

"How're you feeling?"

"Mad," replied Boysie hoarsely.

Jason sat up. "Good thing you've got a thick skull."

"Thanks for keeping an eye on me."

"Eyes to the soul--"

"--Brothers to the bone."

Boysie sat down slowly on the chair opposite.

"Can you give me a ride so I can collect Celeste?"

"Sure but don't you think you should have one of your guys go up there?"

"No. I don't want anybody to know what happened."

"Understood. Cuppa?"

"Please."

Jason busied himself making the tea and some hot, buttered toast. He handed him a mug and sat opposite. "What the hell happened?"

"Someone offered me a different point of view."

"That's original."

"That's what I said."

"And I assume they didn't like your response?"

"Correct." Boysie took a sip of Earl Grey.

"So now what?"

"So now I have to play hardball."

Jason took a bite of toast. "Is this the jam you made?"

"Yeah, you like it?"

"Mmm. Very good."

"It's an old German recipe. Oma used to make it all the time."

"You need to see a doctor."

"I need to find those Muppets who worked me over."

"You want me to go with you?"

"I appreciate your fourth degree black belt skills, but no, thanks."

Jason stood up and placed the dishes in the sink. "I have a twelve o'clock at CAA. But nothing this afternoon."

"I'll be fine." Boysie got to his feet and, heading for the bathroom, said, "I'm gonna be out and about this afternoon. If I get done in time, you wanna have dinner?"

"Sure. Where?"

"There's that great vegetarian place, Electric Lotus, in Los Feliz."

Jason shook his head. "Too far, bro. What about the Chateau Marmont?"

"Alright. I'll give you a bell when I have a better idea."

"I'm going for a run and then I'll take you to get your car."

"Celeste."

"Celeste," grinned Jason.

Boysie took a long, hot shower and when he got out, Jason was gone. He got dressed in a black, all cotton tracksuit, laced up his Jordans and checked his email.

A sun gold, 1969, Dodge Coronet, rumbled up Highway One. Its powerful engine a testament to the legacy of Detroit muscle. Jason pulled up to the booth at Sycamore Cove and Ranger Willis smiled.

"Mr. Blake, right?"

"Yeah."

"I thought that was your Jag."

"Ranger Bruce Willis," Boysie nodded at Jason, "this is my mate, Jason."

"I'm a big fan of yours, man."

Jason, always humble, looked genuinely surprised. "Thanks, man."

"Could I get your autograph, please?"

"Sure."

"Coincidence, but I was just playing it this morning," the Ranger replied as he handed him an INXS CD and magic marker. "I watched you all the way through the show. I voted for you."

"It's Bruce Willis," said Boysie.

"Who is?"

"I am. That's my name," said the Ranger.

"Cool," replied Jason and signed the CD, handing it to him. "Here you go."

"Thanks," he beamed.

They rumbled onto the parking lot and Jason pulled up next to Celeste. "You want me to wait?"

"No, I'm cool. I'll see you tonight."

"Okay."

"Thanks, for the ride, bro."

Jason smiled and stomped on the gas. 550 horses of American muscle snarled to life. Burning rubber, the Dodge accelerated at blinding speed and joined the southbound traffic.

Boysie grinned and was about to start Celeste when a sudden chill rippled down his spine. He got out and checked underneath the car. Much to his relief, no bomb, but just to be sure, he popped the hood. Nothing.

He closed it and Ranger Willis, a quizzical look creasing his friendly face, joined him.

"Everything okay, Mr. Blake?"

"Yeah. Just checking."

"How'd you come to leave her here last night?"

"I wasn't feeling too good."

The Ranger took and involuntary step backward. "Not the flu, I hope?"

"No. Gun metal grey."

"Huh?" Boysie turned around and showed him the wound on the back of his skull. "You should get that looked at."

"I will."

"That happened here?"

"Uh-huh."

"Robbery? Did you report it?"

"No, it was a message. No point reporting it, no witnesses and beside, not the way I do things."

With a thick, stubby thumb, Ranger Willis pointed over his left shoulder, toward the ticket booth. "Actually, there is a witness."

Boysie saw the small, almost hidden security camera perched on the top of the booth. "HD?"

"Yeah."

"Can you access the hard drive?"

"I can. Come on." He followed him over to the booth. Inside, the Ranger scrolled through the computer's video commands. "About what time?"

"I'd say it was around six, six thirty."

Ranger Willis typed in the time and date. Instantly, the choppy footage appeared. "Quality's not that great."

"Maybe I can get the license plate though." The Ranger scrolled forward and a moment later, Celeste drove past the camera and parked. "Can you fast forward again please?"

"Sure."

"There. Right there," said Boysie as the black Escalade came into view and parked, blocking in the E-Type Jag. Using his iPhone, he videoed the computer screen as the three men got out and headed for the beach, leaving the camera's sightline. "Can you punch in on the license plate?"

Ranger Willis shook his head. "No, sorry. Only in the movies."

Boysie squinted and, peering at the numbers, nodded as he remembered having seen the license plate before in Beverly Hills. "MS 9. Right?"

"Yeah, I think so," agreed the Ranger, "but I wouldn't swear to it."

"It's a start."

"Anyway, it's no good unless you know a cop or someone in the DMV."

"Part of my business is towing."

"Got'cha. But that's still illegal unless you own the vehicle, isn't it?" Boysie grinned and using his iPhone, took a snapshot of the license plate. Ranger Willis nodded appreciatively. "Smart."

"Just using available technology."

"Yeah, same as my kids. They have cell phones, video games, iPods, anything they could want. But sometimes I get the feeling they're just not happy."

"Too much of a good thing, mate. You have to do without to really appreciate what you've got."

"Yeah, but they're good kids. Anyway, it's a changing world and sometimes I feel like I just can't keep up."

"I'm only thirty-five, but if anyone had said to me when I was a kid that I'd be drinking water from plastic bottles and paying for it, I'd have thought they were nuts. Star Trek, right?"

Ranger Willis laughed. "Yeah, for sure and they're always on Facebook, Twitter or You Tube, making videos and uploading them for their friends to see."

"Social Networking can be a very good thing. Provides a creative outlet for a lotta people that would otherwise be stifled."

"I guess," he replied reluctantly.

"I've also reconnected with friends that I haven't seen in years and never would've otherwise spoken to. You tried it?"

"Naw. Not for me."

"Do you monitor your kids?"

"Of course."

"That's good." Boysie held out his hand. "Again, thanks for your help."

"No worries," he grinned.

Boysie turned away, stopped and turned back. "How far back can you go?"

"The video?"

"Yeah."

"Seventy two hours and then it records over." Disappointed, Boysie nodded his thanks. The Ranger asked, "You wanted to see if there was anything with your dad on it."

"Stepdad. Yeah."

"Sorry I couldn't help you with that."

"You've helped a lot. Thanks."

He fired up Celeste and waited for her to warm up. A few minutes later, he pulled up next to the Ranger. "Boysie. My name's Boysie." He handed him his card, "If there's anything I can ever do for you, let me know."

The Ranger nodded and watched as Celeste accelerated hard into the flow of traffic heading back toward Santa Monica.

Harry, sipping a glass of white, was propping up the bar again watching his mum serving a couple at the other end. Boysie walked in, sat next to him and asked, "How's she doing?"

"Good afternoon to you too."

"Just answer the bloody question."

"Who took the jam outta your donut?" squawked Harry. Boysie glared at his brother who offered quickly, "She's fine. Seems to be her old self again."

Toni came over and pursed her lips in the way that mothers do when they're about to scold a child. "So nice of you to make an appearance."

"I see you're on the mend," observed Boysie.

"No thanks to you."

Harry let out a small chuckle, not very loud or very long, but enough to really annoy Boysie. He gave him an icy stare and got up. "I'll come back when I have less time." He headed into the restaurant section and sat in his booth.

Amanda came over. "Pint?"

"Please."

"Anything else?"

"Fish and chips."

"Okay," she smiled and left.

Boysie took out his iPhone, scanning through the photos until he found the one of the license plate. He wrote it down on a napkin and then used License Plate Search to track down the owner of the Escalade. It came up as being registered to Midnight Security Corp., out of San Pedro. He keyed it into his iPhone as Amanda returned with his food and the ice-cold pint.

"Thanks."

"Sure," she casually tossed over her shoulder, sailing over to another table.

His ribs still ached, so he ate slowly and planned his visit to Midnight Securities.

Heading Southbound, Celeste's throaty V12 chewed up the 405 Freeway and, much to everyone's astonishment, it was relatively empty. On the world's busiest freeway, sometimes it just happened like that. Boysie merged onto the 110 and continued on down to San Pedro, cruising into the dockland warehouse district. The GPS showed him exactly which warehouse belonged to Midnight Securities. He pulled through the gate and parked next to the line of nine, identical, black Escalades, lined up in military fashion. Each with a sequential MS license plate, beginning at one.

The warehouse bristled with security cameras tracking his every movement. He smiled up at them and wiggled his fingers in a sarcastic greeting. What surprised him, was that there were no guards at the main gate. He headed toward the steel door set in the middle of the building and suddenly realized why, turning just as the gate electronically slammed shut.

"Bollox," he thought to himself.

At the far end of the building, a massive gate rolled up and six black-clad, heavily armed men appeared. Of course, the one in front was his old acquaintance, Blondie. "Nice to see you again, Mr. Blake."

"Wish I could say the same."

"Oh come on now, that's not very nice," he sneered in his best Mid-Western.

Boysie cast a glance at the other five thugs now surrounding him, two of whom he recognized from his previous encounter. He smiled at Meathead. "How's the throat?" Meathead took a step forward, but Blondie waved him off. He contented himself by restlessly fingering the trigger of his assault rifle. Boysie turned back to Blondie. "Bit melodramatic, isn't it?"

"What?"

"All this Black Ops stuff. You should try some pastel colors. Liven things up."

Blondie choked back his disbelief at Boysie's lack of respect, especially when they so clearly had the upper hand. "You should've stayed away, bro."

Boysie nodded. "Yeah, but you and me, we have unfinished business."

"I should've killed you last night."

"That's not very nice," smiled Boysie.

"Shut the fuck up and get inside."

Boysie's iPhone buzzed. He looked at Blondie, held up his index finger, pulled the phone out of his pocket and offered it to him. "It's for you."

Blondie's mouth fell open. "What?"

"Do answer it, ol' bean."

He hesitated for a second, took the iPhone and snarled into it, "Yeah?"

"This is Detective Lawton, Santa Monica PD, and you are?"

The blood drained out of Blondie's face. "Is this a joke?"

Boysie could hear Detective Lawton's angrily raised voice. "Listen, asshole, you can either answer the question there, or I can have you brought here. Your choice."

"How the hell do I know you're who you say you are?"

"Because the unmarked that's now turning onto your street has two San Pedro detectives in it."

Blondie looked at the black police car pulling up at the gate. "Fuck," was all he could spit out, adding, "Paul Windsor."

Boysie smiled at him and snapped his fingers repeatedly, holding out his hand for the iPhone. Paul Windsor hesitated at the insult and clearly wanted nothing more than to make good on his threat. Instead, he snorted and handed it back to him. Boysie grinned and said to Lawton, "Yeah, I'm cool." He looked at Windsor, "I'm cool, right?" He nodded slowly and Boysie said, "Yeah, he thinks I'm cool. I'll call you in ten." He hung up, waved at the cops in the unmarked watching him and turned his attention back to Windsor. "Who hired you?"

"That's confidential."

"Paul, I can call you Paul, right?" he grinned.

Paul Windsor glared at him.

"As of right now, Paul, I can have you and those other two Muppets arrested for assault with intent to commit murder."

He smirked. "On whose say-so?"

"On the say-so of the security camera you so obviously missed. Know what I mean?"

"Then do it."

"In good time."

"You don't have dick."

"My ex might agree with you. However, I want to know his, or her name."

He shrugged. "I dunno and don't care. I only follow orders."

"Just a cog in the wheel, huh?"

"Anything else?"

"If there really was no camera, how did I get this?" He held up his iPhone and showed him the snapshot of the license plate taken from Ranger Willis' computer screen. Windsor tried to hide his surprise, but it just made him look like he had really bad toothache. "Here," added Boysie, handing him his card, "if you wanna keep your arse outta jail, gimme a bell."

He climbed into Celeste and drove slowly toward the reluctantly opening gate, and pulled up next to the San Pedro detectives. "Thank you, gentlemen. I owe you."

"What do you have on these clowns?" asked the grizzled veteran, Detective Rodriguez.

"At the very least, attempted murder."

"Who's?"

"Mine."

"I don't understand."

"Neither do I, yet. But as soon as I can figure out what's going on, I'll give you everything you need to pinch 'em."

Detective Chang nodded toward Paul Windsor. "We've been trying to take 'em down for years, but they're protected by someone at the State Department."

"How do you know that?" asked Boysie, unable to hide his surprise.

"That blond asshole just came back from Afghanistan, doing private security."

"Let me guess, for US diplomats?" said Boysie.

"Yep."

"Isn't that fascinating."

"Midnight Securities has multi-million dollar contracts in Iraq and Afghanistan with the State Department, sanctioned and watched over by the CIA."

"This is getting awfully deep."

"Watch your back, Jack," added Detective Rodriguez.

"Always, mate." Boysie winked knowingly and handed him his card. "Bring your families up for lunch or dinner on me."

Detective Rodriguez grinned. "I thought British food sucked?"

"Porky pies, detective."

"Huh?"

"Lies," said Boysie and drove away.

Rodriguez looked at the card and turned to his partner. "What d'ya think?"

Detective Chang glared at the retreating black clad, security guys. "If he can help us pinch 'em, that's reward enough for me."

Driving back to Santa Monica, Boysie kept going over everything, ending up with the same conclusion; Midnight Securities, sanctioned by the CIA, are the ones who murdered Michael. But why? Why would the CIA bother or even care about a squabble between partners over a small parcel of land in L.A? To what avail? Obviously, they didn't know about the hit, especially as it served no purpose or national interest. For the most part, he didn't buy into conspiracies. He believed that Neil Armstrong did walk on the moon. He didn't believe that the government had anything to do with 9/11, but mostly he didn't believe that Sid Vicious killed Bambi.

Boysie pulled up at the Georgian and the valet, Juan, cracked out the corner of his mouth, "Popo's looking for you, man."

"Uniform or plain?"

"Him," pointed Juan with pursed lips.

Boysie looked over at the entrance. Leaning casually against the wall, a toothpick in the corner of his mouth, fedora pushed to the back of his head, was Detective Lawton. The police officer shook his head in mock disapproval and waited as Boysie tipped Juan and ambled over to him.

"I feel so much safer now the coppers are here."

"Didn't you guys invent the language?" smirked the Detective.

"We did."

"Then speak English, will ya?"

"Drink?"

"Now that, I understand."

They entered the bar, found a quiet booth and waited as the waitress smiled over to them. "Boysie, what can I get you?" she said breathlessly. Her full lips full of red gloss promise.

"Two double Woodford Reserves, please."

"Ice?"

"No thanks."

"Ice," said the Detective.

"Sure." She slinked off toward the bar, watched by the Detective as Boysie watched him.

"To what do I owe the pleasure, Charlie?"

Detective Lawton pulled himself away from committing the waitresses measurements to memory. "Dr. Kantor has made an official complaint."

"The Coroner?"

"Yeah."

"What is it?"

"That you broke into her office and--"

"--While she was in it?"

"While she was in it and sexually harassed her."

Boysie smiled and shook his head. "That's the best they can come up with?"

The cop snapped the toothpick in half, dropping it onto the table. "This ain't no joke, Boysie. It starts out as sexual harassment with intent. Then she, they, find a friendly DA and remember, she is the Coroner, and before you can say Honolulu, you raped her."

"Come on."

"I told you not to go there."

"You did, and when were you gonna tell me about Midnight Securities involvement with the CIA?"

Detective Lawton shrugged his massive shoulders. "I only found out today. Same as you."

"Yeah? And how did you find out?"

Lawton frowned and was about to respond when the waitress delivered their drinks. "On your tab, Boysie?"

"Please," he replied, not taking his eyes off his friend.

She smiled. "Already done."

"Thanks."

Detective Lawton took a mouthful of Woodford. "I can't protect you on this one."

"I'm not asking you to."

For the first time in their decade long friendship, Boysie saw something in his eyes that he had never, ever seen. Fear.

"Look, man," leaned in the veteran cop, "you have got to back-off. Let it go. Tell your momma that Michael's death was an accident. Nothing more."

Boysie nodded thoughtfully and rolled his lower lip between his teeth. "And if I don't?"

"Do I gotta spell it out for you?"

"What happened between me leaving San Pedro and now?"

"I gotta go." The detective drained his bourbon, placed the glass down quietly and said, "The Jackson Pollock thing? It's done too."

"What?"

"Walk away."

"You know that's not gonna happen."

Detective Lawton slid out of the booth, placed the fedora on his head, looked at him and left. Boysie slid a twenty under his glass and headed for the elevator.

The hot water showered over him, relaxing the tension in his shoulders and back. Toweling off, he carefully examined the purple and red bruises on his ribs, presumably from Windsor's combat boots. He slipped on his robe and went out into the kitchen. Grabbing a pint mug, he filled it with triple filtered water from the Culligan water cooler and drank it slowly. He made a pot of tea and sat on the balcony, watching the people milling around below on Ocean Boulevard.

Boysie had been in some close scrapes over the years and violence was nothing new to him. But if the CIA's involvement were true, then this was entirely something different and very, very dangerous. He couldn't get the fear in Lawton's eyes out of his mind. A sense of foreboding was beginning to creep into his being and he didn't like it. Not one bit. He went back into the kitchen as the elevator door slid open and Jason strode in.

"You feeling any better?"

"Yeah, thanks," replied Boysie.

"Is there any more tea?"

"There is."

Jason poured himself a cup. "We still on for dinner?"

"Yeah. How'd it go at CAA?"

"You ever watch Entourage?"

"Yeah. Cool show."

"Then you know how it went," he stated with a grin.

Boysie sipped his tea.

The Château Marmont loomed over Sunset Boulevard as Jason rumbled his Dodge up the narrow side street and stopped at the waiting valets. He and Boysie, both dressed to the nines, climbed out and a hungry looking valet gave Jason a ticket. Boysie looked at the sign that smugly stated; '$35 Parking Fee.'

"Thirty-five dollars to park? Are they mad?"

"It's Hollywood. What do you want, bro?"

"I'd at least like to see the gun when I'm getting robbed."

"What do you care? You're not paying for it," teased Jason.

"Not the point, mate."

"Come on, let's go have some fun."

Jason and Boysie entered the legendary and much hallowed Château Marmont. The beautiful, twenty something hostess, Jasmine, they were soon to learn, was a singer-songwriter. Recognizing Jason, she became very nervous.

"Hi, J.D. May I call you J.D.? I love you, I mean INXS. You guys are amazing. Pretty Vegas. What an incredible song. You wrote that, right?"

Jason smiled graciously. "Yeah but--"

"--I knew it. Did you want in or out?"

"Sorry?"

"In or out," she pouted suggestively. "If I had to guess, I'd say out. Am I right? Yeah? I guessed it, huh?"

"Yes. Outside, please," replied Jason, casting Boysie a sideways glance.

"Sure, follow me. I can't believe I finally met you. I mean, sorry, but I've been hoping to meet you for such a long time 'cause you're so amazing. I just love your voice."

"Thanks."

Jasmine showed them to a table. "I'll send the waiter right over and if you need anything, anything at all, please let me know and I'll be happy to take care of you."

Jasmine left and Boysie observed, "Enthusiastic."

Jason was sparking a cigarette when an errant laugh burst from his mouth, extinguishing his Bick. The waiter, Greg, a pleasant guy in his twenties, came over.

"Hey, guys. What can I get'cha?"

"A bottle of Pinot Grigio, please," said Jason.

"And a menu, please," added Boysie.

"Be right back."

Boysie sank back into his chair. "This is great. Just what the doctor ordered."

"And the night has only just begun, mate," grinned Jason.

"I'm scared."

Jason looked across the patio and saw his friend, the incredible actor Jeremy Renner, sitting at another table.

"I'll be right back."

He went over and, moments later, he and Jeremy came back together. That evening, the three of them drank, ate and laughed into the early hours.

11 ~ QUE SERA, SERA

JASON WAVED GOODBYE AS HE entered the departure terminal at LAX. Boysie smiled, got into Celeste and that's when he saw it on his seat, another shiny, brand new, nine-millimeter, hollow point bullet. He picked it up, looked at it and slipped it into his suit jacket. Because of the elevated terrorist threat, heavily armed police patrolled constantly, keeping a watchful eye on anything and everyone they considered suspicious. Since 9/11, paranoia had seeped into the American psyche.

Celeste joined the traffic heading out of the airport, and it was then that Boysie noticed the black SUV following at a distance. He drove north on Sepulveda and kept it in his rear view, making sure that the driver could easily follow him down on to Lincoln Boulevard. The traffic, as usual, was heavy as they headed toward Santa Monica. Up ahead was Marina Del Rey Hospital. He made the right onto Mindanao Way and then left into the main entrance. The SUV obligingly followed and Boysie pulled up at the main drop-off, around which there were numerous people. He jammed on the brakes, screeching to a halt, attracting the attention of several armed security guards. Grinning, he climbed out and made a beeline for Paul Windsor and Meathead. They, on the other hand, didn't seem quite so pleased to see him. Using the bullet, he tapped on the driver's side window. Windsor glanced at it with a curious expression of anger-tinged humiliation and lowered the window, but couldn't quite bring himself to look at him in the eyes.

Boysie held up the bullet. "I like it. It's direct, just not very subtle."

Windsor shrugged. "Nothing to do with me."

He smiled as he dropped the bullet onto his lap. Windsor left it there. "I want you to go back to San Pedro and if I see either of you two, or anybody from Midnight Securities following me again, I'm gonna send 'em home in an ambulance."

Windsor snarled, "Don't threaten me!"

"It's not a threat. It's a fact."

"You ain't in no position to do anything, asshole."

"Subjective."

"Huh?"

"That means it's a matter of opinion," smirked Boysie.

"I know what it means," he snapped defensively.

Two of the security guards, sensing something was wrong, started heading in their direction. Boysie nodded toward them and said, "Unless you wanna trade bullets with them and the LAPD, I suggest you bugger-off."

"This ain't over."

"Now that I agree with."

Boysie headed back toward Celeste and smiled at the two approaching security guards. "Sorry, just leaving."

The larger of the two asked, "What's the problem?"

"Nothing. They just needed directions," he replied, waving at the black SUV as it drove past them and out of the exit.

"You have to move, sir, or I'll have your vehicle towed."

"No worries."

Boysie nosed Celeste up to the entrance of Marjorie's canyon home. The gate slid open and he parked on the long driveway underneath the swaying palms. Carla opened the front door and smiled.

"Señor Boysie."

"Hola, Carla. Como esta?"

"Bien, gracias. Y tú?"

She gave him an appreciative once over. He had learned long ago that women are born with an uncanny ability to completely analyze a prospective mate. Can he keep her safe? Is he confident, groomed and is he marriage material? They all did it. Just not all of them realized that they were doing it. She stepped to one side as he entered, taking off his Ray Bans.

"The señora is on the patio."

"Is she sober?"

"She only had two martinis with lunch."

"Thanks."

"Buenos noches."

"Have a good night, Carla."

"Gracias, Señor Boysie."

"You know, you can just call me Boysie. If you want, that is."

"Thank you, but out of respect, not at work."

He watched her as she smiled and left, leaving the suggestion hanging in the air.

"Is that you, Boysie?" called out Marjorie from the patio.

"Yeah."

Dressed in another flowing, silk housecoat, she was leaning against one of the brick support pillars. He joined her, and together they gazed at the setting sun, melting into the arms of El Pacifico. Sunset, commonly known in the film business as "Magic Hour," bathed everything in a warm, golden hue. Marjorie's auburn hair glowed copper red, flowing across her shoulders. The lightest hint of Eau de Violet drifted on the evening air and mixed with the perfume from the Jasmine bushes that edged her property. She glanced at him and smiled, then went back to watching the last of the sun as it slid into the ocean. That's when he realized that his heart was beating faster at the sensation of being so incredibly attracted to this woman. Normally confident, he felt nervous and licked his suddenly dry lips. He tried to not look at her in that way. She was, after all, his mum's closest friend. He swallowed and looked down at his shoes. Then at the coyote slinking along in the canyon below. Anything to distract him, but it was all to no avail. She turned and looked at him, her eyes penetrating into the very depths of his being. He was immediately aware that she knew exactly what he was feeling.

Then all life ceased. Nothing moved. No sound except the blood pounding in his ears. It was that perfect moment. The memory of which would be forever embalmed in his heart, like a butterfly in amber.

The underlying urgency of sexual desire, made sublime by the purity of a kiss. Their lips met, soft, slow and warm. Both pulled back and looked into the void that they knew was but a momentary separation. Again, they kissed. Her mouth opened and he slid in his tongue. She accepted and passion overtook hesitancy. He sat on the softly padded chaise longue and pulled her to him. Willingly, she straddled and they continued to kiss. There was no going back from this. They both knew it and both wanted it. Breath, hot, sharp, urgent. She reached down, unzipped his fly, pulled him out and moving her panties to one side, guided him into her. He was as hard as her nipples that he sucked and kissed. He had known a lot of women in his life, but the way she made love to him was something completely new. At sixty-three, she was neither shy nor remotely embarrassed. This brought out of him a depth of emotion he had seldom known. He laid her on the chaise longue, her body glistening with beaded sweat. Kissing her mouth and body, he tasted her womanhood. She shuddered, moaning in the perfumed night as he brought her to the beauty of release; then himself.

After, Marjorie, savoring the moment, remained curled on the chaise longue, wrapped in a soft Mexican blanket. Boysie stood, shamelessly naked, watching the twinkling lights of Bel Air far below. He looked over at her, smiled and sensed that she had been watching him all along. He lay down next to her and she curled into his arms.

12 ~ DEAD DOG ROVER

THE DELICATE SCENT OF MUSK incense greeted Boysie as he entered the kitchen. He felt refreshed after the shower, made a cup of Earl Grey and sat on the balcony. Santa Monica was still asleep and the pre-dawn light made everything look flat. Even the Homeless camping out on the grassy area that divided Ocean Boulevard from PCH, seemed to be enjoying, if that were possible, a lay in. A few souls were exercising, taking full advantage of living in one of the greatest cities in America. He sipped his tea and thought back to the previous night.

"How the bloody hell do I tell mum?" he said out loud.

The experience with Marjorie had been amazing and for his part, he wanted to very much see her again. He had tried to tell her about his visit to the art gallery, but she didn't want to hear it. Didn't want to spoil the moment. He finished his tea and got dressed in jeans and a Bengal Brompton, light tan, houndstooth shirt, topped-off with a soft, brown, faux suede jacket.

Boysie crossed Ocean and decided to stroll north toward Malibu, to gather his thoughts. The air was crisp and clean, tinged with slight ocean saltiness. He loved these fall moments; the smell, temperature and light breeze singing through the swaying palm fronds. Despite everything that was going on, it was good to be alive. He was oblivious to the friendly smiles from some of the girls walking their dogs, which was unusual, as he really liked dogs.

A Muslim family ambled toward him, enjoying family together time. The mother was wearing a hijab. The pretty face of their young daughter, worry free and oblivious to the ignorant stares as she played with her dog. Yelping with delight, it pulled away from her and came bounding over to Boysie, running around in excited circles. He tried to stand on the end of the leash, but lost his balance and, laughing, ended up looking like a scarecrow flapping in the breeze. The girl laughed with him, also trying to pin the leash to the ground. She and Boysie looked like they were involved in this fantastical, modern dance, centered around the happy dog.

Her head exploded like an over-ripe watermelon, spraying blood and brain matter over him and the confused pooch. Her lifeless body seemed to hesitate for a moment and then crumpled to the grass, now stained red. The second bullet screamed past his face, close enough for him to feel its energy, slamming into the tree next to him. Boysie just stood there, looking at the dead girl, her blood running down his face and into his mouth. Her parents, unable to comprehend what was happening, screamed as they cradled her.

Pandemonium.

People started running for cover, whilst others were either oblivious, or, too horrified to move. Multiple bullets started slamming into the ground around him, ricocheting off the sidewalk. The tree next to him shuddered several more times. Quickly, he crouched behind it, trying to figure out where the shots were coming from. He couldn't see the shooter or hear the crack of the rifle and, as suddenly as it had started, it stopped. The silence slammed into him, snatched his breath and held it in a vice grip of fear. It wasn't being shot at that had frozen him. It was the screaming silence. With dread clawing its way up his throat he turned, and what he saw would forever change the course of his life.

Huddled together as if peacefully asleep, with the father trying to protect them from the horrors of the world, were the Muslim family and their dog; except the oozing pool of blood spoke otherwise. Boysie leaned against the tree and broke down. Overhead, seagulls hovered and screamed. Around him, people stood and screamed. Others cried. All he could do was weep as he stared at the murdered family.

Detective Charlie Lawton looked at Boysie in a long, strained silence; jaw muscles flexing angrily as he exhaled through his nose. He sat on the chair opposite, squeezed his eyes shut and pinched the bridge of his nose with finger and thumb.

Finally, he said, "I didn't take the call on this one. I asked the captain to let me take it over, but he refused 'cause of our friendship."

Boysie, lost in misery, looked up. "Who's got it?"

"Some hot-shot who just made detective."

"Can you at least make sure he's thorough?"

The detective shrugged. "It's not my jacket, but his partner's a good cop. Very smart."

The door opened and in walked two Detectives. The female cop was the older of the two. She smiled at Boysie and held out her hand.

"I'm Detective Hampton and this is my partner, Detective Watson."

Boysie asked, "Did you find out where the shots came from?"

"Not yet."

Detective Lawton opened the door and looked at him. "Call me later?"

"Okay," he replied and watched as his friend left.

He turned his attention back to the two detectives that were watching his every move. He ignored that and said, "The angle of impact suggests that it was a roof top shooter."

Detective Watson was clearly chomping at the bit to get stuck in and show the world how clever he was. He put on his best tough guy face. "You a weapons expert?"

"No."

"Then how about you leave the detective work to us?"

Boysie considered him for a moment. Detective Watson bristled.

Detective Hampton asked, "What were you doing there?"

"What?"

"At the crime scene?" snapped Watson.

"It wasn't one when I decided to go for a walk."

Watson nodded thoughtfully as if they were playing chess and he was about to call check. "I see."

With the hot flush of annoyance surging through him, Boysie glared at the rookie cop. He, in turn, whispered something to his partner. The only snippet that he caught was, '*Al-Qaeda*.' "What did you say?" Boysie asked. The two cops turned around. "You think this was a terrorist hit?"

Watson's mouth curled into a sneer. "No."

"Then what're you on about, Al-Qaeda?"

"I was talking about people like them, you know? Not that I need to explain myself to the likes of you."

Boysie could feel his stomach tighten. "People like them? What does that mean, exactly?"

Watson gritted his teeth. "Listen, asshole, they're immigrants from some Third World, oil rich, sand box that murders innocent people in the name of Allah. Who the hell knows what they've done. Far as I'm concerned, they were most likely whacked by someone's brother or cousin as an honor killing."

Boysie stood up, towering above the two detectives. "And you're basing that on what?"

"You watch the news? These people kill each other all the time."

"So to you, they're just Rag Heads, right?"

"That's enough, Mr. Blake," intervened Detective Hampton.

Watson shrugged. "Hey, you said it. Not me."

Boysie took a sudden step toward him, balling up his fists.

Watson involuntarily jerked backward and reached for his gun, stammering out, "Back off."

"What were their names?"

Detective Watson looked like a deer caught in the apple orchard by some angry farmer. Quickly, he looked at his partner for reassurance.

Hampton tried to smile, but it just came off as a nervous tick. She gave up on that and said, "Relax, Mr. Blake."

Boysie ignored her, taking another step toward Watson. "Their names. What are they?"

Watson was beginning to sweat. "I don't need to answer you!"

Hampton put a nervous hand on the can of mace on her belt and snarled, "That's enough!"

Boysie continued to press her partner. "What're their names?"

"Sit down!" Watson stammered and started to pull his gun.

Lawton flung open the door. "Boysie!"

"Their names, you racist fuck!" he growled and took another step toward the scared cop.

"Freeze!" yelled Detective Hampton, aiming her mace at him.

Lawton stepped in between Boysie and Hampton, effectively shielding him from the impending spray. "God damn it, Boysie! Chill the fuck out!"

He looked at his friend. "I just watched that little girl get her brains splattered all over the sidewalk and this asshole wants to insinuate what, they're unwanted immigrants not worthy of his respect? He doesn't know their names and even if he did, doesn't give enough of a rat's ass to use 'em!"

"Go home. I'll call you later," said Lawton.

Boysie, his face and neck red with anger, glared at Detective Watson. Fear was running down the cops twitching face. He looked at Lawton, grabbed his blood stained jacket and left.

Fists slammed into the heavy bag like sledgehammers busting rocks. Boysie grunted from the effort as much as the steel chains that held it up on the beam. He continued to pound on it until his lungs burned and his knuckles were red raw. The gym was full but no one watched or said anything. There's a massive difference between someone who's training or when they're letting off steam. All men know the vibe. All men know not to interfere. At least if they want to keep their teeth in their mouth. Drenched in sweat, he stopped and sat down, his heart threatening to pound its way out of his chest. He couldn't get the little girl's face out of his mind, or the taste of her blood out of his mouth. He watched his own blood seeping out of his skinned knuckles. His friend, 1988 world champion boxer, Larry 'The Shadow' Musgrove, glanced at him but didn't speak as Boysie headed for the showers. He knew well enough to leave well enough alone.

The elevator door closed silently as the remnants of frankincense greeted Boysie. He drank a large glass of water and was about to pour another, when his iPhone buzzed.

"Yeah?"

Harry asked, "You alright?"

"Yeah."

"It's all over the tele."

"I suppose it must be."

"Someone must've really had it in for those Muzzies."

Boysie didn't respond and fought the urge to smash the iPhone at his brother's ignorance.

Harry added, "Mum's been really quiet all morning. At one point, I caught her crying. When I asked her what was wrong, she ignored me and carried on wiping down the bar for the umpteenth time."

"She'll live."

"That's not very nice."

Boysie hung up. He pulled on a grey Fred Perry, black pants, black shoes, black, faux calf skin jacket and left.

Outside, rolling black clouds threatened a deluge. In L.A., the rains don't usually start until January, but there was talk of another El Niño. These had been happening more frequently. A sign of climate change or perhaps just the weather behaving as it always did, despite what humans predicted or wanted. The yellow police tape vibrated in the on shore wind as numerous cops and forensic scientists swarmed the area. Boysie glanced to where the bodies had been, now thankfully removed. Soon the rain would wash away any evidence of the horror they suffered and life, at least in Santa Monica, would return to some semblance of normality.

He entered the pub that was packed with the usual Sunday punters sipping pints. Many chomped on fish and chips, steak and kidney pie,

Welsh Rarebit or English Coastal Cheddar and Branston pickle sandwiches. A football match, broadcast from England, beamed from the numerous flat screen TV's. Boysie made his way to the bar, occasionally acknowledging greetings from regulars that momentarily dragged themselves away from the game.

Harry was in his usual spot, sipping on a glass of white, nibbling on a sandwich. As fast as Summer and Autumn pulled pints, so the wait staff rushed them off to their thirsty customers. Peter, working the cash register, nodded at him.

"You alright, Boysie?"

"Yeah, thanks. She in the office?"

"She is."

He closed the door behind himself, climbed the stairs and found Toni sitting at her desk. She looked up at him and tried to smile, but her mouth just quivered.

"What's wrong?"

She took his hands in hers. "How are you?"

"I've been better."

"It's terrible."

"I can't stop thinking about 'em, Mum. Poor sods."

"Terrorists in Santa Monica. What has the world come to?"

He squinted his incredulity. "Terrorists?"

She nodded and let go of his hands. He sighed his irritation and rolled his bottom lip between his teeth. She asked, "Have you found out anything else about Michael?"

"A lot of conjecture, but nothing definitive."

"He was murdered. I know it in my heart."

"Perhaps."

"Perhaps?" Her eyes lit up and bored into him. "You know something. What is it?"

"I'm not sure yet."

"For Chris' sake! I want details!"

"Mum, it's complicated."

"Murder usually is." Boysie looked at her evenly but all his lack of response did, was to imply much more than he intended. She added, "But I know something about you."

"Many people know things about me."

They stared at each other across the void of suspicion. Exactly what she knew, or thought she knew, was unknown to him and he very much wanted it to stay that way. For a second he thought he could smell the slightest hint of Eau De Violet. Sudden panic curdled his stomach as Marjorie's face flashed before him. He smiled weakly and ran a nervous hand across his mouth.

His mum squinted inquisitively. "Why so nervous? That's not like you."

"I have to go."

"Just like your dad."

"Wouldn't know."

He opened the door and was about to escape, when she asked, "How's Marjorie?"

The most dangerous questions are often asked as an innocuous afterthought. He knew his mum well enough to know that duplicity runs in her veins, and he had to be very careful with his response.

"Worried."

"Ah."

The subtext of, "Ah," was specifically designed to imply that she knew more than she actually did, in hopes that he would tell her something. He closed the door and left.

The rolling, black clouds made good on their threat. The rain hammered down, bouncing off the sidewalk like staccato machine gunfire. Boysie stood there, mesmerized by the sound, caught in the memory of the ricocheting bullets from that morning. By the time he reached the Georgian, he was soaked through. People looked at him curiously, but he was oblivious as he got into the elevator.

He took another shower, poured himself a large glass of Beaulieu bourbon and smoked a cigar. Sitting in front of the open French windows, the occasional errant raindrop found a way under the overhang and ventured in. He called Marjorie, but she didn't pick up, so he had another glass. Detective Lawton called, but he let it roll over to voice mail. He didn't leave a message.

Boysie looked at his cigar and said out loud, "Who was the shooter and why kill the family? To cover his tracks 'cause he missed me. Fucker. I'm gonna find you."

He finished his bourbon and ordered eggs and pommes frites from the hotel kitchen, with an extra side of Bordelaise sauce. He washed it down with a bottle of Cote Du Rhone and tried desperately to forget the events of the day. It didn't work.

13 ~ NASTY BASTARD

5 AM FOUND BOYSIE POWER hiking up the trail toward the summit of Mount Hollywood. The rain had kept most hikers away, except for the hardcore few. Once at the peak, after tapping the green pole, he sat down to catch his breath as the misting rain cooled him off.

The sun was still an hour away from clocking in for the day, although it would have a hard time peeking through the rain clouds. However, the coyotes rewarded everybody with a song. This was quite something to experience as first one, in the canyon below, began to howl. Then another on the other side joined in. Another in a different canyon and so on until the whole of Griffith Park echoed with their howling choir. Amazingly, just as suddenly as it started, it stopped. It always made him smile and was an added bonus to the strenuous hike. He tried some knuckle pushups on top of one of the concrete picnic tables, but his ribs still hurt too much. Instead, he stretched and began the downward journey.

Celeste gobbled up the 10 freeway, spitting out the residue from her twin exhausts. The air, crisp and clean from the rain, whistled overhead. Miraculously, behind him, the sun smiled through the slowly dissipating clouds, casting its warming glow over the land. Santa Monica was just starting to wake up when he pulled up at the Georgian.

After the shower, Boysie made some oatmeal and took a nap. He had not intended to sleep as long as he did, but the stress from the last few days was beginning to wear on him. It was almost nine forty when he finally got up and, after checking his email, dressed and headed out.

Walking north on Ocean, he crossed Arizona and again glanced over at the crime scene. The police tape had been removed and because of the rain, all evidence that an entire family had been wiped out, had, in fact, been wiped out.

Most of the high-rise buildings that faced the Pacific were constructed in a similar architectural style, to resemble a ship's bridge; some even had bows, and 1221 Ocean Avenue was one that did. A couple were just leaving as Boysie held open the door, and walked in as if he owned the place. No one questioned him as he rode the elevator up to the roof. The access door had an alarm on it, but obviously the police had been there the day before. Someone had forgotten to reset it and remove the yellow tape. Pulling it off, he stepped onto the roof, cautiously making his way toward the seaward side of the building. He looked for spent shell casings, but Forensics had been very thorough and all had been tagged and bagged. He tried to figure out where the shooter had been. If anybody could have seen him, or her, and if so, had anyone reported it; but he already knew the answer. Most people do not want to get involved, either out of fear or apathy. He rode the crowded elevator down, lost in his thoughts.

"You're Boysie Blake, aren't you?"

"Sorry, what?"

The voice belonged to a middle-aged woman, who had obviously spent way too much time at the plastic surgeons. "You helped my niece, Janet Myers."

"I did?"

"Yeah. She spoke highly of you. Said after you spoke to her ex-husband, he never hit her again."

"Right."

The other people in the car that had been politely minding their own business, were now no longer minding it. The women smiled at him. Their men suddenly looked very defensive, as if their own manhood had been challenged. He went back to his thoughts.

Janet's aunt was having none of it. She held out her hand. "Millicent." Boysie smiled thinly and shook the offered hand. She continued, "What did you say to him?"

"I don't remember."

"Oh come on now, don't be shy." Boysie ignored her and slid his hands into his pockets. Millicent didn't like being ignored. She smarmed, "Whatever it was, it worked."

The elevator reached the ground floor and everyone poured out of the claustrophobic car. Brilliant sunshine and cool ocean air rewarded him as he left the building. Millicent hurried out behind him, holding out her business card.

"I might have a job for you." He let that, along with her card, hover in the air. In spite of this, she was not the type of woman to be easily dissuaded. "Did you hear me?"

He sighed wearily and smiled. "Darlin', I don't work for just anyone."

"I'm not just anyone and I pay awfully well."

"Have a beautiful day."

She called out after him. "You're a fool!"

He thought about that as he strode down Ocean and agreed that she might, indeed, be correct. Only time would tell. He walked into the pub and sat in his booth.

Amanda came over. "Pint?"

"Coffee, please and Welsh Rarebit."

"Okay."

His iPhone rang. "Yeah?"

"The two detectives that are handling the case have a warrant for your arrest," said Detective Lawton.

"Is that right?"

"The Coroner's made her case against you. You're to be transported to Ventura for processing."

"Not for more sexual harassment?"

"This ain't funny. I told you to back off."

"Tell 'em I'm in the pub and to give me an hour to finish my food."

Lawton hung up. Boysie called his attorney, Matt Sugarman. "How's tricks, Matt?"

"Great. You?"

"I'm about to get pinched."

"For?"

"Attempted rape."

"So the Coroner made good on her threat?"

"Apparently."

"Lawton have the jacket?"

"No, two dicks, Hampton and Watson."

"You at the pub?"

"I am."

"Okay. Don't go anywhere otherwise they might add evading to it."

"No worries."

"I'll call the DA and see what can be done."

"Thanks."

He hung up and Amanda returned with his coffee. "Harry and Crystal are at it again."

He could hear their raised voices in the bar. "Over what this time?"

"Who knows?" she shrugged wearily.

He slid out from behind the booth, took the coffee with him and went into the bar. Harry was by the dartboards. Crystal was holding a fistful of darts that she agitatedly rolled around in her hand. Boysie casually leaned against the doorjamb and sipped his coffee. Crystal glared at him.

"What the hell do you want?"

"Nothing."

Harry spun around. "I tried to get her to calm down, but she's not 'avin' it."

"He called me a rotten bitch!"

"She was flirtin' with the delivery guy."

"No I wasn't!"

"Bollox!"

Boysie had heard enough. "Knock it on the head you two."

"Don't tell me what to do!" snapped Crystal.

He looked at her and took another sip of coffee. "If you wanna continue this nonsense, then please do so in private."

"Screw you!" she screamed.

"Crystal!" yelled Harry.

"You may be scared of him, but I'm not afraid of Boysie Blake."

He took another sip of coffee. "Aren't you supposed to be at work?"

"That's none of your damn business," she replied, a little calmer.

Harry pleaded again, "Crystal, please."

Boysie finished his coffee and put the cup on the nearest table. "I'll make a deal with you. Put down the darts, calm yourself and I'll give you an exclusive."

This was too tempting of an offer. Crystal's journalistic glands were beginning to salivate. "What's the story?"

"Me, being falsely charged with attempted rape."

Silence swept through the bar like the bubonic plague. Crystal's mouth fell open and she dropped the darts onto the floorboards. "Holy shit! Deal."

"You have your camera with you?"

"Yeah, why?"

"They'll be here soon to arrest me."

Toni came out of the office. "What's going on?"

Harry blurted out, "He's getting arrested for being a pervert."

"What?"

Boysie looked at his brother, shook his head and went back to his booth. As he told a rapt audience about his visit to the Coroner's Office, a breathless Crystal snapped some shots. When he finished, they all nodded in silence, except Crystal, who was now furiously scribbling notes. She stopped and looked at him.

"I have to ask, did you, I mean, you know?"

Boysie shook his head at the stupidity of her question and said, "So if that makes me a rapist, then I'm a Monkey's Uncle."

"As Darwin said to the good Lord."

Everyone turned to look at Father Murphy, who had been standing quietly by the back door.

"Indeed," replied Boysie.

"I'll get this out asap," said Crystal.

Peter said, "Okay, back to work."

He, Amanda, Toni and the regulars who felt that as they spent so much time there, they were now part of the staff, all headed back into the bar. Father Murphy sat down opposite Boysie.

Harry slid into the booth next to him and said in a conspiratorial hush, "I didn't want to say anything in front of mum, but three really hard looking geezers came in last night."

"What did they want?" asked Boysie.

"You."

"Was one of 'em around thirty, blond?"

"How did you know that?"

"Just a hunch. What did he say?"

"He wanted to bubble in me ear, but I pretended I was too busy."

"You should've listened. Might've been interesting."

Harry looked apologetically at him. "He was a bit scary. Well hard. Know what I mean?"

"Why didn't you call me?"

"I did, but it went to voicemail."

They both knew that was a lie. Boysie let it go and said, "If they show up again, call me straight away please."

"Okay," he replied, sliding out of the booth and heading back into the bar.

The watery blue eyes of the old priest that were beginning to show the telltale whiteness of cataracts, searched Boysie's face. "It would seem invisible forces are conspiring to cement you in."

He knew that his friend was three sheets to the wind; the most likely explanation for his abstract dialogue. "Perhaps you're right."

"Who do you think it was?"

"Midnight Securities."

The thick, white, ridiculously overgrown eyebrows that had the appearance of hairy caterpillars stuck onto his forehead, suddenly became animated. The good Father flicked them up and down in dramatic emphasis. Boysie, mesmerized, couldn't help but stare. Father Murphy stopped the hypnotic dance.

"Are they the same ones that gave us them bullets?"

"That would be my guess," Boysie replied and finished the last bite of Welsh Rarebit.

Amanda delivered a pint of Guinness and a glass of Bushmills Irish whisky for the priest. He looked up at her and smiled, a sudden twinkle in his eyes. "Thank ya, darlin'."

"You're welcome, Father," she replied. "Boysie?"

"No, I'm good thanks." She went back into the bar. He added, "Have either Bergman or Martinez contacted you again?"

"No."

"Surprising, considering how badly they want the land?"

"Aye and--" Boysie's iPhone interrupted the priest. "--Excuse me please, Father."

"Sure," he replied as Boysie took the call.

"Yeah?"

Matt said, "I called the DA. You are getting pinched and he can't, or won't, help."

"Are they on their way here?"

"Yeah, any minute."

"Bail?"

"Depends who the judge is. I'm on my way to the Ventura Court House to take care of it now."

"Thanks." Boysie hung up.

Father Murphy said, "I want to put the land in your name."

"Why?"

"Bargaining chip."

"I'll be fine."

"Ya sure?"

Before Boysie could reply, six heavily armed SWAT Officers, their guns leading the way, stormed into the pub, immediately surrounding Boysie and Father Murphy.

The lead SWAT officer screamed, "FREEZE! HANDS WHERE I CAN SEE 'EM!"

Boysie remained calm with his hands flat on the tabletop. He smiled at the SWAT Officer. "Don't look now, but they're in plain sight."

Father Murphy chuckled. The SWAT officer did not. Detectives Hampton and Watson walked in and Crystal started snapping pictures. Boysie's mum, Harry and everyone from the bar, crowded into the doorway.

Detective Watson stepped forward. "Mr. Blake?"

"Can I safely assume that was rhetorical?"

"Answer the God damned question."

Father Murphy, no stranger to the police, chuckled, "I can confirm that it's him."

Detective Watson ignored the priest and glared at Boysie. "You're under arrest for rape."

Boysie called out loudly, "Suspicion of attempted." He stood up and was immediately handcuffed by a SWAT officer. As they led him outside, several eager, tabloid reporters accosted him.

"Mr. Blake, did you do it?"

"What do you have to say?"

"Are you guilty?"

He calmly smiled as they led him over to the waiting detectives police car, sitting him in the back. Hampton and Watson got in and flashing the emergency lights, pulled into traffic. They made a hard left onto 2nd Street, sped three blocks to California and took that down to PCH.

"Not so smug now, are you, tough guy?" sneered Watson. He was riding shotgun, sitting sideways, looking at him through the reinforced, steel mesh partition.

Boysie ignored him, instead looking out of the window at the glistening Pacific.

Detective Hampton, who was driving, asked, "Are the cuffs too tight?"

"No, but thanks, anyway."

"If your hands get numb, let me know."

Watson was not going to have any of this. "I don't give a crap if they cut off his circulation and he gets gangrene."

"That's not very friendly, is it?" asked Boysie.

Hampton allowed herself to smile.

"Shut up," snapped Watson.

"Have we ever met before?"

"I told you to shut up."

"Okay but it's just, you know, you seem unreasonably hostile," said Boysie.

A Harley that was coming toward them, slicing the double yellows, blew by and narrowly missed hitting them head on. "Idiot," she threw after the biker.

"So have we?" repeated Boysie.

"Not directly," replied Watson.

"Ah, the mystery unfolds. Pray tell?"

Detective Hampton glanced at Watson. "Yeah. I'd like to hear it too."

"He dated my ex."

Hampton snickered. Watson's face flushed pink.

"I did?"

Watson regained his composure. "Sarah Levine."

"Oh," said Boysie knowingly.

"Yeah, 'oh,'" asshole."

Silence filled the car as they continued northward. Detective Hampton's mouth was twitching as she fought to gain control and lost. An errant giggle leapt out, exploding with happiness at being free.

Watson growled, "It's not funny."

"No, sorry. You're right."

"Was she your ex at the time?" asked Boysie.

"No, but shortly after that she was."

"This may or not matter to you, but I didn't know she was married."

"Just another notch in your belt, huh?"

"It wasn't like that."

"How the hell was it then?"

"I met her at a party up in the Hills. We hit it off."

"Yeah, you hit it alright," snapped Watson.

"Look, mate, if it were me, I'd be pissed too; but the fact remains that I was unaware she was married. You can't exactly blame me for that."

Detective Hampton nodded. "He does have a point, Corky."

"Corky?" grinned Boysie.

"You got something to say about that to?"

"No, no. Not me, mate."

"Yeah, I didn't think so and don't call me mate."

"How did you find out?" Hampton asked.

"Never mind."

"Okay, if you don't wanna talk about it, no worries," agreed Boysie. He went back to looking out of the window, contemplating his situation.

Detective Watson took a deep breath and sighed. "STD." Boysie and Hampton looked at him. He continued, "She gave me crabs."

"Wow," exclaimed Hampton.

"She didn't get 'em from me."

Watson nodded and replied, "I know."

Boysie knew that the detective's manhood had long since taken a vacation. He felt bad for him. "It happened to me too."

"Who cares."

"I did. I was really in love with this girl. We'd been together for a while and you know, I thought she might be the 'one.' She moved in and everything was cool, but then little by little, something just started to not feel right. You know?"

"Yeah, man, I know that feeling," confirmed Watson begrudgingly.

"Turns out, she was pulling tricks."

Watson's eyes grew large. "Wow, dude. A hooker?"

"Yep. I had no clue."

"Uh, how did you find out?"

"My brother."

"Your brother?"

"We decided to have a dinner party one night. He comes over with his fiancé and the second he meets my girl, he looks like he's seen a ghost."

"Why?"

"A few months before, he and his girl had been fighting and he got mad and called an escort service. They sent her over and--"

"--Your old lady?"

"Yeah and now here she was, my girlfriend."

"Three degrees."

"Anyway, he pulls me to one side and tells me after making me promise not to lose me rag."

"Did you?"

"No, because if I had, his girlfriend would've found out. It was bad enough that my relationship was over. I didn't wanna screw theirs up too."

Detective Hampton hissed, "How gallant!"

"What could I do?"

She glared at him in the rearview. "Hey, from your perspective, nothing. From a woman's, your brother is so typical of men that can't keep their peckers in their pants. It's why the divorce rate is fifty percent."

"You're not wrong, but he's my brother."

"So what?" she retorted, adding, "his girlfriend deserved the truth."

Boysie nodded and rolled his bottom lip between his teeth. Detective Watson looked much happier. Detective Hampton did not. She pulled into the Ventura police station and killed the motor.

"Corky, go see if they're ready for us."

"Why wouldn't they be?"

"Just do it." Watson headed into the police station. Hampton opened the back door and helped Boysie get out. She looked at him and pursed her lips in the way that women can, when doubt invades. "Was any of that true?"

"Not a word."

She smiled. "Didn't think so."

Boysie nodded toward the entrance of the police station. "Shall we?"

"First, tell me why? Why would you do that after he's been such an asshole to you?"

"We've all been there. Perhaps not to the same degree, but most of us have been through heartbreak at some point in our lives. We all recover at different rates. Some not at all. He just needed a helping hand. That's all."

Detective Hampton considered Boysie for a long moment. "And the part about his wife?"

"That was true."

Allowing him the dignity of walking into the lion's den of his own volition, she smiled and un-cuffed him.

Matt Sugarman turned to the desk sergeant as they entered. "That's my client."

The desk sergeant, who looked like a twisted New York pretzel and turned out to be just as salty, replied, "How's about we book him in first?" Matt looked at Boysie and raising his eyebrows, grinned. The desk sergeant was not amused, particularly as Hampton had broken all protocol and removed his handcuffs. He glared at her. "Handcuffs! The prisoner's supposed to be handcuffed!"

Sadly for him, he had no idea who he was messing with.

"And you would be raising your voice at me, why?" she asked with a disarming smile.

"Listen, dick, you're out of your jurisdiction and we have a way of doing things up here in Ventura County."

"Really?"

"Yeah, really."

Detective Watson, who up to now had remained silent, suddenly felt the need to ride to the rescue of the damsel in distress. "Hey!" All eyes turned to the angry rookie. "Watch how you speak to her."

The desk sergeant was about to cut Watson's balls off when Hampton did it for him. "When I can't handle some empty ball bag like him, I'll ask you for your help. Until then, Rookie, shut the hell up."

Watson and the Desk Sergeant now had more in common than they realized and looked at each other in stiff competition of whose face would end up reddest. Watson lost. He remained quietly looking down at his feet. Again, Boysie felt bad for him.

Detective Hampton glared victoriously at the Desk Sergeant. "Process him then bring him up before the magistrate. And don't take all afternoon."

The Desk Sergeant looked as if he had indeed grown some, but thought better of it. He took Boysie into the back for processing.

The magistrate had a kindly face, but not a kindly bone in her body. The D.A. objected to bail and so did she, at first. Matt asked to see her in chambers and before anyone could say Kalamazoo, reluctantly, the magistrate set bail at three hundred grand. Matt posted it after going to the bank.

Outside in the late afternoon sun, a dog that had escaped its leash trotted past Boysie and Matt as they exited the courthouse. The dog looked at Boysie. He looked at the dog. Both happy to be free. Neither with any idea what the rest of the day had in store.

Matt got into his Mercedes and started the motor. "You wanna have dinner up here somewhere?"

Watching them from across the street was Detective Hampton, leaning against her police car. Watson was nowhere to be seen. She locked eyes with Boysie and smiled. He looked down at his attorney. "Have dinner wherever you want and put it on my bill."

He frowned his confusion. "What're you gonna do?" Boysie glanced at Detective Hampton. Matt followed his sightline, smiled and added, "I should've asked who."

"Whom."

"Go to hell," he grinned and gunned the motor.

Boysie crossed the street. "Detective. Still on the job?"

"No."

"Where's your partner?"

"He left."

"And where are we going?"

"My place."

"Lead the way, Kemo Sabe."

He opened the driver's door for her. "I see chivalry's not dead."

Marjorie had said the same thing at Michael's funeral. He felt a moment of sadness, but recovered and replied, "At least not with me." He went around the passenger side and called out. "Front or back?"

"That depends on if you want me to handcuff you or not."

"Later." Boysie got in the front. "So this is what it feels like."

"What feeling would that be?"

"Power."

The detective smiled and gassed the motor. As they cruised south on PCH, she asked, "Did you have any idea that I was gonna be waiting for you?"

"No."

She liked that. He could tell.

As a kid, he had learned that the last thing a woman wants is to be thought predictable. Again Marjorie flashed into his mind. Why hadn't she called him back? But he knew the answer even as he now dialed her number. "Speaking of which, I do have two calls to make."

"Sure, go right ahead."

"Thanks," he replied as he waited for Marjorie to pick up.

"Wallace residence," announced Carla.

"Is she there?"

"One second please, Señor Boysie." Carla put the phone down and he could hear her as she headed for the porch. A moment later she came back on the line, "She is not available right now."

"Thanks," he said and, annoyed, disconnected. He dialed the second number, "Mum?"

"Who else were you expecting?"

"Is everything alright?"

"Yeah. You?"

"I made bail."

"Yeah?" came her curt response.

"What's wrong?"

"You mean besides you being charged as a rapist?"

"Yeah, beside that," he responded tightly.

"Why, nothing. Should there be?"

Boysie shook his head and hung up.

Hampton asked, "You okay?"

"Family."

"Pity we can't pick our family the way we pick our friends."

"Yeah. Anyway, do I call you Detective, Ma'am, Officer or what?"

"Jackie."

"You married, Jackie Hampton?"

"Does it matter?"

"Yeah, as a matter of fact it does."

"You're charged with attempted rape and what, now your morality meter is ticking?"

"If you believed that I was guilty, I wouldn't be here, would I?" he stated.

"Are you?"

"That would be redundant."

"And so is asking me if I'm married."

Up ahead was Sycamore Cove. Boysie pointed toward it. "Do you mind pulling over please?"

"Sure," she smiled.

A cold ocean wind had begun to blow, further twisting the old, gnarled, sycamores. The park was deserted as Detective Hampton pulled into one of the spaces facing the ocean. Boysie glanced over at the booth, but there was no sign of Ranger Willis. They got out and ambled toward the beach.

She said, "I've driven past this place many times, but never actually been here."

"I used to love coming here on my own, but not so much anymore."

"Why?"

"My stepfather was killed here, not too long ago. It's sort of tainted it for me."

"Michael Santoro." Boysie looked at her quizzically. "Lawton told me. Only he said it was an accident. Maybe even suicide."

He shook his head emphatically. "It was murder and the Coroner that did the autopsy, is the same one that's accusing me of rape."

"You're suggesting what, a conspiracy?"

"You're a detective. Make up your own mind."

Hampton looked at him evenly. "That's a very serious charge."

"I haven't accused anybody of anything, yet, but you'll be the first to know when I do."

They sat at one of the wooden picnic tables. Above them, forever scavenging, opportunistic seagulls, now alerted by the presence of humans, started to congregate. Hovering on the salty air, the more that joined them, the more irritated they became.

Detective Hampton asked, "So what proof do you have that it was murder?"

"Surfers don't come here. At least not experienced ones and he was very experienced."

"That's your proof?"

"He was also involved with some dodgy business partners."

"That's not exactly gonna get a guilty verdict, is it?" she pointed out rhetorically. "Do you at least have some sort of motive?"

"A strip of land worth nine million dollars between The Bergman and Cassa Del La Martinez."

"He owned it?"

"He did but just before he was topped, he signed it over to Father Murphy."

"Father Murphy, Father - wait a second. You mean that Catholic priest that's always advocating for the Homeless?"

"Yeah."

A giggle escaped her full lips. "He now owns the land?"

"He does, yeah."

A sudden gust caught them. Hampton shivered and pulled her jacket tight. "Who was the will's beneficiary?"

"My mum."

"And she doesn't want it?"

"She doesn't care about the money. She cares about the murder."

"Nine million dollars cuts an awful lot of family ties," replied Detective Hampton.

Boysie frowned. "You suggesting she's involved?"

"No, but whoever stands to gain the most from his demise, could be."

"His ex-partners are in process of disputing the will, claiming he was mentally unstable."

"But what do they have to do with it, if they're not family?"

"Apparently there's something in their partnership agreement that Michael violated by selling the land to the priest, for a buck."

"How much?" exclaimed Hampton.

"A dollar," he replied with a shrug and a wry smile.

"Jesus." She kicked some sand around and added, "What's he plan to do with it?"

"Build a rehab."

"No wonder they're pissed."

"Indeed."

The detective looked up at the gathering seagulls, some of which had landed and were beadily eyeing them. "They remind me of The Birds."

"This whole mess reminds me of a Hitchcock movie."

"Come on, I'm cold. Let's go eat."

Boysie nodded and was about to stand, when she leaned in and kissed him. "What was that for?"

"Just because." She held his hand as they made their way back to the police cruiser. The seagulls glared at them for wasting their time and took off, screaming their annoyance. Driving back toward Santa Monica, Hampton asked, "Do you have any favorite places to eat around here?"

"Yeah, the Carbon at Malibu Beach Inn's good."

"Great. I love that place," she said cheerily.

"You eat there a lot?"

"Enough."

"Not that it's really any of my beeswax, but how does a cop afford the prices?"

"How do you?"

"I'm not a cop."

"No, you're not, but you are a suspicious character."

"Me?" he smiled innocently.

"Or as my ex, who's also English, liked to say, 'a nasty bastard. A wide boy. A villain. A man of spurious character.'"

"Thanks. I got it."

Sally, the perky, surfer-type waitress, brought them a bottle of South Australian, 2005, Claire Valley Riesling. She gave their order of seared North Atlantic salmon to the chef and sailed off to another table. The Pacific, illuminated by the moon, had turned choppy and whitecaps could be seen against its rolling darkness. Boysie took a sip of the delicious wine and peered at her across the rim.

"What?" she asked with a not so innocent shrug of her shoulders.

"I read a lot."

Bemused, she said, "And?"

Boysie took another sip, savored the wine and put the glass down. "In fact, I love to read the dictionary. I'll open it to a random page, start at the top and work my way down."

"On the John, where all men like to read?"

"Glad I'm not a stereotype." She smiled and he continued, "Providence."

"Providence?"

"The act of providing or preparing for future use or application; a making ready; preparation."

"And this is interesting, why?" Her hazel eyes were beginning to turn cold as he maneuvered the chess pieces across their dialogue.

"I'd like to flatter myself and believe that with us, it was the Blind Hand Of Fate. You know, two people meet and there's sparks?"

"I thought so."

"But the truth is, that you're not divorced and, in point of fact, you know more about this whole mess then you would like me to believe."

"Wow. Are you suspicious, or what?"

"How's the food?"

"Screw you."

"Was that a denial?"

"Yes, I'm still married, but separated. My ex is a great guy, just not a great guy for me. Like you, he didn't trust me and let me tell ya, that wears out pretty fast. So thanks for dinner and kiss my ass."

Boysie's tongue probed her hot, willing mouth. Her breath came in short, sharp rasps as she pushed up against him, feeling him hard against her. They stopped kissing and he gently placed his large, bony hands on her shoulders and held her away from him.

She frowned, wiped her mouth and asked, "What's wrong?"

"Nothing. It's not you, it's me."

"I don't understand." He took a couple of steps back and slid his hands into his pockets, signaling that there would be no more intimacy, at least not on this night. "Contrary to what people may think or say about me, I'm not a promiscuous guy. Sort of old fashioned, really."

She sat on the bed and looked at him.

He continued, "I believe I'm involved with someone, or at least I thought I was and now I'm not sure and the signs are that we might not be, but until I am sure, I don't want to mislead anyone, myself included."

She crossed her legs and nodded thoughtfully. "I can respect that."

"Thanks."

"You do realize that this just makes me wanna bed you all the more?"

He smiled and headed for the door. "I was right, wasn't I?"

"About?"

"Come on, Lawton bubbled me to you, didn't he?"

She frowned and looked down at her shoes as she considered the question. "You and him've been friends for a long time, he tells me."

"Uh-huh."

"A couple of years ago, we were undercover, downtown L.A. Someone was decapitating homeless women. It went bad and he saved my life."

"That was you? He told me about this."

Detective Hampton opened the top buttons on her blouse, revealing any ugly scar across the right side of her neck. "I was passing this alley just off Third."

"Skid Row."

"Yeah and I catch a glimpse of something. Lawton was nearby, checking out someone else. So I radio him and make my way into the alley. I see this guy, he had to be three hundred pounds of, 'Don't know who the hell I am,' dribbling over something in the rat infested garbage. It's a woman. Another victim. He's holding her head back, slicing through her neck like he's cutting a steak. I pull my piece and yell for him to freeze, only I don't see his accomplice in the dark. Next thing I know, he's smacked me across the head with a brick and I'm rolling on the ground with him and now I'm in the fight of my life with both of 'em. The one that jumped me, holds me from behind while the other begins slicing me above the carotid artery. You know, like one of those Taliban videos?"

Boysie nodded.

"I'm screaming and kicking him enough that he doesn't manage to penetrate my neck too deep. There's blood spurting everywhere and,"

Hampton paused, sighed and continued, "and I'm trying desperately to avoid the blade that he's trying desperately to stick in me. I start to black out and that's when Lawton appears outta nowhere and pumps two in his head. Then pops the accomplice right in the face. Two down and I'm still breathing. I would've been dead if it wasn't for him."

"Jesus."

"I was in hospital for a week and when I got out, I couldn't work for a while. I fell into a depression and things got bad in my marriage. You don't get to make detective and not learn how to tussle. I've been in some bad scrapes and have mostly held my own, but nothing quite like that."

"That must've been hell."

"Yeah, it was."

He held her for a while and they listened to the surf rolling onto shore.

Eventually, she said, "Could you, I mean, would you please stay the night? I won't try anything and we can keep all our clothes on. I just don't wanna be alone."

He looked at her and instead of the tough, street hardened cop, he saw a vulnerable little girl. "Sure," he replied and kissed her softly on her forehead.

14 ~ CASTLE GANDOLFO

IT WAS EIGHT A.M. WHEN Boysie pulled up at Marjorie's gate and pressed the buzzer. He smiled into the camera and her disembodied voice slid out of the intercom.

"Yes?"

"Open the gate please, Marj."

The gate remained closed and he remained where he was. Stalemate. He stared into the camera and a few moments later, it quietly slid open. He drove Celeste up to the front door, killed the motor and climbed out. Marjorie drifted around the side of the house.

"Bon jour," she slurred.

He glanced at the martini in her hand. "Kick starting the day?"

"Every day," she noted and took a sip.

The sunlight was just beginning to probe its way across the hilltop. It found something to gleam off, the nine-millimeter bullet that was rolling around in the bottom of her glass. She looked at it and giggled drunkenly.

"How many of those have you had?"

"Bullets or martinis?" Dismayed, he shook his head. This irritated her, so she poured the rest of the drink down her throat and glared defiantly at him. "You do not lecture me."

He followed her as she drifted around to the back patio. "I'm not, but I am curious why you haven't returned my calls."

A sudden sadness swept over her and an errant tear leaked out, tumbling its way down her normally composed face. She wiped it off and unsteadily sat down on one of the wicker chairs. "What happened the other night, what we did, was both beautiful and wrong."

"Wrong?" he asked, surprised.

"You should be with a woman more your own age."

"Isn't that for me to decide?"

"Not if I'm the woman."

"We're consenting adults and being with you was amazing. I'm not sorry."

Another tear leaked out and she smiled, trying hard to control her lips that were beginning to tremble. He reached forward to wipe it away and she pulled back. Cheated of the touch of her warm skin, he rolled his bottom lip between his teeth.

Her Savannah accent and societal constraint kicked in. She moved her head back, adjusting her body into what she obviously felt was a more regal stance. "Your mother is my closest friend and would be very embarrassed to consider our illicit affair."

"My mother is in no position to judge anyone as you, of all people, should know."

"Yes, she's had indiscretions and with younger men, but you're her son and despite how I feel, it cannot happen again."

"This bloody well sucks."

"After today, we never speak of this again. Promise me?"

"Is that what you really want?"

"Yes."

"You're sure?"

"I am."

Boysie shook his head as he tried, in vein, to fight the sense of loss sweeping over him. She, in turn, was doing the same, but with a lot more self control. "Alright, if that's what you want, then that's what we'll do."

"Thank you."

He picked up her glass and retrieved the bullet. "Has Gandolfo contacted you?"

"Not unless he's switched business cards," she said pointedly looking at the bullet.

From his pocket, he retrieved its two companions. "Father Murphy was donated one in his collection plate. Two were left for me in my motor on separate occasions."

"In case you didn't get the message the first time?"

"Apparently."

"It would seem we're part of an exclusive club," she drawled.

"Do you think Gandolfo did this, or at least had it done?"

"I have known David for many years and can tell you that he is a very secretive man. Not only is he in the top echelon of Hollywood power brokers, but, he also has a lot of very powerful friends in Washington."

"CIA friends?"

She nodded. "His fingers run long and deep into many, many pies. Not all of them, if any, are sweet."

"That would explain why the FEDS aren't involved and that he doesn't really seem to care about losing a hundred and fifty mill."

"Are you any closer to resolving the issue?"

"I'm working on it."

She tried to smile, but it was to no avail. Clearly, the stress of possibly losing everything that she had worked so hard for over the years, plus the pressure of their intimacy, had taken a heavy toll.

"I made you a promise that I would fix this mess, Marjorie. I'll take care of it. Believe me."

She rubbed her forehead in the way that people do when worry envelops them, and stood up. "I'm tired, Boysie. I'm going to bed."

He nodded and watched as she drifted past him. The sadness he felt was as oppressive as the heady mixture of her Eau De Violet and gin scented breath. Together, they wrapped cloying arms around him. He would always remember that feeling and that scent.

Opening the front door, she stopped and stared at him. In the silence, their emotions were palpable and conveyed more than words ever could. Tears filled her eyes as he wandered past her and, now outside, turned to look at her. She closed the door, leaving him alone in the early morning still. The buzzing of a fat bumblebee drew his eyes as it seemingly defied physics, flying from flower to flower. So, too, it had seemed, that the love he felt for her should have defied the odds. Only now the pain of loss, would forever live in his heart.

David Gandolfo wasn't prepared to see Boysie leaning against the side of his E-Type Jaguar, blocking the end of his driveway. He applied the brakes on his mid-night blue, Bentley Mulsanne and stopped without effort. The only sound, the wetness of rubber as the tires gripped the blacktop. Confused, he watched as Boysie pushed himself up off Celeste and languidly, dragged an appreciative index finger along the Bentley's front fender. Upon reaching his window, he tapped it gently. Flustered, Gandolfo lowered it.

"What're you doing here?"

Boysie paused and fought hard to control the anger clawing its way up his throat. "Have you seen Avatar?"

"What?"

"You know, the James Cameron flick? It's really good, mate."

"This is why you're here, to talk about a movie?"

"Not just any movie."

"I'm sorry, but I'm late for a meeting."

"You should see it in 3D. It makes things pop out from the screen and-_"

"--I know what 3D is," he snapped tersely.

"It really puts it in your face."

Gandolfo, beginning to sweat, inched his hand toward the gun that he kept hidden by the side of his seat. Boysie smiled with all the warmth of a cobra about to kill its prey. Gandolfo thought better of it and retracted his hand.

"Boysie, why don't we meet at the Ivy for lunch and we can talk about whatever you want."

"Cameron really hit it out the park this time. The premise of things not being what they seem is not new to Hollywood, but his presentation is really unique. Groundbreaking. Know what I mean?"

Gandolfo wiped the beads of sweat away from over his mouth. Boysie's blue eyes, as cold as glacial ice, bored into him. Abruptly, he turned and got back into Celeste. He kicked the motor to life and drove off along the leafy, secluded lane toward Sunset Boulevard. David, shaking in a puddle of his own fear, leaned back and tried to calm down.

Boysie was sitting in his booth at the back of the pub, sipping on a pint of Newcastle, when Gianni strolled in and sat down.

"Morning," he said with a grin.

"Thanks for being so prompt."

"Aye, no worries." He cocked his head slightly to one side and asked, "You alright?"

"I've been better."

"Anything you wanna talk about?"

"No."

Gianni looked around at the near empty pub. "It's quiet this morning."

"For now, thankfully."

Gianni's cell phone buzzed and he pushed it over to voicemail. "So what's up?"

"I've ordered you a pint and the Queen sized breakfast."

"That's very nice. Thank you."

"Tell me what you know about Valentine and Gandolfo."

Amanda arrived with Gianni's pint and his breakfast. She placed them down and glanced at Boysie. "You okay?"

"Yeah, I'm fine."

She smiled at Gianni. "Need anything else or you good right now?"

"This is great. Thanks."

Harry, with a glass of white wine in hand, drifted up behind her.

Amanda asked, "You want any Coleman's?"

Harry piped up, "Of course, Amanda, he'd love to dip his banger into something hot."

Boysie, sipping on his pint, almost choked. Amanda glared at Harry, who slapped on a stupid, drunkard's grin and wobbled away.

Gianni, trying hard to remain composed, smiled sweetly up at her. "Please. That'd be fantastic."

"I'll be back in a sec," she replied and sallied forth to obtain the mustard.

Gianni was really annoyed. "Your brother's a tosser."

"Yeah, sorry."

Amanda placed down the pot of mustard, smiled at Gianni and went over to another table. He watched her and took another sip. "She's a lovely girl though."

"Ask her out. She's single."

"No, I dunno."

"Are you dating someone?"

"No."

"Then what's the problem?"

"We're not here to discuss my non-existent love life."

"Her last name's Fitz," grinned Boysie.

"She's Scots?"

"Never asked her, but sounds like it, or maybe French."

Gianni contemplated this and when he had contemplated it enough, he said, "Anyway, to answer your question, I did hear this story once and I don't know if it's true or not, about how someone, some speculate Valentine, screwed Gandolfo out of the Da Vinci Code." He took a sip of beer and continued, "It was around the time that it was still a galley. You know, an unpublished manuscript?"

"I know what a galley is."

"Anyway, a bidding war had started and suddenly Gandolfo makes this outrageous offer. It's so much money that everyone cries foul."

Boysie looked bemused. "How ironic that in a bed of snakes, the one with the sharpest fangs is deemed to be out of order."

"Bidding wars get ugly, mate."

"Moving on."

Gianni nodded. "So the story goes that the agent handling the deal, gets a call from someone in the CIA, who basically tells him that if Gandolfo wins, he has absolutely no intention of ever making the film and, will use his wealth and power to ensure that the book never gets published."

Boysie scratched the back of his head. "Why?"

"I dunno, exactly, but apparently he's an ultra-conservative Catholic with--"

"--Ties to the Vatican."

"How did you know that?"

"Just a guess."

"Maybe you should become a detective."

"Maybe you should eat your breakfast."

Gianni grinned and placed some of the mustard on his plate, dipped a piece of sausage into it and took an appreciative bite. "Mm. There's nothing like bangers and Coleman's."

"So the deal never happened?"

Gianni swallowed. "At least not with him."

"It's a good book. Very intriguing premise."

"Aye and one of the few times a movie didn't screw it up."

Boysie took a sip of beer. "CIA?"

"It was all a bit Cold War. Freaked a lotta people out."

"So who put the bubble in?"

Gianni replied after an appropriately dramatic pause, "Your stepdad."

"What?"

"That's what I heard. I don't know if it's true or not. Remember, I also heard it was Valentine."

"That sounds more likely to me. I mean, when has Michael ever had dealings in the business?"

"I dunno. That's a question for your mum."

"Yeah, you said that right."

Harry wobbled past them, another full glass of wine in his hand. Gianni put down his knife and fork. "What's the deal with him lately?"

"I dunno. He's drinking more and more."

"Is he still going out with Crystal?"

"Far as I know," replied Boysie.

"I saw her the other day in Beverly Hills."

"Oh, yeah?"

"She was sitting with this young Hollywood type looking all gooey eyed. I think he's got a hit TV series, or something."

"Did she see you?"

"No, or at least I don't think she did." Gianni's cell phone buzzed again. "Sorry, mate, it's Shannon."

"Tell her I said, '*Allo.*"

He stood up, "Will do."

Boysie took another mouthful of Newcastle as Gianni went outside. Harry swayed out of the kitchen, looked at Boysie, gave him the finger and came over to the booth, sitting down heavily.

"What's going on with you?" asked Boysie.

Harry was having a hard time focusing. He put the glass down with a thud, slopping wine over the white tablecloth. He angrily barred his teeth at Boysie. "You're a bastard."

"Oh, yeah?"

"You can get women anytime you want."

"Actually, that's not true."

"Bollox. You snap your fingers and they just fucking fall at your feet."

He went to take another drink and Boysie slipped two fingers onto the base of the wineglass, keeping it firmly where it was.

"Let it go," Harry snarled drunkenly.

"Keep your voice down," growled Boysie.

His puffy face was creased with angry red lines. "Gimme my bloody wine!"

Trying to ignore the growing argument, embarrassed silence started to spread across the few customers that were there.

"Calm yourself, Harry."

He sneered. "Or what? You'll kick me head in?"

Trying to reason with a drunk is an exercise in futility. He let the glass go. Harry grinned triumphantly and lifted it to his mouth, sucking down the wine.

Gianni hurried back in. "Sorry, but I've gotta go put out a fire."

"Everything alright?" asked Boysie.

"Aye, it'll be fine. The stars agent of one of my films wants more money, or he won't do the show, except he's not worth it anymore."

"Go handle it, mate."

"You can bet on that."

Harry finished his wine and looked at Gianni. "Amanda likes you, you know? You should shag her."

"Shut up," snapped Boysie.

Harry spat alcohol laced fury at his brother. "Don't tell me to shut up."

"I'll talk to you later," Gianni said and left, glaring at Harry.

Boysie turned his attention to his brother. "You need to go and lay down."

"Fuck you!"

SMACK! Boysie slapped him across the face. Not hard, but hard enough to get his attention. Stunned and humiliated, despite the booze, he just sat there. His cheek, reddening and his bottom lip quivered as if he wanted to cry.

Despite feeling sorry for his brother, Boysie leaned in on him and growled very quietly, "I've had enough of your boozing and constant shit stirring, and embarrassing Amanda crossed the fucking line. Now go into the office and sleep it off."

"But--"

"--Now."

"Okay," he replied meekly and stood up.

Peter was hovering by the back bar and came over. "Come on, Harry."

"Thanks, Pete," he said and cast a mournful look at Boysie, and went with Peter up the stairs.

Toni walked in, glanced at Boysie and turned away. In no mood for her nonsense, he said, "Sit down."

"Don't tell me--"

"--Do it."

She glowered at him and sat. "What do you want?"

"He's going into rehab."

"Rehab?"

"You deaf?"

"I don't think so."

"Then shut up and listen."

"Don't talk to your mother like that."

"You birthed me but you've never been a mother."

Tears began to fill her eyes. "You've always hated me. Ever since your father--"

"--My father?"

"You've always blamed me for what happened," she sniffed. Tears as fake as veneer, sliding down her face.

"I don't wanna talk about that right now."

"You don't love me." She picked up a napkin and blew her nose, leaving the trail of tears.

All too familiar with her injured bird act, his patience was fast running out. "I'm not gonna sit by and watch my brother drink himself to death. Understand?"

She snarked, "You're the one that's always enabled him, letting him be the bar manager."

"We're both guilty of that, but no more. I'm done with it. So are you." He waved her away like an annoying fly. "You can go." She sat there and began to smirk. He felt like slapping her too, but restrained himself. She was, after all, still his mum. "What?" he asked through gritted teeth.

Triumph glistened in her eyes as she laid down her trump card. "Gandolfo is suing Marjorie for the money."

"When did this happen?"

"The letter from his attorneys arrived this morning. She's terrified, so what are you gonna do about it and don't tell me you're handling it. I see no progress."

"I can't tell you everything that's going on. You're just gonna have to trust me."

"When? When will all this be resolved?"

He shrugged. "I don't know."

"I've already given up on Michael. His killer will never be brought to justice, will he, Boysie Blake?"

He sat back and considered her for a long moment. Suddenly aware that this part of the pub had quietly emptied out, he realized that she had played him perfectly. "Do you know anything about Michael having stopped Gandolfo from buying a manuscript?"

"Which manuscript?" she asked innocently.

"There's more than one?"

"I don't know of any."

"Really?"

"Really."

"Keep Harry away from the wine."

She smirked and watched him leave out the back door.

Father Murphy, alone in the church, was lighting the frankincense in the thurible, readying for evening mass. Fingers of incense smoke drifted upward, enveloping the priest like embalming fluid. Boysie let the huge, ornately carved, wooden front door of the church close with a boom. Startled, the priest glared at him.

"What the hell's wrong with you, Boysie?" The marble and granite expanse echoed his voice.

Boysie, his face set hard enough to bust bricks, said through gritted teeth, "Come over here." Father Murphy put down the matches and went over. "At what point where you gonna bubble me about Michael, Gandolfo, the manuscript and the Vatican?"

Father Murphy's face sank. "I was waiting for the right opportunity."
"It's now."

An elderly nun, Sister Marguerite, drifted out of a side door, carrying some fresh flowers. She smiled at Boysie and began replacing the older ones that had been consigned to die on the altar. Father Murphy pointed toward the front doors. Once outside, he lit a cigarette and looked apologetically at Boysie.

"Nuttin' in life is as it seems. Ya ought to know that."
"Save it."

The priest knew better than to try and bamboozle him. He blew out a lungful of smoke and flicked the butt toward the curb. A spray of embers showered the sidewalk.

"Michael," he hesitated, "he was given to fits of irrationality."

"Yeah, and now he's dead and you, Father, know a lot more than you're telling. And I bloody-well wanna know why."

"It's not that simple, Boysie."
"Bollox."

The priest shrugged, indicating his reluctance to talk about it anymore. However, Boysie knew just how to pry it out of him. "You're eighty-sixed from the pub until you tell me what's going on."

Father Murphy was horrified. "Ya can't be serious?" Boysie turned on his heel and started to walk away. "Okay, wait. Stop!"

He kept on walking.

"Jeasus! Alright!" He stopped and turned. The distressed priest went over to him, looking furtively over his shoulder. "You're a cold man, Boysie Blake."

"And you're a sneaky old bastard."

The priest grinned sheepishly, looped an arm through his and led him toward the beach. "How did you find out?"

"A rumor introduced itself to me."

The priest nodded. "As you know, Michael, Martinez and Bergman were partners. What you don't know is that Michael owned all of the land."

"Wait. You mean the land their hotels are built on?"

157

"Aye. He'd leased it to 'em for ninety-nine years, with a buy-out percentage deal if they ever were of a mind."

"So for the going market rate, they could buy the land off him, but he would still own a percentage?"

"In perpetuity."

"Smart."

Father Murphy nodded slowly. "Michael kept the center piece of land for himself. He was going to build something or other, a spa, I think, but Bergman got pissed off and wanted him to give him the land for the same deal. Michael said no, of course, and as things got more and more tense between them, he decided to just sit on it and let it become an eye-sore to spite Bergman."

"And how does the manuscript fit into this?"

"Ya know how Hollywood functions, everybody knows everybody. At least those that have any kind'a heat. One of his friends was an agent--"

"--The one that handled the deal?"

The priest nodded. "Aye and it was him that told Michael about it. He knew it was gonna be a best seller and wanted it for himself. So he asked him for a loan."

"And Michael gave it to him?"

"He would have, only Gandolfo outbid everybody."

"But I heard he lost out on the buy," said Boysie.

"He did, for two reasons. One, when Michael agreed to back the agent, he did so with a million dollars which sent a shock wave around the town. It's illegal for an agent to purchase an intellectual property because that makes 'em producers, even though it goes on all the time. So when Gandolfo came back with two million, Dan Brown knew something was rotten in Denmark. He's nobody's fool. He writes about conspiracies and when the rumor started about the CIA and all the rest of it, he withdrew the manuscript."

"You know this first hand?"

"No. I heard it from Michael, of course."

"So none of that could be true."

The priest shrugged. "It's L.A. Who knows for sure."

Boysie was silent for a moment as they crossed over Ocean Avenue; the crosswalk beeping out its imitation cuckoo call, urging everyone to hurry. They leaned against the concrete railing, staring out at the surf breaking on the deserted beach. A crescent moon hovered in the darkness and for a moment, one might almost have believed in fairy tales. Almost.

"How does the Vatican fit in?"

"The cold slap of irony, huh?" replied the priest with a twinkle in his watery blues.

"Just answer the question."

"Obviously, they didn't want the book published or a film made. So they bank-rolled Gandolfo's bid."

"Bugger me." Boysie mulled that for a moment, "And the CIA did want it made?"

"No. The Anglicans did."

Boysie stared at the priest and suddenly the penny dropped. "They wanted to keep their ten percent vig."

"Now ya got it."

"And how many are there?"

Father Murphy raised his eyebrows. "Seven hundred million, give or take."

"And at ten percent tithing, that's an awful lotta shekels."

"From your mouth, to God's ears," the priest chuckled, pulling his black frock coat tight against the evening chill.

"But I read how the Archbishop Of Canterbury said he didn't have a problem with it."

Father Murphy nodded. "Us and the Anglicans had been under the same roof for fifteen hundred years. But they split from the Vatican and formed the Church Of England and various other factions. Over the years, there's been a lotta in-fighting and recently a lotta've 'em became disillusioned with the admittance of female bishops and gays."

"After everything, everybody's suffered, you'd think they'd know better than to be so bloody prejudiced."

"I'm not here to debate the whys and wherefores of the church wit'cha, Boysie. Especially as you're a lapsed Catholic yaself."

"So the CIA had nothing to do with it?"

"Just a scare tactic. Unless someone high up in the Church Of England had a whisper in the Queen's ear and she had a whisper in someone's ear at MI5 and--"

"--They bubbled in someone's ear at Langley."

"Unlikely, but ya never know," offered the priest.

"So someone wanted to embarrass the Vatican, effectively blocking the potential defection of millions of Anglicans, into becoming Catholics?"

"Aye, in a nutshell."

"And the Da Vinci Code made that possible?"

"There's a few other incidents of late that come to mind, but me cloth prevents me from saying 'em."

"Do me a favor, squire."

"As her ladyship said to the gardener."

Boysie grinned. "Anyway, the book came out in two thousand and two. So what am I supposed to believe here, that Nostradamus predicted all this?"

Father Murphy grew red with anger. "What the hell does that blasphemer have to do with it?"

"Exactly."

"You're missing the point."

"Then enlighten me."

Father Murphy drew himself up. "The decision to offer Anglicans an open door wasn't made overnight. It took years. Somehow it got out so when Angels and Demons was published, the Cardinals had their knickers in a twist."

"Thanks for the visual."

"But they figured it would die down. Then along comes the Code and all hell breaks loose and the decision was made to hold back on the offer."

Boysie chuckled sarcastically. "Bad publicity effecting the Catholic brand."

"Are ya done?"

Boysie nodded that he was indeed, done.

Father Murphy muttered something under his breath, took out his hip flask, had a nip and continued, "So the film does good but the Holy See plays up negative publicity, using bloggers all over the world to write more bad reviews, trying desperately to discredit the book and the film."

"But it had the reverse effect."

"Aye, much to the church's chagrin because the Anglican Council and the Vatican might be friends on the surface, but are deadly enemies underneath."

"And Gandolfo's right in the middle." Father Murphy nodded. Boysie put a foot up on the first rail and stared out to sea, watching the distant lights of passing tankers on their way to San Pedro. He looked at his old friend and said, "In the end, who did buy the rights to the Da Vinci Code?"

"Not sure. Ron Howard directed it, I think."

"Yeah, that's right, he did."

"I doubt ya man there had anything to do with it."

"I dunno. Gandolfo may be many things, but he's not stupid."

Father Murphy took another belt of whisky and offered the flask to Boysie. He took a sip, handed it back to him and said, "I'll bet you a pound to a penny that with Michael outta the way, the land would've become theirs by default in their partnership agreement."

"Aye, that's right."

"You knew this? You knew that they had motive?"

"I did."

"And by selling it to you for a dollar, he safe-guarded himself."

The priest wiped an errant tear away from his grey whiskers. "In a manner of speaking, I s'ppose."

"But doesn't church law dictate that any of its servants that receives a gift, it automatically becomes the property of the Church?"

"It does."

Boysie laughed. "So the Church now owns the land?"

"They don't know about it."

"That's not very honest of you, Father."

"It is so long as I don't sign the bill of sale."

"So if I understand correctly, you would transfer it back to him when the time was right?"

The priest shook his head, had another nip of Ancestral Mist and said, "No. The idea was for me to transfer it to you and then at the right time, you'd transfer it back to him."

"I see. Use me to keep them at bay." The priest nodded. Boysie considered this for a moment and said, "Why play me like that when all he had to do was ask?"

"It wasn't my idea, Boysie."

He was suddenly grim as he rolled his bottom lip between his teeth. "My mother's."

The priest sighed and looked away. "Aye."

"And what're the odds that makes Gandolfo their silent partner?"

This startled Father Murphy, who wiped a shaking hand across his grey whiskers and said, "Jeasus. I never even thought about that."

"Do you remember the name of the Castle that the Pope stays at during the summer months?"

"Gandolfo."

He nodded slowly. "Castle Gandolfo."

The priest looked at him in the pressuring silence. "You do realize what you're suggesting here, Boysie?"

"I do."

"I always thought it was just a coincidence."

"There are no coincidences, mate." Boysie returned to watching the slow rise and fall of the distant tanker lights. Finally, he added, "Mum knew this all along and said nothing. I can't believe it."

"She knew about the land, but not the manuscript."

"And what about you? Why didn't you tell me all this before?"

"Because Marjorie made me promise not to."

"Marjorie?"

"Aye. When those bullets got left for us, I told her that if you ever started to figure it out, I'd have to tell ya."

"But what's she got to do with this?"

Father Murphy paused, took a deep breath and said, "She and Gandolfo used to be married."

Boysie shook his head, trying to wrap his mind around this new revelation. "Of course they did and if the top of your head popped off and Saint Peter jumped out singing Yankee Doodle Dandy, that wouldn't surprise me either."

"You can be a blasphemous bastard, Boysie."

He looked at the priest, swallowed his anger and walked away. Father Murphy had another nip of ancestral mist and leaned against the railing, contemplating.

15 ~ BAIT AND SWITCH

DETECTIVE HAMPTON PULLED HER UNMARKED to the curb, placed the police placard on the dash and got out. Even though it was a red zone, no one was going to issue any tickets to a cop. She walked into the Georgian and over to Concierge.

Jimmy looked up and froze. The smile fell off his face and flapped around on the desk, gasping for air. "How may I help you?" he asked thinly.

The detective grinned her recognition. "Jimmy The Fingers, right?"

"Sorry?"

"Come on, Jimmy, my partner and I banged you away for a three to five when I was working Robbery, a few years back."

Panic creased his brow and he whispered hoarsely, "Please, I need this job."

"Relax, I'm not here to bust your chops. I'm going up to see Mr. Blake."

"Oh, okay. Is he expecting you? Sorry."

"He is."

"No disrespect. I have to ask, that's all. It's my job."

Detective Hampton pointed to the elevator. "That one?"

"Yes, ma'am."

The ornate brass door opened silently and Boysie smiled at Detective Hampton. "'Allo, darlin'." He kissed her on the cheek.

"That was a disappointment," she pouted.

"Glass of wine? It's an incredible zin, made by some friends of mine, Robert and Pat Nadeau, up in Paso Robles."

"I'd love to, but I'm on the clock."

"So this is an official visit?" He poured himself a glass of the deep ruby red wine.

The detective sank down on the sofa, crossed her legs and said without blinking, "It seems you have a natural talent for pissing people off."

"Who've I annoyed this time?"

"Besides me?"

"Didn't realize I had, but yes." He took a sip of wine and sat opposite her.

"David Gandolfo." Boysie smiled. She continued, "It seems you paid him a visit this morning and threatened him."

"Anything else?"

"He was granted a restraining order."

"Okay," replied Boysie indifferently.

"Okay?"

"This wine is called Critical Mass." He laughed and added, "Seems quite appropriate, considering."

The intermittent twitching of her foot displayed her growing annoyance. "Lawton warned me that you can be a hard-head."

Boysie put down the glass of wine. He sat next to her and brushed a curl away from her eyes. "You didn't come here to tell me what I already know, did you?"

She tried to hold his gaze, but couldn't and shyly looked away. "No," she whispered.

"Then tell me why you did," he asked gently.

She looked at him, her breath coming in short, expectant rasps. Boysie kissed her and she melted into his arms, and to her, the kiss lasted forever. He stood up, held out his hand, which she willingly took, and led her into the bedroom. Loneliness can be the fuel of passion and their lovemaking was a testament to this. Release came quickly, as it sometimes does, and flowed from her in what felt like a never-ending stream. They lay entwined in their exhaustion; bodies glistening in the candlelight. As they fell asleep, Detective Hampton couldn't remember having felt so safe in a long, long time.

Ramon, waxing and polishing the nineteen sixty-eight E-Type Roadster that Steve had backed out of buying, watched as Boysie pulled up in Celeste. He got out, grabbed his grey silk sports jacket and slipped it on.

"Morning."

"Hola, Señor Boysie," replied Ramon.

"Where's Pedro?"

Ramon shrugged and lowered his eyes suspiciously. Boysie went into his restoration facility and found Jose working on a black on black, bone stock original, nineteen sixty-one E-Type.

"Where you been, Boss?"

"Busy. Everything alright?"

"Not too many customers."

"Recession has a way of doing that, mate."

"Sí." He picked up a grey rag and wiped the oil off his hands.

Boysie watched him do this and asked, "What's going on? What's with all the long faces?"

"ICE snatched up Pedro yesterday. They got him locked up downtown."

"Where the hell did they grab him?"

"Here."

Anger surged though Boysie. "The INS came here?"

Jose nodded, "Semone."

"But he had a Green card."

"I'm sorry, Boss, but it was a fake he bought in East Los."

"Then this might be one problem I can't solve."

"They gonna give you plenty shit, man. Be careful."

Boysie nodded, "Why didn't you call me?"

"For what? You can't fight the INS. Too much bullshit on the news, man," Pedro said and shrugged his acceptance, wiping his hands again on the oily rag.

There was no point in saying anything else. Boysie got back into Celeste and drove away. "It Comes Down To This," a song from Jason's latest CD, pounded out of the stereo. He pulled up to the red light, lost in the music, and didn't notice the bright yellow Ferrari or its driver, Collagen Lips, cruise slowly to a stop next to him. It didn't matter, she noticed him and her overpriced face twisted into ugly knots. Sitting next to her was her tattoo-covered boyfriend; a twenty something, wannabe Hollywood tough guy.

She said loudly, "Hey, look, it's that asshole I told you about."

Tough Guy snarled, "Is that right?"

She nodded and he glared at Boysie. "Yo, fuck-face!"

Boysie pointed innocently to himself. "Moi?"

"Yeah, you, dickhead. Pull the fuck over!"

The light blinked green and Boysie stomped on the gas. Not to be humiliated again, Collagen Lips screamed the yellow Ferrari off the line and was instantly on his tail. Tough Guy was flipping him off, angrily pointing and yelling for him to pull over. He did better than that. He took the next left and pulled into the alley behind the stores on Arizona Avenue. He turned Celeste off and leaned against her, waiting for the yellow Ferrari to appear. The high-pitched whine of its powerful engine announced its imminent arrival moments before it nosed into the alley. A smirking Collagen Lips turned the motor off, blocking the exit. Tough Guy leapt out, as well as anyone could leap out of a Ferrari and, glaring at Boysie, pulled off his tank-top, revealing a muscular body entirely covered in ink. He tweaked his neck as if cracking it in preparation for combat.

"I'm gonna fuckin' beat the fuck outta you, motherfucka for fuckin' disrespecting her!"

"Could you say that again without the curse words please? It's a bit difficult to understand you."

Tough Guy hesitated, shook his head in disbelief, bowed up and stepped forward,. "Fuck you--"

CRACK! He didn't see the lightning fast, hard left hook, but his jaw felt it. Tough Guy buckled and sank to the ground, out cold. Boysie calmly walked over to Collagen Lips, whose face twitched fearfully as she tried desperately to start the Ferrari. He leaned in and grabbed her hand, forcing it away from the car keys and removed them. She sat frozen, trying unsuccessfully to stop her twitching face that now resembled a bowl of vibrating Jell-O.

"What's wrong with you?"

She wiped the nervous sweat away from her upper, overly inflated lip. "What do you mean?"

"All the plastic surgery, loud car, obnoxious boyfriend, can't hide you from yourself, darlin'. Know what I mean?"

"What?"

"Mirror, mirror on the wall?"

"Screw you."

"See? That's no way to behave. Learn to love who you are, not what you think you should be." Stunned, tears filled her eyes. He handed her back the keys. "Go home. Get therapy. I'm in therapy. In fact, the whole damn world needs therapy." She glanced over at her still unconscious boyfriend. "Especially him," added Boysie.

"Will he be alright?" she asked, wiping her eyes.

"Yeah, he'll be fine."

Collagen Lips started her car, backed slowly out and looked at Boysie one last time before driving away. He got into Celeste and pulled out of the alley as Tough Guy started to wake up.

Marjorie, her eyes glassy, sat and stared out over the reservoir. Boysie looked at her, barely able to contain his annoyance. He shook his head and poured himself a glass of Beaulieu. She took a sip from her martini.

"We were kids, just barely out of high school. The marriage was doomed to failure from the start."

"What sort of a relationship have you two had over the years?"

She shrugged. "Friendly. Polite."

"Animosity?"

"Not from me, but he was very bitter about the divorce. We were both dirt poor back then, struggling from pay-check-to-pay-check. He was working in the mail room at William Morris and I was a waitress at Mel's Drive In."

"Happy Days, huh?"

Marjorie looked at him. "Yeah, at first we were happy. We didn't have a dime. We lived in a studio over in Koreatown, in one of those pre-war buildings that kind'a look like they belong in New York? Anyway, we were very much in love and had our whole future planned out. He was going to become a super agent. I was going to become a famous actress and eventually we'd have our own film company." She drained her martini. "Just didn't work out that way."

Carla appeared with a fresh martini and placed it on the wicker table next to Marjorie, taking the empty with her. As she passed Boysie, she threw him a guilty look and shrugged. He nodded his complete understanding.

"I thought you were gonna take it easy with those?"

"Do not rob me of one of my last pleasures." She took a sip and unsteadily placed the glass down.

"What about his involvement with the Vatican?"

"I was pregnant and so his parents sent us on vacation to Italy. It was wonderful. Romantic. What every girl dreams of. Almost."

"Almost?"

She nodded. "We had been to Florence and Tuscany and not one argument. Then we visited Rome and at first, it was great. It was nineteen seventy-one. The young and beautiful café society. Mopeds and Alfa Romeos. Wine and cappuccino. It was a whirlwind of excitement and we were having a ball. Then one day we went to Saint Peter's Basilica and everything changed. He was mesmerized by it and sort of had this spiritual awakening, an epiphany. He was a lapsed Catholic, so I guess it was always in him. He had this really strange look on his face and told me that he was going to devote his life to God. I thought he was just caught up in the moment of all that incredible art and history--"

"--Stendhal syndrome."

"What?"

"It's a psychosomatic disorder caused by seeing so much incredible art. The person becomes overwhelmed and can even have hallucinations."

"Is that a fact?" she asked dryly.

"Sorry."

"Anyway, I was wrong. For the remainder of the vacation, he spent all of our time prowling the Vatican, meeting with whomever he could. He told me that he had met with some Cardinal, uh, Christoforo, I think. Apparently, he was very intrigued by the possibility of having one of their devoutly faithful working in Hollywood, especially as it's mostly Jews that run the business. You know, he would run interference for them if any films or shows were being pitched that the Holy See didn't want made."

Boysie finished his bourbon and put down the glass. "Is this real? I mean, it sounds so bloody far-fetched."

"You don't know the half of it, Boysie."

"I'm not sure I want to."

"Ignorance is bliss?" she asked sadly.

"There's a lot to be said for it. Anyway, go on."

She drained her martini and went back to gazing out over the reservoir. "David rose up through the ranks very quickly. Over the years, I heard rumors that he'd nixed this show or buried some book or whatever and he seemed unstoppable. Hit movie after hit movie. Money just flowed to him and as his power grew, so too did his reputation for ruthlessness."

"How did the Vatican reconcile with him being a divorcee?"

"I don't know, but apparently anything can be forgiven if it's for the good of the church."

"Apparently."

Marjorie looked at him. "Religion and politics. It's a global business."

The growing unease in the pit of his stomach mocked him. He dug his hands deep into his pockets looking for the comfort of warmth, but it did no good. "What's the tie-in with David's last name being the same as Castle Gandolfo?"

"He said that when he told the Cardinal his surname, he just smiled and blessed him."

Boysie poked at a dry twig with his shoe. "Yeah, must've been a real sign from God."

"He works in mysterious ways?" she said bitterly. "He wants either the painting or the money returned by noon, tomorrow. If that doesn't happen, he's instructed his attorneys to not only sue me for it, but also for additional damages and," she cleared her throat, "and they're going to contact the FBI and have me investigated for fraud."

"Yet he told me that under no circumstance, did he want the police involved."

"He did?"

"Yeah because of that takeover he's negotiating." Boysie, suddenly lost in thought, drew in some air, adding, "You know what this is? Bait and switch."

"Sorry?"

"Has he ever bought anything from you before?"

"No."

"Then he must've waited a long time for the right situation to repay you for the divorce."

"You think David set this whole thing up just to get at me, for revenge?"

"That'd be my guess."

"He's capable of a lot of things, but I do not believe he would do that. Not to me."

"Marjorie, think about it; all the cops have to do is have both paintings examined. Valentine has the real. Gandolfo the fake. It's not rocket science. They check the bank accounts and verify the transfer took place and Bob's your uncle, Valentine gets banged up for fraud and you're off the hook."

"But I can't have the police involved. I already told you that."

"Yeah, you did, but you didn't tell me why."

She sighed and took a moment. "Last year I brokered a couple of deals where the payment was in cash."

Boysie nodded, "And so was your percentage and let me guess, you never paid taxes on it?"

"How could I? That would've meant informing on my clients and that would've been the kiss of death for me."

"Were they friends of David's?"

The blood drained out of her. "Yes."

"Christ, Marjorie."

"Oh, my."

"That's tax evasion. He knows it."

Fear coursed though her, momentarily sobering her up. "But why wouldn't they also charge Valentine then?"

"Technically he's the one that pulled the theft, so they obviously will."

"Should I call him?"

"Who, Valentine?" asked Boysie.

"Yeah. Perhaps he can--"

"--No, forget it. I'm gonna pay him another visit. See what's what."

"Please, be careful."

"Valentine can't afford to have the Ol' Bill or the Tax Man snooping around. So why do it? Why would he risk that, knowing he could spend the rest of his life in nick? It doesn't make sense."

"Wish I had the answer."

Boysie studied this still defiantly proud, but now vulnerable woman that he admired so much. "I don't mean to pry and if you don't wanna tell me, it's cool. But what happened to the kid?"

"Carla!"

The housekeeper popped her head out of the back door. "Sí señora?"

"Another for me and whatever he's having, please."

Carla looked at Boysie who shook his head. She disappeared inside to make the drink.

"Well?"

"Just a second, my dear. I need a little fortification."

"You need to tell me," he replied impatiently.

Carla brought out the fresh martini, but this time with three olives in it. She handed it to Marjorie who smiled her thanks and took a sip. "So, where were we?"

"The kid?"

"Aborted."

She said it so matter-of-factly, that it caught him by surprise. He said, "One of the gravest sins a Catholic can commit."

"I'm not Catholic," she replied tersely.

"No wonder he's pissed."

"You're siding with him?"

"I don't respond to stupid questions, Marj."

"Don't call me stupid!"

"Not you. The question."

"Semantics. You may go."

"Listen, by omission, you, my mum and Father Murphy have involved me in something that can put me in jail for a very long time."

All the alcohol she had consumed was winning the battle with reason. Anger steeled her eyes and she snarled at him viciously, "And so does being a Fence."

He held his tongue. She didn't.

"You deal in stolen goods, diamonds, gold and God only knows whatever else and a lot of your friends are very unsavory characters. You've had your hands in a lot of shady deals and you're going to lecture me about morality and breaking the law? Please, don't make me laugh."

"You done?"

"Yes and so are you."

Carla's nervous face appeared in the doorway. She stepped to one side as Boysie passed her on the way out.

Valentine was in the Jacuzzi, nibbling on caviar as the eighteen year old redhead nibbled on him. Bruno, his right leg in a cast, wearing shorts and a sweater, sullenly sat nearby.

"Hey."

He ignored Valentine and carried on sulking.

"Bruno!"

"What?"

"We need more champagne and get me a cigar while you're at it."

"Alright." Bruno got painfully to his feet and started the slow trudge to the kitchen.

Valentine shook his head and got out of the Jacuzzi. "I'll get the cigar." He turned to the redhead and undressed her with his eyes. Not that there was much left to take off. "I'll be right back, babe."

She smiled and Valentine kissed her, fondling her breast. As he headed for the French doors that led into his office, he didn't see her quickly wipe her mouth, or the shudder that coursed through her. He walked in and stopped dead in his tracks, his jaw hanging open like a Venus Fly Trap. Lighting one of his cigars, feet up on his desk, looking at the Jackson Pollock, was Boysie.

Valentine swallowed hard. "Jesus Christ."

Boysie blew out a long line of smoke. "Not exactly."

"What the hell are you doing here?"

He swung his legs off the desk. "Isn't that redundant?"

"How did you get past my security system?"

"There you go again."

Valentine glanced at the desk drawer where he kept his .38 snub nose. Only it wasn't there anymore. It was in Boysie's fist, pointed straight at him.

"Boss," called Bruno from outside.

"He calls you Boss?" Flies were starting to settle in Valentine's open mouth. Boysie couldn't help but laugh. "Get him in here, but do it easy, mate."

"Bruno."

The Samoan limped his massive frame into the doorway. He peered past Valentine and unable to hide his surprise, fixed his glare on Boysie. Clearly, his deepest desire was to repay him for the busted kneecap, in spades.

"Don't be shy, Bruno." He waved the big man in with the .38. He limped past Valentine and made for one of the huge leather chairs. "I didn't say sit, did I?"

"No, but--"

"--What? Your knee hurts?"

"Yeah," he replied, embarrassed.

"Not my problem. But what is, is that Pollock. Right, Valentine?"

"Beats me."

"If you insist." The redhead appeared in the doorway. She saw the .38 and opened her mouth to say something, but fear closed her throat. Boysie stood up. "Take a seat, darlin'."

Meekly, she complied. Bruno was starting to shake from the effort of supporting himself on his good leg. Boysie pointed at the other seat. He nodded and sat down, the leather groaning under his weight.

Valentine began smirking, "Ain't you a couple of days late in collecting your vig?"

Unmistakable and completely fear inducing, is the sound of a gun being cocked. The trio held their collective breath as they focused on the end of the barrel aimed right at Valentine's flabby gut. Boysie, mad enough to chew lead and spit bullets, glared at him.

Fear had apparently robbed Valentine of reason. He took a step forward. "What're you gonna do, shoot me in front of witnesses?"

Boysie rolled his bottom lip between his teeth and continued to glare at him. Then something in him changed. It was the detached, cold look in his eyes, the lack of expression, that Bruno instantly recognized.

Stupidly, Valentine did not. "You ain't gonna do shit, Problem Solver."

"Boss, shut up."

"Don't tell me what to do, you useless fuck. This idiot's not gonna do anything."

"Boss, please."

Emboldened, Valentine barked at Boysie. "Do something. Only you won't, will you? No. So get the hell outta my house and tell that stupid bitch, Marjorie, she better make good on the money and pay back Gandolfo, or strap a mattress to her back and head to Skid Row."

Boysie got to his feet and took a step forward, the gun leading the way. Valentine's bravado evaporated. The redhead tried again to scream. Bruno gritted his teeth. Boysie pulled the trigger but instead of the explosion of gunpowder, there was only the explosion in Valentine's Speedo as he defecated. Bruno launched out of the chair with his one good leg. Valiant effort. All for naught. Boysie sidestepped and cracked him on the temple with the gun. Unconscious, he stumbled sideways, knocking everything off the desk and crashed to the floor with a three hundred and thirty pound thud. Tears poured out of the redhead as she desperately looked around for help that wasn't going to appear.

Humiliation had just introduced itself to fear and Valentine, shaking, said, "Let her go."

"Oh, now you wanna be Sir Galahad?"

"She's got nothing to do with this."

Redhead looked at Boysie pleadingly. "I promise I won't say anything. Cross my heart."

The growing stench from Valentine was beginning to suffocate the room. Boysie looked at her. "Get your stuff and get out of here. You ever say anything to anybody, and I will find you."

She shook her head vigorously. "No, I mean okay I won't. I promise."

"Go."

"My clothes are in his bedroom."

"How old are you?"

"What?"

"Eighteen? Nineteen?"

"Eighteen, yesterday."

"Actress?" She nodded. "Darlin', giving head doesn't get you ahead. Not in his business and certainly not with a sleazebag like him."

Redhead glanced at Valentine, lowered her eyes and went into the bedroom. She returned a moment later wearing jeans and a pink cashmere sweater, with pink, sparkly sandals. She was somebody's daughter and still, for now, at least, retained her high-school innocence. Sadly, he knew that in all probability, she would soon enough bear all the hallmarks of another desperate actress willing to do anything to get a part.

"You have a way to get home?" She shrugged. He pulled a wad of bills out of his pocket and handed it to her. Wide-eyed, she hesitated. "Take it."

She took it.

"Bye," she said with quivering lips and left by the front door, without another glance at Valentine.

A brown mass was seeping out of his Speedo, sliding down his right leg. He looked at it, not sure what to do.

"You're beginning to stink up the room, mate. Go on, get in the Jacuzzi."

"Let me shower."

"Get in."

Very reluctantly, Valentine climbed back into the cooling water and sat down. "I swear, I'm gonna repay you for this, so you better kill me."

"That's not a bad idea and always an option but for now, I want information."

"Go to hell!"

"Tell me all about you and Gandolfo."

"There's nothing to tell."

"I'm not gonna ask you again."

"Fuck you."

"You've got balls, I'll say that for you, but not much sense. So I'll tell you what I'm gonna do; either you tell me what's going on, or I'm gonna pistol whip you."

Valentine dropped his eyes onto the hard steel .38 in Boysie's fist. His mouth moved as if he wanted to say something, but the words remained stuck in his throat. He dragged his gaze away from the gun and looked at him. "Take the painting. That's what you came for, right? It's yours. You can have it. I'll even give you a bill of sale."

He looked at him pointedly. "For a dollar?"

"What?"

"That's what Michael did. He sold the land to Father Murphy for a dollar."

"Who sold what land?"

"Father Murphy? Martinez? Bergman?"

"I don't know what you're talking about."

"Sure you do."

"No," he replied innocently, "I don't. I swear."

He was telling the truth and Boysie knew it. "Okay, let's forget about that for a minute. You were about to tell me why you and Gandolfo pulled the bait and switch on Marjorie."

Valentine swallowed hard. The once clear Jacuzzi water was beginning to cloud. Bits of brown debris surfaced, floating like pond scum. "Just take the painting, please."

"What's really going on with you and Gandolfo?" Boysie's iPhone buzzed. "Where are you?"

Tommy answered, "On Coldwater by the Fire Station."

"Then come up to 1311 Lago Vista."

"Alright."

"Did you bring an opo?"

"Yeah. He can handle himself and he'll keep his north shut."

"Excellent." Boysie hung up. "Jack Valentine, you've done a lotta devious things, mate and gotten away with it. But shafting a friend of mine is not gonna be one of 'em."

"I didn't screw anybody."

"Marjorie doesn't count?" Valentine shrugged. "Tell me what's really going on."

Bruno stumbled out of the office doorway, rubbing the side of his head. Boysie grinned. "Come over here."

Bruno meekly complied, limping across the grass. "I don't feel so good."

"I can see that, me ol' son. You need to cool off. Get in."

He looked at the cloudy, foul smelling water. "In there?"

"That is water, right?"

"Yeah, but--"

"--Then yes, get in."

"You son-of-a-bitch."

"I've been called worse by better. Now, if you please."

Bruno glanced at the .38 and sneered. "It's empty."

Valentine could see the brass tips of the bullets in the cylinder. "No, it's loaded."

"Only one chamber was empty, Bruno." Boysie waved the gun. "Now get your arse in the water."

"But my cast'll get wet," he whined.

"I'm not gonna tell you again." Bruno looked at his boss, gritted his teeth and very unwillingly, lowered himself in. "Good boy." Boysie's iPhone rang again. "Outside?"

"Yeah," replied Tommy.

"The code's *74263."

He hung up and Valentine asked, "How did you get the code?"

Boysie looked at Bruno and grinned. Valentine looked suspiciously at the big man. "You gave it to him?"

"No."

Boysie, tiring of this, snapped his fingers in front of Valentine's face. "Oy! Focus!"

"Take the painting and go so I can get outta this shit," he said, beginning to shiver.

"You'll be happy to know that I'm gonna deliver it to Gandolfo."

Valentine tried to hide the sudden smirk and glanced at Bruno. "You do that."

"Now why do you find that funny?"

"For the same reason you wouldn't," replied Valentine as Bruno tried to suppress a giggle.

"What I'm having trouble wrapping my head around, is you knowing that all the Ol' Bill have to do is examine the painting and you're done for. Yet it doesn't seem to bother you."

Valentine shrugged.

Tommy and his opo, a hard looking geezer in his late twenties, with hands the size of shovels, walked in. Tommy looked at the gun in Boysie's hand.

"Bit 'eavy innit, Boysie?"

"There's a painting above the desk in the office. Stick it in the van, but be very careful with it."

"The real Pollock?"

"Yes, the real Pollock. Now if you don't mind?"

"Alright, keep your shirt on," replied Tommy as he and his opo went into the office.

Valentine and Bruno were shivering in the cold, putrid water. Boysie picked up one of the larger, thick towels and began slowly wrapping it around the gun. The two men in the water understood full well his intent and fear flushed the remaining blood out of their sweaty faces.

Valentine managed to croak out, "You're not serious?"

"You don't wanna tell me what's going on? Okay. Then I have to make it look like a robbery."

"But that doesn't make any sense."

"You're right, none of this makes any sense." He finished wrapping the towel into what was now a poor mans silencer.

Bruno licked his dry lips. "Wait, just wait! I know the whole deal."

"Shut up," snapped Valentine.

"Fuck you. I'm not getting whacked because of some stupid painting."

"You idiot. You'll get us both killed."

Boysie cocked the gun. Bruno looked at it and blurted out, "It was Gandolfo!"

"What?" asked Boysie, stunned.

The big Samoan looked at the painting that Tommy and his mate were carefully carrying out. "That's the fake."

"Shut up," screamed Valentine.

"Gandolfo has the real painting. He always has. It was--"

"--You're dead. You're finished. Fired. I'm gonna--"

CRACK! Bruno head-butted Valentine so hard it broke his nose and knocked him out cold. Boysie couldn't help but admire the speed and accuracy of the blow. Blood started to turn the brown water a dirtier shade of red. He pulled Valentine back and rested his head against the side of the Jacuzzi.

"Nice," admired Boysie, unwrapping the towel and dropping it to the ground.

Bruno spat contemptuously, "I never liked the fucker anyway."

"You were saying?"

"Can I get out?"

"When you've told me."

"It was Gandolfo who set the whole thing up."

"But I thought they were mortal enemies?"

"They are, but he told Valentine that he would give him a hundred million dollar film fund and distribution with his company."

Boysie nodded as everything was beginning to come into focus. "Did he say why he hates Marjorie so much?"

"No, but I was never at any of the meetings. All I know is what he told me."

"Okay, you can get out."

Bruno hauled himself out of the Jacuzzi, the soggy cast now covered in slimy, brown goo. "Christ, man, I'm gonna have to get it redone."

"It'll reset when it dries out. Although it might stink a bit."

Tommy came back out of the office. "It's loaded."

"You have safe parking for the van, right?"

"Yeah, but isn't that a little too expensive to leave in it?"

"Not as expensive as you might think."

"Alright," shrugged Tommy.

"I'll give you a bell in the morning."

"Laters," he replied and left with his opo.

Boysie turned to Bruno. "If you need a job, come see me at the pub."

"No, I'm alright. He's a prat but the pay's good."

"Shit's gonna hit the fan, mate. You may not wanna stay around."

"Yeah, you got a point there, except that I still owe ya," he said with malintent.

Boysie nodded. "When you're ready, you know where to find me."

He opened the chamber on the .38, dropped the bullets into the Jacuzzi, followed by the gun and left.

16 ~ DEAD MAN DOWN

DETECTIVE LAWTON LOOKED AS CRUMPLED as his sports jacket. In the breast pocket was the ever-present, shiny, silver pen. Sitting opposite Boysie, he nibbled occasionally on his Jack and rocks. The bar at the Georgian was quiet and the waitress, sensing that these two had something to talk out, stayed away, casting an occasional eye.

"There ain't no case to be made," said Lawton.

"What about attempted fraud?"

"No money changed hands and anyway, all he has to do is push the blame onto the gallery owner. Legitimate mistake," shrugged the detective.

"So that's that?"

"Yeah. That's that."

"You are a detective, right?"

"Don't push your luck, Boysie."

"How about you interview David Gandolfo? Maybe lean on him a little? Talk to the gallery owner. Know what I mean?"

"I told you to drop it."

"I remember," replied Boysie caustically.

"Don't look at me like that. You don't understand."

"I understand, alright. What I don't, is what happened to you."

"Reality set in. I've got a family, for Chris' sake," he spat through gritted teeth.

"Yeah, I'll bet they'd be real proud."

"That's funny coming from someone who's looking at ten to fifteen on a rape beef."

Boysie snorted his contempt across the rapidly growing void of their friendship. Lawton, unable to look him in the eyes, drank down the glass of Jack Daniels and wiped a nervous hand across his mouth.

Boysie rolled his bottom lip between his teeth and asked, "Who got to you, Charlie? What did they threaten you with?"

"I know your card says problem solver, but this is one problem you can't solve. Believe me."

"We've been friends a long time and have helped each other whenever we could. There used to be trust between us. What happened to that?"

Charlie Lawton shook his big head a couple of times as if trying to exorcise whatever it was that had him so scared. He gave up on that and instead wrung his hands in the way some men do when fear becomes their new dance partner. He stopped and looked at Boysie.

"That Muslim family that got whacked? You were right. The shooter was after you. They just happened to be in the wrong place at the wrong time."

"How do you know that?"

"I just do. Okay?"

Boysie pushed his untouched glass of Jack across the table. The detective looked at it, picked it up and slugged it down. "Was it that blond haired guy, Paul Windsor, from Midnight Securities?"

Lawton swallowed the last of the bourbon and replied, "I dunno. Maybe."

"You knew it was gonna go down, didn't you?"

"No," he lied and they both knew he just had.

Boysie looked over at the waitress and signaled for another round, but doubles. She nodded and ordered the drinks. "What's the connection between Bergman, Martinez, Valentine, Michael and Gandolfo?"

"You know I'm Catholic, right?"

"No, I didn't."

"Weird, huh? You'd expect me to be Baptist," offered Lawton.

"And sing in the choir every Sunday?"

The detective snorted at the stereotype. "Yeah, something like that." He toyed with the empty shot glass. "I was adopted by a white couple when I was seven. Wasn't easy for them, or me, but they were good people and loved me. They had strong faith and were very involved in the church. They're dead now. Drunk driver."

The waitress delivered the two glasses of Jack and drifted away.

"That's a touching story."

The cop paused and glared at him. "You're one cold son-of-a-bitch."

Boysie let out a short laugh at his hypocrisy. The cop glared at him. "So what did 'they,' whoever 'they' are, threaten you with, Detective?"

Lawton gulped down half of the bourbon. "They told me to tell you to walk away."

"How? How did they tell you?"

"Does it matter?"

"Did they come over your house at four, one sunny afternoon for High Tea? Was it delivered via carrier pigeon? Email? Text? How?"

"You're unbelievable."

"That's funny. That's just what I was thinking about you."

Lawton nibbled some more on his bourbon. He took a deep breath and said, "Two days ago, one of the neighborhood kids, an eleven year old boy, was found raped and beaten to death. I got a call the next day and was asked if I got the message."

Boysie had been holding his breath and let it out as the disgust coursed through him. "Jesus." They looked at each other across the silence. "Did you report the call?"

"To who? What am I gonna say?" replied the detective, staring into his bourbon. "Some anonymous asshole threatened me? How can I fucking prove anything? No, I'll just get my sons killed. The hell with that."

"But you knew someone was out to whack me. You could've warned me, but you didn't and that's okay. Right?"

"That kid, he was the same age as my boys. What the fuck would you do?"

Boysie didn't know what to say. The horror of it all was pressing down on him. He picked up his glass and gulped down the bourbon. "What were you saying about you being Catholic?"

"That's what they asked me, the caller. If I was willing to sacrifice my family by going against the will of the church."

"I'm no lover of religion, but I can't believe that the church would knowingly participate in something like this. I mean, it's just -- I dunno." Boysie fell silent.

The detective shifted in his seat. "Have you ever known me to say anything I don't mean?"

"No."

"Then give me your word you're gonna let this go. All of it."

"You already know I'm not gonna do that."

Lawton sighed and nodded. "Yeah, I know." He tapped the underside of the table with the barrel of his gun. "You know what this is, right?" Boysie nodded. "Get up and be real easy about it."

"You're gonna have to pop me right here, right now."

"Harry's on his way to meet Crystal, or so he thinks."

Boysie resisted the urge to gouge out the detectives eyes with the whisky glass. "I leave with you and you make the call to him. Deal?"

Lawton nodded. Measuring each other carefully, they stood up. The cop hid the gun inside his fedora that he held about waist level.

The waitress called out, "On your tab, Boysie?"

"Please and add the usual."

"Thanks," she smiled.

"My car's right outside," said Lawton stiffly. Boysie led the way. The unmarked police cruiser was parked in the alley by the side of the hotel. He and Boysie walked down the steps, past the gathering Brunchies sitting on the restaurant patio. Lawton opened the back door. "I'm gonna cuff you. You make a move and I'll kill you." Boysie glared at him and nodded. The cop took out his handcuffs and snapped them on him. Allowing him to keep his hands in front, Boysie got in. The detective started the car, turned and stared at him through the reinforced wire mesh partition. "God damn you. You should'a just walked away."

"Your place or mine?" asked Boysie.

Lawton opened his mouth to respond, changed his mind and stomped on the gas, squealing into traffic. He didn't see Jimmy the Concierge having a quick smoke, watching them from the side gate that opened into the alley. Lawton took Ocean, made a left and a right on to Lincoln and dropped down onto the East bound 10.

Boysie said, "Make the call."

"I left my phone at home."

"Use mine."

"You're too gullible. He's probably at the pub, drunk, as usual."

"You being straight with me?"

"Ultimately, does it matter?" he asked rhetorically. Boysie snorted his contempt. Lawton added, "What about the painting?"

"It's safe."

"Not that it really matters any more, but Valentine's not gonna press charges."

"Is that right?"

"Yeah, but I gotta wonder why?" asked the detective.

"It's as you said, no money changed hands. Gandolfo has the real Pollock and the fake actually could be used against him, if someone had any desire to press it, that is."

"Yeah, I guess so. No evidence. No crime."

"But you had to know all this, right? Isn't Gandolfo pulling your strings?"

"Shut up."

"Am I gonna be the cliché, buried in the desert?"

"A lotta problems get solved that way," replied the detective with a knowing glance.

"So I hear."

"You think you're the first one that I've had to take care of?" smirked Lawton.

Boysie shook his head in disgust. "I've known you for ten years and don't know you at all."

"All you had to do was let it go. But no, not the great Boysie Blake."

"Does that make you feel better, working yourself up into a lather to justify what a scumbag you are?"

Detective Lawton glared at him in the rear view and for the next two hours, they sat in thick silence. Both knew what was going to happen and had to make themselves right with it. As usual, it was blustery as they sped past the ever-expanding windmill farms, generating power for California. Just after the Morongo Casino, they veered off onto Route 62 toward Yucca Valley, located at the base of the Sawtooth Mountains. Quickly, civilization became a distant memory. In this part of the High Desert, there are many dirt roads that lead into desolate mountain valleys. It was on one of these that Lawton now turned, just off Pioneertown Road. At around three hundred yards and well hidden from the highway on which the occasional Harley roared past, he stopped the car. Grim faced, he got out and opened the back door.

"Get out." The detective took a shovel out of the trunk and handed it to him, but couldn't look him directly in the eyes. "Move." Lawton gestured with his gun and they headed deeper into the silent valley.

For the next fifteen minutes, they crunched across the hard packed sand. The wind picked up and moaned balefully through Joshua Trees. Dark clouds began to roll in, carrying with them the threat of a storm and super-charging the already tense atmosphere. The detective stopped to catch his breath and leaned against the rocks as a thorny tumbleweed rolled past.

Boysie looked at him. "Here?"

The detective took off his fedora and wiped copious amounts of sweat from inside the brim. "Dig."

Boysie dropped the shovel.

"Ain't gonna tell you again." Lawton aimed his gun at him.

"What're you gonna do, shoot me?"

Lawton pulled back the hammer. "You can either die quick. Or I can cause you a lotta pain first."

"You wanna put me in the ground? Then you're gonna have to dig the hole."

BANG! The bullet screamed past Boysie as the gunshot echoed off into nowhere. "Next one'll be in your gut."

Boysie held up his hands for the detective to take off the cuffs. He took out the keys, but kept the gun in his left and stepped forward. He inserted the key and as the ratchet clicked open, Boysie quickly grabbed Lawton's massive hand, spun to the left and back elbowed him in the face, hard as he could. His head snapped back and blood spurted out of his nose. BANG! This time the bullet found flesh and tore through Boysie's right side, knocking the wind out of him. Spitting blood and teeth, Detective Lawton pistol-whipped him so hard that he almost blacked out, then staggered back against the rocks.

The cop stopped to catch his breath, wiped the blood away and yelled, "You son-of-a-bitch!"

Blood poured out of the bullet wound and Boysie sank to his knees, holding his side. Lawton bent down and retrieved his gun. Glaring death at him, he pressed the barrel hard into Boysie face and jacked back the hammer. They locked eyes and the moment trudged by like molasses in January. Much to Boysie's surprise, the detective took the gun away.

"Dig."

In later years, Boysie would contemplate if what happened next, had been deliberate on the cop's part. He held out his hand for Lawton to help him up. He nodded, leaned in and as he heaved him to his feet, Boysie cracked him with a hard left, knocking him off balance. The detective stumbled backward, fell onto his ass and fired again. The bullet ricocheted off the rocks, whining harmlessly through the desert still. Boysie grabbed the gun, jamming his index between firing pin and the next bullet. Simultaneously, he snatched the silver pen out of Lawton's breast pocket.

Rage, fueled by fear, propelled a primal scream from Boysie's mouth. He pressed down onto Lawton's massive hulk, forcing him onto his back and using the pen like a knife, furiously stabbed him multiple times in the throat, prison style. Blood bubbled out of the gaping wounds, running onto the parched, silver sand that greedily drank the crimson offering. The look of surprise on the cop's face changed to his death grimace. Eyelids fluttered rapidly like the wings of a dying bird, and he made wet sucking sounds as the life force oozed out of him. His massive frame heaved a couple of times. He coughed once and then it was over, his last breath hissing out of him like a busted airline.

Boysie picked up the gun, grabbed the keys and stumbled back toward the distant road. Several times, he almost passed out from the intense pain and blood loss. As if claiming another soul, a murder of iridescent crows squawked as they flew across the valley, hungrily eyeing the scene below with black, beady eyes. Finally, he reached Lawton's car. With a shaking hand, he pulled out his iPhone, only to find that the screen had been smashed. Grimacing with pain, he hauled himself back out of the car and stumbled the last three hundred yards to the main road. A group of bikers roared toward him out of the shimmering heat haze as he crawled into the middle of the road, fading into unconsciousness.

17 ~ COP KILLER

BOYSIE WOKE UP TO FIND himself handcuffed to the hospital bed, with tubes sticking out of every orifice. A burly and very pissed off cop, glared hatred at him. He yanked on the handcuff, clanging it against the rail.

"Keep still, cop killer," snarled the police officer.

Boysie tried to speak but his throat was too dry, so he relaxed and fell back into a fitful sleep. A couple of hours later, Nurse Garcia woke him up.

"I need to check your wound," she said with animosity.

"Water, please." She handed him a sippy cup filled with ice-cold water. He took a drink and handed it back to her. "Thanks. Where am I?"

"Riverside County."

"How long have I been here?"

The police officer stuck his head in the door. "Cop killers don't got no rights, so shut the hell up."

The nurse continued, "Two days. You'd lost a lotta blood."

Boysie called out, "Officer."

"I told you to be quiet."

"Why am I handcuffed?"

"Cop killer mean anything to you, stupid?"

"What about my rights? Innocent until proven guilty, mean anything to you?"

"Like I said, asshole, you don't got none."

191

A sudden flash of pain shot through his right side. Boysie grimaced and replied, "Don't have."

"What?"

"It's, don't have."

"You don't have what?"

"Not me. You."

"What don't I have?"

"A brain, command of the English language, ability to reason?"

The cop covered the distance in three strides. He loomed over Boysie, his face twisted with hatred. "Say it again!"

Despite Nurse Garcia's feelings toward Boysie, this was still her domain and he was, after all, her patient. She glared at the police officer. "Get out."

He looked at her. "You don't tell--"

"--Get out or I'll call your Watch Commander myself."

"And he's a rapist."

"Out."

The police officer sneered down at Boysie. "In a couple of days we're gonna transport you to holding and then you'll be mine."

"Can't wait."

All this served to do was to annoy Nurse Garcia even more. She came around the bed and got into the police officer's face. "Mira!" she hissed through clenched teeth, "Get out, now."

The cop looked at her and knew that arguing with a pissed off Latina was probably not a good idea. Abruptly, he went back to his post outside the room.

"I need a phone please," asked Boysie.

"After I check the wound." She gently lifted the gauze, looked at the sutures and nodded with satisfaction. She opened the nightstand next to his bed, pulled out his wallet and handed it to him. "You'll need a credit card to make any calls."

"Thanks."

She nodded and left the room. Sliding his handcuffed arm up the rail, he opened his wallet and took out a credit card. Nurse Garcia came back in. "He said I can't let you have the phone."

"No worries, but thanks anyway." She turned to leave. "It was self defense."

She stopped and looked at him. "What?"

"I'm not a rapist or a cop killer."

"My husband's a Sheriff."

"It was self-defense."

"You raped her in self-defense?"

"I'm investigating a murder."

"You're a cop?"

"No. Civilian."

"Oh," she said with disdain.

"The Coroner, a woman I believe to be involved, made the accusation."

"And the dead lieutenant?"

"He was a friend of mine for over ten years. He told me the same people behind the murder, had hired him to whack me."

"Quite a conspiracy."

"I don't expect you to believe me. I don't even believe me."

Nurse Garcia opened her mouth to respond but before she could, two grim faced detectives entered. The more senior, Escalante, was a twenty-year vet of the Homicide Division and his partner, Stoneham, had served fourteen.

Without taking eyes off Boysie, Lieutenant Escalante said, "Nurse, we need some alone time with the prisoner."

She nodded and left, closing the door behind herself. The lieutenant considered him for a long moment and after the moment had quietly plodded by, he said, "I'm Lieutenant Escalante and this is my partner, Detective Stoneham."

Boysie flicked his eyes from one grim face to the other.

Detective Stoneham asked, "Why did you kill him?"

"Because he was gonna kill me."

"Bullshit."

"No. It's the truth."

Escalante leaned forward. "And why was he gonna do that?"

"Money."

Stoneham hissed through clenched teeth, "You're on bail on a rape beef, so don't feed us any crap, okay?"

"I don't have to. Look at the evidence; I'm out in the middle of nowhere with an SMPD detective that has no authority or reason to bring me there. Why? Why would he do that?"

"I don't know," replied Lieutenant Escalante.

"It's his prints on the shovel, as well as mine. What do you think we were doing there, gardening?" The detectives looked at each other. Boysie continued, "Call his captain and ask him if he was authorized."

"We already did."

"So I guess you earned your Lieutenant's shield then?"

Escalante smiled grimly. "His captain told us that you two used to be good friends."

"Used to be."

"What happened? You bang his wife?" sneered Stoneham.

"Why, you want me to bang yours?"

Stoneham balled up his fists and darted forward, but the Lieutenant shoved an arm in the way. "Let it go."

Stoneham growled, "You get the hell outta our county and if I ever catch you here again, you're gonna wish I hadn't."

Boysie smirked. "You'll be lucky if I don't sue you for wrongful arrest. Now take these bloody cuffs off me and get the hell out."

Stoneham looked as if he very much wanted to make good on his threat. He eyed the Lieutenant and left. He, in turn, pulled up a chair and sat down.

"You have a key?" asked Boysie.

The lieutenant reached over and unlocked the cuffs. "I saw your business card. So what are you, the poor man's Marlow?"

"You read. It's a miracle." The detective smiled. Boysie said, "No, not hardly."

"Then what?"

"Just like the card says, someone has a problem, I help 'em resolve it, if I can."

"For a fee?"

"No, I work for free."

"Robin Hood. Right?" he sneered.

"What you think of me means nothing. I help those that can't help themselves and only after they've exhausted all other legal avenues, including being turned down by the police and judicial system."

"So you're some kind of unlicensed dick?"

"If that makes you feel better."

Escalante took out a pack of smokes. He slid one out and began tamping down the tobacco on his broad, flat thumbnail. "Off the record, what really happened out there?"

"I already told you."

"There might be some truth in what you said, but I'd bet a month's pay there's so much more in what you didn't."

Boysie looked evenly at the police lieutenant. "Now why should I trust you?"

"Because I'm a slow, methodical cop and I'll just keep on digging until I find something and from what I hear, you might have a skeleton or three you don't want discovered."

Boysie considered this for a moment. "Off the record?"

"Yeah, Scouts honor," replied the detective and made the Cub sign.

"He was saving up for a sex change operation and needed money."

Escalante tried hard not to laugh and managed to choke it down. He cleared his throat and said, "Is that right?"

"I've made a few enemies along the way and I guess someone offered him a lotta wedge to whack me."

"Interesting."

"I suppose the temptation proved too much, what with kids, family. You know?"

"Yeah, I guess so." He stuck the smoke behind his ear and stared at Boysie. "Did he say who?"

"No."

"And you have no idea who they could be?" Boysie gave him a look of, *"You really expect me to tell you and implicate myself?"* Escalante nodded his understanding and snorted, "That's your story?"

"That's what happened, if that's what you're asking?"

"A sex change."

Boysie smiled.

The cop stood up and straightened his jacket. "My partner was right, stay out of our county." Detective Escalante ambled over to the door and looked one last time at Boysie. "Maybe he was a dirty cop and had it coming. I dunno. My advice to you, don't come back."

He left the door open and disappeared down the hallway.

18 ~ WANTED DEAD OR ALIVE

DR. NEWCOMB PACKED UP HIS medical kit, slipped on his jacket, headed for the elevator and pressed the call button. He turned to Boysie who was lying on the sofa.

"After today, please find yourself another doctor."

"Don't believe everything you read."

The doctor couldn't look him in the eyes and kept them glued to the floor. The elevator door quietly slid open and he quietly slid inside it.

Boysie got up slowly and made a cup of Earl Grey and sat on the balcony overlooking the choppy whitecaps that surged toward the beach. The house phone rang and he picked up the extension on the small table next to him.

"Yeah?"

"It's Jimmy."

"What's up?"

"That five-oh chick's on her way up to see you."

"Thanks."

"You need anything?"

"No, I'm good."

"Okay," he replied and hung up.

Ever since Boysie had returned home, the newspapers and TV had been all over the story. Some had automatically labeled him "Cop Killer," whilst others called him a "suspect." Apparently no one wanted to hear the truth; it doesn't sell prime time. If it wasn't for the fact that the Paparazzi couldn't get past Jimmy, they would have been banging on his door. A couple of times a helicopter had hovered over the Georgian, but he had quickly lowered the remote controlled blinds, thwarting their intrusion. He was waiting for the first surveillance drone to appear. It didn't. He knew that Gandolfo had won, no longer needing to have him killed as he was now effectively discredited. But this just nagged at him. Why would one of the most successful and famous film producers of all time, indulge in murder and fraud? Didn't make sense. He had too much to lose. Everything that he had spent years building, would be ruined. No. There was something Boysie had missed. Something he needed to discover, even if he never did anything with it. Except, perhaps, clear his name as a rapist and cop killer. It's funny how this town works, he thought to himself; one day I'm everybody's friend when they need me. The next, I'm a leper and everyone's got amnesia.

Detective Jackie Hampton drifted out of the elevator. She saw him on the balcony, came over and stood next to him. He smiled at her, but she kept her distance; the icy wall around her an unexpected and impenetrable barrier. He got the message and together, they looked down at the afternoon humanity on the boulevard below. He finished his cup of tea and slowly lowered himself into the whicker chair.

She turned to him and leaning against the railing said, "My partner knows I've been seeing you."

He didn't look up at her. "Yeah, I'm okay. Thanks for asking."

"No matter how the inquest turns out, you have no more friends in the Santa Monica or LAPD, and if I continue to see you, it's career suicide. I'm finished."

"Guilty even if I'm not?"

"You killed a twenty-three year, decorated vet who also saved my life. Doesn't matter if it proves out, most cops'll never forgive you."

He looked up at her. "Including you?"

"Me most of all."

"Thanks for that."

She shifted uneasily, glanced around at nothing and looked at him. "I just got out of a meet with the Captain and the Chief."

"Bet I know what's coming next."

"The evidence does support your claim, so they've instructed me to ask you for a favor."

"That's a joke, right?"

Nervously, she cleared her throat. "They want you to say that he was a rogue cop and does not, in any way, represent the attitude of the Santa Monica, or the Los Angeles Police Departments, toward its citizens."

"Wag the dog."

"What?"

He thought for a moment. "No."

"That's a mistake."

"I tell you what. I'll do it on two conditions."

"Which are?"

"The request has to be personal, from you. Not from them." She knew exactly why he had done this. The burning anger in her eyes told him that she completely understood his maneuver. She nodded. He smiled. "You're gonna have to say it."

She flexed her jaw muscles angrily. A moment passed and she said, "Please do it as a favor to me."

Check. He got ready for his next move.

"Certainly, detective. And I trust that when I need to call in the marker, you'll pay it back." She said nothing and turned away, looking out to sea. He added, "It also wouldn't do for a much decorated detective to be implicated in a conspiracy to pervert the course of justice, meaning my rape beef, would it?"

"As far as we're concerned, there's no connection to be made with that," she spat angrily.

Boysie smirked. "No, I bet there isn't." She shifted uncomfortably. "Now that you owe me, here's the second demand. What's the department gonna do for me?"

"Nothing."

"Wrong answer. I want the rape case to go away."

"Not possible. We have no jurisdiction over the Ventura County Sheriff's Office."

"Then we're done here."

Annoyance narrowed her eyes. She glared at him, took out her phone and went inside out of earshot. He gazed out to sea, trying to ignore the increasing pain from the bullet wound. She came back out, opened her jacket revealing her gun and detective shield clipped onto her belt, and stuck her hands on her hips. Unknown to her, he had previously initiated a video recording of their entire meeting. Dotted around his loft, including the balcony, were tiny, high-resolution, HD security cameras, with audio.

"The mayor's agreed to do whatever it takes to make the rape case go bye-bye."

"Attempted rape of which I'm innocent anyway."

"Agreed."

Check mate. Boysie smiled. She didn't.

"Thank you, Jackie and it sucks that it had to come to this."

The softness in his voice, wrapping itself around her name, caught her by surprise. So did the tears that were beginning to form in her eyes. "I like you, Boysie, more than I've liked any man in a long, long time."

"Yeah, me too. I really felt we connected."

"We did. It's just, you know, I've struggled for years in the Department to make detective. I love what I do and don't wanna lose my job."

"It's okay. I get it."

She wiped the tears away and in doing so, the hardness returned. "Anyway, they'll make it happen. You have my word."

"Not that I doubt anybody, Detective Hampton, but just as soon as I get conformation, I'll issue the press release."

"You'll have it tomorrow." She spun on her heels, stepped into the doorway and stopped. "I came by to tell you to your face, about you and me, that is. I wanted to do that."

"And now you've done your civic duty, you may go."

"I thought you'd understand."

"Oh, I do, Detective."

She didn't like the underlying accusation in his voice. "You can be such an asshole."

"Yeah, I suppose I'll have to live with that," he replied and yawned loudly.

She left.

He called the pub and Harry answered, "You're not coming over, are you?"

"Why?"

"Paparazzi have been here all day."

"Is Crystal there?"

"She's been camped out here since it hit the five o'clock news yesterday."

Boysie poured himself a glass of red. "Are you two back together?"

"I'm not sure. She came in acting like nothing bad had happened between us."

"Opportunity knocks," he said cynically and added, "where's Mum?"

"She doesn't wanna talk to you."

"Why not?"

"You know why. They were close friends."

"And he tried to murder me."

"Yeah, so you say."

Boysie hung up, sipped the wine, sat at his computer and checked the recorded meeting. Detective Hampton could be seen and heard in crystal quality.

Swarez called on Skype. "You alright?"

"Bit weak but I'll survive."

"It's all over the web. Uh, sorry to say this, mate, but they're calling you a cop killer."

"So I hear."

"Not that I believe you did it."

"I had no choice."

"Bugger me," replied Swarez, shocked. "So now what happens?"

"I dunno. It feels surreal. I never---- I mean----."

Swarez looked sympathetically at his friend. "Sorry."

"There it is, right? I'll forever be known as that."

"Can't you tell your side to the press?"

"What?"

"Tell the world, mate. Once it's on the Internet, it becomes true anyway. Yeah?"

Boysie grinned. "You're a bleedin' genius."

"I am?"

"Press conference. That's exactly what I'll do. Beat 'em at their own game." The house phone rang. "Hold on a sec." He picked it up. "Yeah?"

"You've got a special delivery from the Apple Store," said Jimmy.

"Can you bring it up please?"

"I'll be right there," he replied and hung up.

Boysie turned back to the computer. "I've gotta go but thanks, I believe you've just leveled the playing field."

"Glad I could help," Swarez grinned.

"Me too."

Boysie disconnected Skype as Jimmy strolled out of the elevator, carrying the package. "Here you go."

"Thanks." He opened it and took out the new iPhone.

"If you need me to, I'll stand up in court for you," offered Jimmy.

"Thanks, mate, I appreciate that but hopefully it won't be necessary."

"Okay," he replied and headed for the elevator. "But just in case, tell your lawyer that I saw him cuff you and put you in the car."

He looked at Jimmy as if he was Saint Nick just bringing him his only Christmas present. "Where were you?"

"I was having a smoke--"

"--In the alley?"

"Yeah."

"Bugger me sideways, Jimmy, I could kiss you."

"I'll pass," he grinned.

"Did you see the gun?"

"Yeah, he had it in his hat, but had to holster it when he put the bracelets on. That's why I called the detective."

"Who?"

"The one that just left, Hampton."

Anger flushed away the excitement. "Interesting. Anyway, I owe ya, Jimmy. Thanks."

Detective Jackie Hampton had known all along that he was innocent and must therefore have corroborated his story to her superiors. They, in turn, had conveyed it to the Chief Of Police and the Mayor. He put that thought to one side and connecting his new iPhone to the iMac, downloaded his contacts. He poured himself another glass of wine while he waited for this to finish.

For the most part, Boysie had always shunned the limelight. Even when he went with one of his celebrity friends to a premier or red carpet event, he always waited in the background. He liked the relative anonymity and it helped with his high profile clients. Only now he was, at least temporarily, infamous. He had to use that to his advantage. There was no better venue to accomplish that, than the Georgian Hotel's own, Speakeasy Restaurant. The fabled room had once played host to notorious mobsters, Bugsy Seigel and Al Capone, along with Hollywood legends, Clark Gable, Carol Lombard, Fatty Arbuckle and a host of others. During Prohibition this was considered the "hide-out" of Hollywood; private and secluded. He chuckled at the irony of using the Paparazzi, the very ones that had so hastily condemned him, to clear his name. He took a shower and redressed the healing wound. Putting on a taupe cotton shirt, he added a beautiful, dark blue suit, made by Huntsman of Savile Row. A pair of bespoke, calf leather Bontoni shoes, completed the ensemble and the finishing touch was his Tag Heuer watch. He looked and felt like a million bucks and nothing like his new "cop killer" moniker. He picked up the house phone.

"Jimmy, is the Speakeasy available?"

"Yeah, right now it is. At least for the next hour."

"Please ask all the reporters to meet me there."

"You sure?"

"Yeah." He hung up, sent a text to Crystal to come over for the press conference and left.

The cacophony in the Speakeasy died a dramatic death as he entered. The twenty or so photographers, reporters and camera operators, lit the room in a blaze of flash and video lights. Smiling and confident, he let them take all the shots and footage they wanted, turning left and right to accommodate them.

When everyone was satiated, he cleared his throat and began. "Hi and thanks for meeting me on such short notice."

Four wait staff entered pushing dining carts laden with coffee, tea, sandwiches and pastries and quietly went about distributing the fare.

A reporter, Mitch Earl, called out, "Mr. Blake, I, for one, appreciate the coffee and cake, but can't help but wonder if you're gonna be as generous with your answers."

"Ask and ye shall receive."

Some of the reporters laughed.

Mitch asked, "Did you kill the detective?"

Boysie took a deep breath and the room fell silent. "Yes."

Feeding frenzy; an explosion of shouted questions from every corner of the room. He waited until they had all asked whatever they wanted, without answering any. Slowly, one-by-one, they got it and silence again drifted across the proceedings. He was now completely in control and everyone knew it.

"I was abducted at gun point by Detective Lawton and taken out to the desert to be executed. I have a witness that saw him force me into his car and is willing to testify at the hearing, should that become necessary. As you can see, I don't have a publicist, or a manager or an agent in tow, so what I'm telling you, is the unguarded truth."

Another reporter, Sara Blackwell asked, "Why did he want to kill you?"

"Before I answer that, I want to state that he was a rogue cop and does not, in any way, represent the attitude of the Santa Monica or Los Angeles

Police Departments." Several of the more seasoned reporters smiled at the obvious promo. "How many of you know who I am?" Most of the reporters put up a hand. "And how many know what I do?" Again, the same reporters put their hands up. "In helping people, I've tried to live a shadow life, but I guess it hasn't quite worked out that way."

Sara blurted out what everyone was thinking. "You didn't answer the question and what about the rape allegation?"

"That's two questions, uh?"

"Sara Blackwell. L.A. Times."

"Sara. My stepfather was recently murdered and--" Again, the room exploded with questions and again, he smiled and waited calmly until they calmed down. "His death was called accidental by the very same Coroner that's now accusing me of attempted rape. I had gone to her office in Ventura County to ask her some questions and the rape allegation is a result of that visit."

An emaciated reporter, with a face like an angry weasel, yelled out, "Why should we believe you? After all, you've got quite a reputation as a thug who always skates away when Johnny Law comes knocking."

Boysie smiled as all eyes rolled back from Weasel Face and fixed hard on him. "You don't have to believe me. The truth will prevail."

Weasel Face was just getting started. "Are you accusing the Ventura County Coroner and their District Attorney of conspiracy?"

"No, I'm not accusing anybody of anything. I'm simply stating the facts and we'll let the courts decide."

Mitch Earl called out, "Mr. Blake--"

"--Boysie."

"Uh, Boysie, are you inferring there's a connection between the Coroner and the deceased detective?"

Everyone held their collective breath. He knew that his answer would be front-page news but instead, he smiled and corrected, "Imply."

"What?"

"Am I implying."

Mitch grinned and said, "I stand corrected. Are you implying that--"

"--No, you're doing that. The police are investigating and will continue to do so until they get to the bottom of this mess."

Weasel Face called out again, "What's it feel like, to be a cop killer?"

Even though most of the reporters groaned and some even glared their annoyance at his question, Boysie knew that secretly they were all glad that he had asked.

He smiled at the reporter. "I thought he was my friend and when I realized that he was going to murder me, I did what anyone of you would've done and fought back."

"Yeah but--"

"--You asked the question, so let me finish." Weasel Face snapped his jaw shut. "Killing anyone, taking human life, is about the most terrible thing anyone could experience. I'm now forever branded and even though it was self-defense, most every law enforcement officer will forever revile me. So how do you think I feel?"

All eyes now turned to Weasel Face who sat there, reddening by the second under the pressure of the open hostility from some of his peers.

"You still didn't answer the question about Detective Lawton," called out Sara Blackwell.

"Sara, I don't know why he tried to kill me. He never told me even though I asked."

"Very clever, you turning the tables on us," she said.

Again, everyone fixed cold, hard stares on Boysie. "You lot have been camped out here for two days and I don't like being a prisoner without being in jail. Not that I wanna be in jail." A few of the gathered throng laughed. Sara Blackman did not. Boysie continued, "Thank you for your time." He stood amid the barrage of questions and camera flashes and raised both of his hands in gesture for them to stop, which, to his surprise, they did. "I'm still really tired from being shot and need to rest. So please, give me a break and in a couple of days, we can do this again."

Weasel Face snarked out, "You say it was self-defense. Then show us the bullet wound, if there is one."

Boysie locked eyes with him and slipped off his jacket. He pulled up the right side of his shirt and showed them the bandaged wound through which blood was beginning to soak. More camera flashes and someone called out, "Jesus." He reached for his jacket and felt the sudden nausea beginning to curdle his stomach. Enthusiastic beads of sweat quickly formed on his face, and the resulting clamminess soaked his shirt. After steadying himself on the chair, he took a deep breath and felt the room begin to spin.

"Are you okay, Boysie?" asked Mitch Earl.

"I'm uh, I'm--" was the last thing he remembered.

He didn't see Mitch or the other reporters grab him as he fainted. Nor did he later remember the ambulance ride to UCLA Emergency on Sixteenth Street.

Boysie woke up to the quiet murmur of people talking in the hallway. The sun had long said goodbye and an evening fog was rolling in off the ocean, amplifying a distant, wailing, police siren. A drain had been inserted into the bullet wound and reddish-brown fluid oozed down the plastic tubing, emptying into a container. Disinfectant hung in the air; a sharp reminder of where he was, not that he needed reminding. He felt weak, exhausted and alone. He expected that his mum and brother would visit, but in reality, he knew better. Closing his eyes, he drifted off to sleep, dreaming of betrayal, love lost, family dynamics and his dead father. He woke up to find the rugged and friendly face of Father Murphy, illuminated by the shadowed, horizontal lines of the Venetian blind. The priest was sitting on a chair in the semi-darkness, a rosary in his blue veined hands, staring at him.

"'Allo, Father," he managed to croak out.

"I thought I was gonna be givin' ya the Last Rites there, Boysie."

"Kicking and screaming."

"Off this mortal coil, eh? That's good. Glad to hear it."

"How's Mum?"

"Alright."

"And Harry?"

"Ah, don't'cha worry about them. They'll be fine. What about you?"

"Me? Yeah, I'm okay."

"I watched you on the news. You even made the BBC."

"Yeah, I'm a regular bleedin' celebrity," he chuckled and stopped as pain flashed through him.

Father Murphy took out his hip flask, spun the cap and had a nip. He offered it to Boysie who shook his head, so the priest took another and put it away. "Now what're ya gonna do, that you're no longer, you know, anonymous?"

"Go on holiday and hope time blurs the collective memory."

"Sounds like a good idea, but in the meantime, did ya get anything resolved?"

"Let me see; I killed a friend. Stole a fake that I thought was real. Saw a family get murdered. Tried to help my mum by looking into the murder of my stepdad. As a result, got accused of attempted rape. Dumped for promotion. Am, as you so rightly point out, no longer able to solve problems as I'm now bloody and infamous. Got myself shot, beaten, abducted, not to mention a sundry of other ills. So apart from that, no, I've not really achieved anything."

"Feeling sorry for yaself there?"

"Yeah, you might say that there's just a tinge of self pity."

"Then what good are you to yaself, let alone anybody else?"

"Kiss my arse."

Father Murphy stood up, opened the door and looked at Boysie. "Ya da' would never have done that. Self pity's for fuckin' losers."

He walked out, letting the door close slowly, trapping Boysie in his burgeoning melancholy.

The next morning Boysie called Marjorie. "'Allo, Marj."

"How are you? I was so worried."

Her concern felt thin. Perfunctory. He let that go. "Better and you?"

"I saw you on the news. It was awful. Simply awful. Are you still in hospital?"

"I'm being discharged this afternoon."

"Do you need me to come and get you?"

He swung his legs off the bed and looked out of the window at the clear blue. "No."

"So what can I do for you?"

With effort, he stood up slowly and looked down at the teeming street. "Nothing. I'm good."

"Okay then," she replied and hung up.

He looked at the iPhone and snorted his surprise at her rudeness.

Doctor Goldfarb and Nurse Parish came in. "How're you feeling, Mr. Blake?" asked the doctor as he glanced at his chart.

"Better, thank you."

"We're going to remove the drain today and tomorrow you should be able to go home."

"Great."

Doctor Goldfarb had kindly eyes. "You've been through a lot, so please, take it easy for a while."

"I will and could you please tell me what caused the infection?"

"There was a very small piece of material inside the wound, probably from your shirt that apparently had been missed."

"At Riverside County?"

"Yes. It's most often the cause of unexplained post-operative infection."

"With fatal results, right?"

The doctor nodded. "If left untreated."

"Thanks."

"You're on a course of antibiotics that you must finish."

"I will."

Doctor Goldfarb held out his hand. Boysie smiled and shook it. "Thanks for everything, doctor."

"My pleasure, Mr. Blake."

"Boysie."

The doctor smiled and left.

Nurse Parish said, "There's someone here to see you."

"Male or female?"

"Eddie Perez."

Boysie grinned. "Send him in, please."

"Sure," she replied and left.

Eddie and Boysie had met through a mutual acquaintance and had been friends ever since. He's one of Hollywood's top stunt coordinators and second unit directors. Having worked on many famous films, he was well liked by both filmmakers and movie stars alike. A few years ago he was doing a stunt on Adam Sandler's, You Don't Mess With The Zohan. The stunt went wrong and he was flamed up, burned over a fifth of his body. Ironically, he had also performed stunts on Angels and Demons.

Eddie walked in wearing jeans, sneakers, a sweatshirt and carrying his motorcycle helmet. His head, clean-shaven and all smiles. "How you doing, bro?"

"Alright, Eddie. You?"

"No one's pulled any lead outta me recently," he grinned.

"What's the word on Bruno and Valentine?"

Eddie sat in a chair. "He's still his bodyguard and he's been asking all over town where you hang out."

"But he already knows where."

Eddie shrugged. "Who cares. He's an idiot."

"And Valentine?"

"Nothing. Not a word. He's not been seen for days."

"He's probably too embarrassed."

"You really made him sit in his own crap?" asked Eddie in amazement.

"Yep."

"That's good. He had it coming. That asshole ripped a writer friend of mine off for a lotta money. He lost his home and everything and ended up staying at my place 'til he got straight."

"Glad I could be of service," grinned Boysie.

"You want me to take care of Bruno?" asked Eddie, not smiling anymore, all business.

"No. I'll handle him when I've recovered." He grimaced as he felt a sudden twinge coming from the wound.

"What's wrong?"

"Nothing. I'm alright."

"Want me to call the nurse?" Eddie asked anxiously.

"No."

"It's gonna take a while for that to heal and Bruno's not gonna wait."

"That's up to him."

Eddie nodded but he couldn't hide his concern or the malintent that momentarily sparked across his eyes.

Boysie shook his head. "Uh-uh."

"What?" Eddie shrugged innocently.

Nurse Parish came back in. "I'm sorry, Mr. Blake, but the doctor wants the drain taken out."

Eddie stood up. "Call me later?"

"Yeah."

He smiled at the nurse and left.

"I'm going to give you a mild sedative before I remove the drain."

Boysie nodded and lay back down. She administered the sedative and a few moments later, he fell into a deep sleep.

Jimmy grinned at Boysie as the cab pulled up outside of the Georgian. He opened the door and offered his hand, gently pulling him out of the back seat.

"You need me to help you up the stairs?"

"No, I'm good, Jimmy. Thanks."

Boysie carefully climbed the steps and entered the lobby, half expecting there to be some Paparazzi. After the meet in the Speakeasy, they had left and as of yet, none had returned. In fact, none had showed up at the hospital either.

Jimmy held open the elevator door until he was inside. "If you need anything, Boysie, let me know."

"Thanks."

Safely back in his flat, he locked off the elevator so that now the only way in would be either by parachute or rope. He opened the window, made a cup of tea and took it into the bedroom. He propped himself up against the headboard of his California King and tried to sort out everything that had happened, but to no avail. Tiredness was beginning to close his lids, so he crawled under the covers and instantly fell asleep.

19 ~ SKIN DEEP

THE iPHONE BUZZED, STIRRING BOYSIE out of sleep. He cracked open an eye, fumbled it off the nightstand and looked at the screen. It was a text from Tommy, "?" He took a shower and shaved. Made some tea with two slices of toast onto which he spread unsalted butter and St. Dalfour blackcurrant jam. Usually, he would have eaten quickly, but today he chewed slowly and methodically and when he was finished, he called Tommy.

"You alright, Boysie?"

"Yeah, thanks."

"How you wanna handle this--"

"--Not on the blower."

"Got'cha."

"I'll meet you in the pub in about an hour."

"Alright."

"And bring your opo with you."

"Will do."

Boysie, dressed in a relaxed Nike tracksuit and sneakers, entered the side door of the Royal Arms and ran his eyes across the contingent of regular punters hanging out in the bar. He sat at his booth and Amanda all smiles, hurried over.

"Boysie, how're you feeling? You okay?"

"Good. You?"

"Me? I'm fine but I was really worried when I saw on the news that you'd been shot. Terrible business."

"Yeah. Can I have a coffee, please?"

"Sure. Anything to eat?"

"No, thanks. Tommy and a friend of his'll be joining me in a few."

"Okay." She sailed off for the kitchen.

His mum breezed in as if nothing had happened, sitting opposite. "Hi."

He made no attempt to return the greeting as they locked eyes. She pouted and pretended to be hurt. It was her way of trying to gloss over the fact that she knew she had screwed up, but would never acknowledge it. He suspected that in truth, deep down, she really didn't care.

She smiled, fake and twitchy, "Are you better?"

Boysie rolled his bottom lip between his teeth. She shifted uneasily, spread her hands wide on the table and tried again to smile it all away.

"Where's Harry?" he asked.

"Am I his keeper? No, I'm not."

"Did you talk to him about rehab?"

She laughed and shook her head. "Why should I?"

Frustration flushed through him. "If you don't mind?" He waved his hand, dismissing her.

"What?"

"I've got some friends joining me."

Venom filled her eyes. She stood up and hissed through clenched teeth, "You can have your stupid meeting here today. Next time, do it somewhere else."

"Somewhere else?"

"Yes. I'm trying to run a business, not a place for you and your friends to hang out."

"Careful."

"You be careful. I own half. Do not forget that."

"You own twenty percent. Harry owns twenty. I own sixty and it was my money that bought it in the first place. In point of fact, you two still haven't repaid the initial loan from almost fifteen years ago. So if anyone has to be careful, mother, it would be you."

She spun on her heel and stormed off.

Amanda tactfully appeared from out of the kitchen with his coffee. "Anything else?"

"No, I'm good. Thank you." She nodded and drifted off. He took a sip of coffee and relaxed into the worn red upholstery.

Harry appeared with the ubiquitous glass of white wine and stood in front of him, but made no attempt to sit. "What's doing?" he smirked.

Boysie took an irritated breath. "Little early for that, isn't it?"

"No."

"How's Crystal?"

"She's good, yeah. Not that you really give a fuck."

Sergeant Pepper's Lonely Hearts Club Band tumbled out of the speakers.

Boysie said, "Did she write the article?"

"Which one?" wobbled Harry and took another sip. The excess leaked out of his mouth, dribbling down his unshaven chin. He grinned stupidly and wiped it away with the back of his hand. "Oops."

Boysie knew that trying to have a conversation with him was impossible. "Let's hang out in a couple of days when I'm feeling a little better."

"Why?"

"'Cause I've been busy and thought we could spend some time together. Maybe catch a flick."

"Best not. Bad for my image, hanging out with a cop killer."

Boysie wanted to strangle him, but just shook his head and let it go. Amazing the liberties that family believe they can take, saying anything hurtful they want. Willfully ignorant of consequence. "Anything else you wanna say, Harry?"

He made a stupid drunk face and wobbled away.

"Alright?" said Tommy as he and his opo sat down, adding, "Chris. Boysie."

They shook hands.

"Good to meet you," said Chris.

"Thanks for the other night," Boysie replied.

"No worries. Tommy says you're alright. Good enough for me."

Boysie took out two envelopes, handing them one each. They flipped through the twenty-five grand each had received.

"Nice," said Chris.

"Very generous, mate," agreed Tommy.

"Where's the painting?"

He jammed an oil-engrained, stubby thumb at himself. "At my gaff."

"I need you to hold onto it for a minute."

"Yeah, alright. No worries. Everything kosher?"

"I'm working on it. But for now, I don't need it around."

"Little toasty, is it?"

"Remarkably, no."

Amanda drifted over. "What can I get you guys?"

Tommy replied, "Pint'a diesel, please."

"And you?"

"Bass," replied Chris.

"Anything to eat?"

Tommy said, "We'll both have fish and chips, please."

"Be right back," she assured them.

He squinted at Boysie. "Word is Bruno's been looking for ya."

"So I hear."

Chris flexed his massive hands. "I'll be happy to take care of him."

"Naw, I'm good." Boysie slid out of the booth.

Tommy asked, "You off?"

"I'll give you a bell later."

"Fair enough." They shook hands. "By the way, that girl's still looking to sell her E-Type. Very fit."

"What's her connection to Gandolfo?"

"I think she's one of his little, you know, <u>friends</u>?"

Boysie nodded his understanding. "Why's she selling it?"

"She's broke and got a kid."

"So I guess she's no longer in favor?"

"I think he was taking care of her for a regular jump about, but got bored and just cut her off without warning."

"Can you give her a bell and set up a meet?"

"When?"

"Now."

Boysie loved the feeling of speed and Celeste supplied it generously; the air whistling overhead as she voraciously inhaled the 10 Freeway. He turned off at La Brea and took that up to Franklin, passing the Magic Castle and parking on Orchid Avenue. He found 1752, rang the buzzer for 3D, marked cryptically with a tiny photo of Marilyn Monroe and waited. The intercom crackled and the disembodied voice of a woman hissed out of the speaker.

"Who is it?"

"Boysie."

"What the hell's a Boysie?"

"I'm the one Tommy just called you about."

"Oh, sure. Sorry," she suddenly purred.

The buzzer sounded, unlocking the door, and he entered the cool, shady foyer. Stepping out of the old elevator on the third floor, the hallway looked like something out of a 1930s movie; dingy paint and yellow bulbs offering smudges of light to whoever would believe them.

Marilyn Monroe opened the door and smiled at him. The unmistakable scent of Chanel No. 5 wrapped its enticing fingers around him like the Sirens' Song. He stopped and frowned his question at the dead-ringer of her namesake. She giggled and for an instant, he couldn't tell the two apart, except that one was dead and she most certainly, wasn't.

"Come in," she said and stepped to one side.

"Thanks." He drifted past her into a large apartment, filled with 1950s furniture. The place looked like a shrine. Numerous photographs of the real Marilyn Monroe and in almost every available space, Monroe knick-knacks held court. She closed the door and sat in one of the large, leather armchairs with curved, wooden armrests. He dragged himself away from drinking in the memorabilia and sat down, instead drinking in her remarkable likeness to the dead American icon. Wearing a white, soft cotton bathrobe, belted at the waist, she crossed her legs, exposing more thigh than he had bargained for. Her blond tousled locks looked like she had just stepped out of the shower, but her bright red lips denied that observation. Marilyn was obviously not one given to subtlety; emphasized by the thoughts now dancing in her light brown eyes.

She said, "Tommy fixes my engine for me, from time-to-time."

"Is that right?" replied Boysie, deliberately ignoring the inference.

"Besides the Jag, I have a 1959 Caddy."

"Beautiful lines."

She smiled. "I think so."

"Can I see it?"

She pulled a smoke out of a silver-plated cigarette box and looked pointedly at him. He reached over, picked up the Zippo and held the flame up to her. Gently, she cupped his hand, drawing in the smoke. He put the lighter down and she flashed her brilliant pearly whites.

"Thanks," she drawled languidly, propelling the word with a thin stream of smoke, which, he knew, obscured more than the nicotine it held.

"Shall we?" he smiled.

The chrome on Marilyn's 1966 E-Type sparkled in the afternoon sun, as did the original paint; Golden Sand. The Jag started on the first try; the engine purring contentedly.

Boysie asked, "How much?"

"Eight six, firm."

"It's nice, beautiful, but not worth that much. I mean, not to me at least." She pouted her full lips. He understood the allure of being with someone so sexually awake, but kept his focus on the business at hand. "The best I can do is sixty-eight five."

She burst out laughing and it resonated around the courtyard like a peal of bells. She gathered herself together, gazed at him and said, "No."

He grinned wryly. "Okay, seventy even, but that's my last offer."

Marilyn leaned over the steering wheel, calling his eyes to her ample cleavage like a humming bird to nectar. She turned the engine off, glided toward the door and without looking at him, purred, "David's even more obsessed than you realize."

Boysie pulled out his checkbook. "Seventy five and you'll tell me all about it."

She poured two glasses of Château Saint Michelle, Eroica Riesling, handing him one.

"Thanks." He tasted it, adding, "Wow, that's delicious."

"Yeah, I love their wines."

"So what happened between you and David?"

She sat down, tugged on another cigarette and sipped her wine. "He got tired of me."

"That's a bit hard to imagine."

"It happens to concubines everyday," she said without the slightest trace of shame or embarrassment and smiled at him, before adding, "Especially in Hollywood Of Excess."

He nodded. "How did you meet?"

"I've made my living for a long time as her impersonator. I had been booked to pop out of this giant cake at his birthday party and--"

"--You melted his butter?"

She giggled. "Yes, the attraction was mutual and instant."

"What were you saying about him being obsessed?"

"I have a medical marijuana card and he loved to get stoned."

"So does half of California."

"You want? I have some great bud."

"Pass, but thanks."

She sipped her wine. "He would get blitzed, I mean, he would toke so much that any normal person would pass out. But not David. It just seemed to level him out."

"Is that right?"

"Yeah, well anyway, we'd just been to the premier of Angels and Demons and he was really angry. We'd had a lot to drink and came back here with a couple of his friends. We started partying hard, I mean eight balls and man, we went skiing, if you catch my drift?"

Boysie smiled. "Was that a pun?"

"What?"

"Nothing."

"Anyway, we were really, really high. His friends left and suddenly David starts crying. I thought he'd lost his marbles, you know? But no, he starts jabbering on about this chick, Walls, or something."

"Wallace?" offered Boysie, all eyes, very alert, his heart beginning to race.

"Yeah, that's her, Wallace. So I'm wiping his tears and he gets this really scary look, like he wants to kill me and tells me that she had his kid adopted."

"You mean aborted?"

"No, I mean adopted and how he only just found out and that he's gonna find her and then destroy this Wally chic."

"Wallace."

"Yeah, her. See, I'm a mom too and--"

"--Where's your kid now?"

"With her loser dad and anyway, he swears that he knows she's alive and that he's gonna find her if it's the last thing he does."

Boysie took another sip of wine, absorbing everything Marilyn Monroe had just unloaded on him. "Does he know this for sure?"

"No, but he had this detective working on it."

"Was his name Lawton?"

"I don't know. Maybe. I never met him."

Boysie put down his wine and made for the door. "Thanks for the info. I'll have one of my guys swing by for the car tomorrow."

She flicked her eyes over him. "It was great meeting you."

"Yeah, you too," he smiled and left.

Even though the sun felt good on his face as he drove the 10 West, Boysie couldn't wrap his head around this new revelation. Marjorie had had a kid, a daughter and if, in fact, this were true, then he, like Gandolfo, wanted to know where she was. He knew why she had concealed her from Gandolfo, but despite his dislike of the man, he also felt bad for him. He needed more info on Miss Monroe and knew exactly who to call.

"My Lord, are you okay?" asked Levi anxiously in his Tennessee drawl.

"Yeah, no worries. How did you know?"

"I may live in Chicago, but I still have many friends in L.A."

"How's Jason?"

"The love of my life. We are very happy, thank you, and planning our wedding."

"The Supreme Court made the right decision, but I get the feeling individual states are still gonna fight it."

"Let them try. Anyway, are you coming to Chicago?"

"Hadn't planned on it, Levi, but that's not such a bad idea as I could really do with a holiday."

"Then come on. It'll be a blast."

"How's your new CD coming along?"

"Thanks for asking," he said humbly, which was the way he always was. He had won the Tony for Best Actor in a musical, Million Dollar Quartet, but unless you knew that, he would never tell you. "I'm writing some of the best material of my life."

Boysie had a special place in his heart for Levi. They had met when a mutual friend had introduced them on the set of Levi's movie, Don't Let Go. Ever since, they had remained close friends.

"That's great."

Levi asked, "What's wrong? You sound so stressed."

"Besides getting shot, you mean?"

"Yeah, besides that," he drawled.

"I am, just a little."

"How can I be of service?"

"I need some info on a Marilyn Monroe impersonator."

"L.A. based?"

"Yeah and she's a dead ringer for her."

"And she's definitely a she?"

That caught Boysie by surprise. "Uh, I think so. I mean you know, she looked all woman to me. Not that I looked in her nickers."

"The wonders of surgery."

"That's scary."

"Something that isn't what it pretends to be in Los Angeles? My, my, how unusual."

"Yeah, you've got a point there," chuckled Boysie.

"And does she go by her name?" asked Levi.

"She does."

"I do know of her, but I'll have to call some friends to get more information."

"I need to know what kind of a person she is. If she's given to bullshit or anything else you can find out about her."

"Does this have anything to do with you getting shot?"

"It does."

"Okay then. I'll call you later today."

"Thanks," replied Boysie.

He hadn't seen the fast approaching California Highway Patrol car, but he definitely heard the siren. He glanced in his rear view and saw the flashing red and blue, and looked at the speedo, sixty-three. The limit was sixty-five and instantly he realized what this was. Pulling off at Overland, he parked by a little patch of green just left of the off-ramp. He killed the motor and sat completely still, his hands on the wheel. The police cruiser pulled up behind him and two CHP officers got out. They glanced at each other and approached him, one on either side, hands on their guns. The first cop was gritting his teeth so hard that Boysie thought they might snap.

"Do you know why I stopped you?" growled the cop.

"We both know why you did."

The cop glared at him, neither admitting nor denying the subtext of his statement. "License and registration."

Boysie glanced at the second cop in the side mirror. She had her hand on her gun, was sweating a little too much and kept glancing nervously at her partner. He, on the other hand, had no such issues. He looked as straight as his neatly pressed uniform, resplendent with its knife-edge creases. A lot of ex-Armed Forces join police departments after their tours of Iraq or Afghanistan. Most have seen combat, some more than others. He fit into the latter category, confirmed by his unblinking, thousand-yard stare and his constantly flexing jaw muscles. Up ahead, the signal flashed red and the line of cars coming off the freeway quickly backed up. Several motorists now "rubbernecked" the unfolding scene. This served one great purpose; they had now become unwitting witnesses, should this go sideways. He knew that he only had seconds to act before the light flipped green. Boysie put his hands straight up in the air. This was a very unusual thing for a motorist to do and caught everyone's attention. One or two would now be using their cell-phone cameras. Boysie grinned, saved by YouTube. The cop knew that by him doing this, it had killed his plan, whatever it had been, because now, it no longer could be.

He glared at Boysie. "Next time."

Boysie pulled a card out of his top pocket and offered it to him. "Take my card, Officer White. Call me anytime you wanna make good on that."

The cop, surprised by the insinuated offer, shook his head slightly, as if unable to fully comprehend it. He refused the card, motioned to his partner and abruptly, they got back into their cruiser. They roared away, kicking up clouds of angry dust.

Celeste turned onto Stone Canyon Road and Boysie pulled her over to answer his cell. "Yeah?"

"It's Levi."

"That was quick. Wha'cha find out?"

"She's a flighty little girl who has all the attention span of a one eyed dog in a meat plant."

Boysie chuckled. "What about her and Gandolfo?"

"Well firstly you didn't tell me anything about him," he drawled with a touch of chastisement.

"I figured you'd find out."

"Thank you, detective. Anyway, he's not such a nice person, so perhaps they were well suited."

"I dunno and don't care. But he's making life very difficult for me and some of my friends."

"He has a deep, dark secret that he wants left that way. My advice is put as much distance between the two of you as you can."

"Wish it were so, mate. Not possible."

"Boysie, we've been friends for a long time and I've known you to get involved in some, shall we say, unsavory situations. But David Gandolfo has ties that stretch all the way from Hollywood to Washington DC, Italy, China and Russia. You need to be very, very careful of that one."

"This I am aware of."

"What you may not be, is that he likes all comers."

"All comers?"

"He has a very broad and eclectic taste in sex partners."

"Wait. You're saying he's Arthur and Martha?"

Levi burst out laughing. "Yes, but so much more."

"Well I'll be buggered."

"A clumsy pun, but quite appropriate and yes, you will be, if he gets the chance."

"Is she a hooker?"

"No. She's just like a lotta girls that go to Hollywood to find their fame and fortune, only to end up with some sugar daddy or other and then realize years later that sadly, they have missed the riverboat."

"Thanks, Levi."

"Except that she isn't what she seems."

"Come again?"

"It is as I suspected. She is trans-gender. In her former life, known as Thomas Arlington, from Virginia, I believe."

"But she has a daughter."

"Really?" he replied, flatly.

"The deeper this gets, the muddier it becomes."

"If you make it through whatever mess this is, come up and stay with us for a while. There's some very lovely girls, real girls, that I'd like to introduce you to."

"I might just take you up on that."

Boysie pulled up to Marjorie's gate, pressed the buzzer and stared into the camera. The gate clicked open and he parked in the driveway. Carla opened the door, but her usual smile was missing. Instead, an air of sadness hung about her. They locked eyes and he went out back to the terrace. He found Marjorie sitting poolside, watching the water lap quietly against the turquoise tiles. She glanced up at him and went back to watching the water. He stood quietly to one side, dug his hands into his pockets and waited. The longer he waited, the heavier the vibe became.

He cleared his throat. "Marj, we need to talk."

She continued to stare at the pool. "Yeah, I guess so."

"I heard something from a very reliable source that I need to run by you." She continued to stare at the lapping water. "Is there any truth to the rumor that David's bisexual?"

She chewed the inside of her lip and nodded. "Yeah, but that's not relevant to anything."

"And you didn't tell me, why, exactly?"

"I just answered that."

Boysie sat next to her and waited until she looked at him again. "And where's your daughter?"

Marjorie caught herself as surprise turned to rage and faster than he expected, she slapped him, hard. He didn't flinch. They sat there in stinging silence as Carla watched anxiously from the living room window.

Tears filled Marjorie's eyes and she gently touched his red cheek, dropping her hand in defeat to her lap. "If being bisexual is the worst thing that David has ever done, then it'd be a cold day in hell. He's obsessed with winning and can't stand defeat. It can take any form; from something as inconsequential as getting the waiter's attention first, to losing a bidding war."

"The Da Vinci Code."

"Yeah. It wasn't the only time he'd lost out to another producer or a studio, but that one embarrassed him the most."

"Because of his ties to the Vatican?"

"And Angels and Demons was more than he could take, or so I heard."

"But what does this have to do with your daughter?"

Carla appeared with a martini and placed it on the table next to Marjorie, who immediately drank almost half of it.

"I knew after our honeymoon that he was dangerous and decided not to tell him that I was pregnant. I was terrified that he'd take her and corrupt her to further the Church's agenda. He had become obsessed with its doctrine. That's all he spoke about, so I couldn't allow it. It would be better not to have her, then to risk exposing her to his madness."

"So you faked the abortion."

She nodded and finished the martini. "He would beat on me for hours on end, but I never told him the truth. I loved her and her life meant more than mine."

He sighed deeply. "I'm sorry."

Marjorie wiped her tears and smiled at Carla as she replaced her drink with a fresh one. "I took her to Mexico and dropped her off at the orphanage in San Carlos. It was the only thing I could do to protect her. For years I would send them money, but then one day she was adopted and that was that."

"You've never tried to find out who adopted her?"

"Not at first. Once I'd signed the release papers, I had no legal hold on her."

Boysie said quietly, "The price we pay."

Marjorie nodded. "Then a few years ago, I had a change of heart and tried to find her, but they wouldn't tell me. I even offered them ten million dollars and they turned me down flat."

"I don't know what to say; except that in light of everything, you probably did the right thing, Marj."

"Probably is right, but I guess I'll never know for sure." She took a sip on her second martini. "Doesn't a day go by that I don't think about her."

"That's what this is about. Ruining you because of her."

Marjorie stood up, a little uncertainly and helped by Boysie, made it over to her chaise longue. "Can you give me my martini please?" He brought it over and handed it to her. She took a sip, placed it down and looked at him. "I'm sorry to have dragged you into this."

"There was never any sale."

"What?"

"It was a set up between Gandolfo and Valentine. When he contacted you to sell the painting for him, it was David who was pulling the strings all along."

"I'm sorry, I don't understand."

"David had both paintings from jump. The real and the fake Pollock."

"But--"

"--He had you broker the deal, but never had any intention of buying the painting because he already owned both. He had given Valentine the forgery to make the deal look real, to you."

"But what about when Stanford Mills verified it?"

"Paid off, I guess and no money ever changed hands from Gandolfo's account to Valentine's."

"Yes it did. The Escrow Company handled the transaction. I signed all the paper work and was emailed a digital receipt once the money dropped. I have hard copies."

"Don't you see? It was a digital transfer of funds. I bet Gandolfo owns the Escrow Company and had someone erase all traces of the deal."

"Wait," Marjorie said, gathering her thoughts. "The fifteen million dollar fee is in my account."

"You sure?"

"Carla!"

She appeared in the doorway. "Sí señora."

"Bring me my iPad please." Carla disappeared into the house. "But why?"

"Revenge."

"Jesus Christ."

"As no shekels were handed over and Gandolfo has had the real Jackson Pollock all along, there's been no crime."

"Oh my."

Boysie let out a small chuckle and said, "It's quite brilliant, actually."

"Could you curb your enthusiasm for him and tell me if I'm liable for the one hundred and fifty million, or not?"

"No, you're not."

She nodded and suddenly, anger sparked across her eyes. "What about what he's put me through? Setting me up, so that my reputation's ruined? Even though you say the deal never happened, nobody'll ever buy anything from me again. I'm finished!"

"Yeah, he's a clever bastard."

"Son-of-a-bitch!" Carla reappeared and handed her the iPad. She logged on to her bank account and just stared at the screen, the blood draining from her face. "It's gone," she whispered hoarsely and turned to him.

"I figured it might be."

"You figured?" She glared at him. The alcohol fueled rage, twisting her face into ugly knots. Her lips pulled back like a snarling dog, revealing teeth that were clamped tightly together. "I want my fifteen million back!"

"Let it go," he advised calmly.

"That money's mine. I earned it. I brokered the deal."

"Technically yes, but--"

"--You promised you'd get it!"

"No, I promised I'd get the theft sorted and it is."

"I want my money, God damn it!"

"Marjorie, this is a very sticky wicket."

"I thought your word meant something?"

Irritation coursed through him and even though he knew he was being manipulated, he said, "Alright. I'll see what I can do but you have to understand, right now, that I reserve the right to back off as I see fit. Agreed?"

"Thank you," she smarmed.

He took a bottled water off the bar and drained it without stopping, placing the empty in the blue recycle bin. He looked at her and said, "Were you involved in helping to block Gandolfo from buying the Da Vinci Code manuscript?"

"No, of course not. I don't give a crap about religion." She sucked down the rest of the martini, some of it dribbling out the corner of her mouth. She wiped it away with her sleeve and yelled, "Carla!"

The housekeeper appeared with another martini and handed it to her, taking the empty glass. As she turned to leave, she caught Boysie's eye and made an apologetic face. He ignored her.

"Ease up with the libation, please?"

Marjorie looked at him, her head slightly wobbling. "What do I do now that I'm broke again?"

"You're far from broke, darlin'."

"Wealth is fleeting and relative to the amount of money you have." Her responses were taking on an alcoholic's irrationality. "Do have a drink, dear boy."

"No, thanks."

"Why's David being so God damn evil?"

"Because you lied about the abortion, stopped him from being her father and you know where she is, or at least he believes you do."

She considered this and when she had considered it long enough, anger puckered her mouth into hard rivulets. "Even if I could, I would never tell him."

Boysie stuck his hands back into his pockets. "And you really have no idea what became of her?"

She emptied her glass, tried to replace it on the table, missed and dropped it onto the concrete where it smashed into a thousand crystal shards. "No," she slurred, her eyes rolling up into her head.

A deep sadness washed over Boysie as he watched her slump back into the chaise longue. Within seconds, she was asleep. Carla appeared with a heavy blanket and gently covered her.

Father Murphy, listening attentively, sat opposite Boysie, nursing his pint of Guinness as punters came and went from the pub. "Jeasus, and ya say ya man there is ambidextrous?"

"Apparently."

"And he looked exactly like Marilyn Monroe?"

"She."

"She's a he, ya said."

"She's trans-gender."

"Takes all sorts, I guess."

"That's very liberal, coming from a man of the cloth."

"Pope Francis is very forward thinking," Father Murphy replied, reverently.

"I wonder how long it'll be before they Kennedy him?"

Father Murphy threw Boysie a look. "Never knew you for a conspiracy theorist."

"Normally, no, but the Vatican does have its share of dark mysteries, does it not, Father?"

The priest sipped his Guinness and wiped the foam off his whiskers. "I'll call the priest at the San Carlos Orphanage, but I doubt very much if he'll give me anything."

"Maybe you can sweet talk him."

Father Murphy soured his face. "You're not funny, although you think you're hilarious and anyways, I don't have the number."

Boysie held up his iPhone. Father Murphy took it, and his beer, and went to the private room at the back of the restaurant. Toni came out of the bar, glanced at Boysie and quickly left. He sipped his coffee as the side door opened and Eddie strolled in.

"Park your bones."

"Thanks," he replied and sat down.

Amanda came over. "Pint?"

"Coffee, and bangers and mash."

"Okay," she left to place the order.

Boysie asked, "What did you find out?"

"It's no secret that a lotta people wanna see Gandolfo crash and burn. But, very few, if any, are willing to say so publicly, let alone offer any info on his dealings."

"What about Bergman and Martinez?"

"They're both heavily in debt to him."

"Is that a fact?"

"Yeah, they wanted a loan to buy the land from Michael to up the value of their own properties and had assumed, you know, that he would sell it to them. So they borrowed the nine mill off Gandolfo, using their hotels as collateral."

"Why not just go to a bank?"

"I dunno. Anyway, they also had previous debts to the construction company that had built their hotels and used part of the loan to pay them off, as there was an impending lawsuit. So after all the madness that happened over the Da Vinci Code and Angels and Demons, Gandolfo was out for Michael's blood. He called in the marker and when they couldn't repay, in exchange for forgiving the loan, he had them whack him."

"They did it themselves?"

"No, they hired some dude out of San Pedro."

"Nine million dollars for a hit's an awful lotta money."

"Not when you've been screwed out of millions on the overall book and film deal," replied Eddie.

"But he never wanted either released, so he or the Vatican wasn't gonna make anything anyway."

"Yeah, he was," grinned Eddie, "because even if Bergman and Martinez did whack him, part of the deal was that Gandolfo would end up being a silent partner in their hotels. They, in turn, through a United Arab Emirate bank, had actually offered him an open Letter Of Credit to fund the film. Although the money was actually coming from Gandolfo, but without the Vatican's knowledge."

"Gordon Bennett!"

"Don't know him."

"No, it's a Cockney expression for----never mind. So let me get this straight; Gandolfo, against the Church's wishes, would've produced the film anyway?

"Yeah."

"But why? He's their Man In Havana."

"What?"

"It's an old spy novel."

"Yeah, I remember that. The one set in Cuba, right?"

Boysie nodded. "How did you find all this out?"

"I'm Puerto Rican, remember? We have our ways."

"No, seriously."

Amanda placed Eddie's coffee in front of him. "The food'll be right up."

"Okay," he smiled and took a sip. She left and he lifted the front of his sweatshirt, revealing the .380 tucked in his waistband. "Martinez didn't like having my gun stuck in his face."

"Subtle."

"Effective," grinned Eddie.

"Don't say anything to the priest yet. I'll handle that."

"Sure."

Amanda placed the bangers and mash in front of him and asked, "Anything else?"

"No, I'm good, thanks."

"Okay," replied Amanda and went back into the bar.

The priest sat back down. "It's as I thought, Boysie, they'll not be giving out any information."

"I suppose I've gotta go see 'em myself."

"Who?" asked Father Murphy.

"The orphanage."

"The one in Mexico?"

Boysie smiled, "Unless they've moved to Beverly Hills."

Eddie swallowed his food. "When?"

"Now."

"Can I finish my food first?" asked Eddie.

"Take your time. I'm going alone."

Father Murphy rubbed his heavily lined face. "Ya want me to go with you?"

"No. You take care of the Wicked Witch."

"That's not a nice way to refer to ya mother."

Boysie left.

20 ~ THE DEVIL'S DISCIPLE

ON THE WAY TO VAN Nuys Airport, Boysie called Marjorie, telling her about his excursion to Mexico. The charter flight took off and quickly ascended to a cruising altitude of twenty nine thousand feet. Boysie relaxed into the luxurious, hand tooled leather executive chair. He glanced at the exotic wood table in front of him, on which the glass of Woodford Reserve rested contentedly. Angela, the flight attendant, a beautiful thirty something with very long legs wrapped in black stockings, smiled at him.

"Would you care for something to eat?"

"No, I'm fine, thanks."

She liked him, he could tell from the smile that never faded to the amber eyes that drank him in. "If you need anything else, Mr. Blake, just let me know."

"Boysie."

"Boysie," she agreed and moved away with some effort.

He went back to his deliberations, trying hard to hide that he was a white-knuckle flyer. He had once mentioned this to Jason, who had used it as the title to one of his songs. He gulped the bourbon and sat back as the warmth spread across him. He looked out of the window at the land spread out, far below and he tried to distract himself by checking his passport. No good. He swallowed the rest of the bourbon. Angela appeared with a fresh glass of the caramel gold and set it on the table. He looked at it, then up into her eyes, the color of which resembled the bourbon. The attraction he had seen in them only minutes before had been replaced by a motherly empathy that was oddly reassuring.

"I used to hate flying, but just like anything, you get used to it," she offered reassuringly.

Boysie nodded. "I try to avoid it at all cost."

"May I sit down?"

"Please," he replied, welcoming the distraction. A soft napkin appeared in her hand that she held out for him. He took it and wiped the misting sweat off his brow. "Thanks."

"I've been flying for fifteen years and never an incident."

"With this company?"

"Yep. The pilot's my ex," she smiled wryly.

"How's that working out?"

"It's cool. We're better friends than we were lovers."

Dutch courage was beginning to calm Boysie. "Yeah, I've been in a few of those. Never easy though. I mean, you know, to go back to being friends after you've been intimate."

"For us there was no other choice. We own the airline."

"Wait. You own this yet you still fly?"

"Sure."

"Why's that?"

She took a breath and relaxed into her seat. "I love it," she shrugged.

"Huh."

"So is this business or pleasure?"

"Business."

"And what type of business are you in, Boysie, if it's not too personal of a question?" He slid one of his cards across the table. She looked at it without picking it up. "Cryptic."

"Discrete."

"And what types of problems do you solve?"

"It depends on the situation. I'm always open."

She narrowed her eyes, rubbed the tip of her nose with her index and pointed at him. "Didn't I just read about you?"

"I don't know. Did you?"

She nodded and looked down at his side. "Something about how some cop tried to kill you."

"Yeah, that would be me."

"Bad business."

"Now there's any understatement."

She nodded and crossed her legs. He wanted to look at her shapely thighs, obligingly exposed by the skirt riding up. He resisted and contented himself with peripheral only. This was the type of woman that didn't miss a trick and she smiled at his self-control. "There's a lot of ex-pats that live in San Carlos. Is this your first trip?"

"Yeah."

"We've flown there a few times. It's an interesting place. Seeing anything in particular?" Boysie smiled and remained schtum. "Got it," she confirmed with a grin.

"Please don't think I'm being rude, Angela. It's very complicated and I've no wish to involve anybody in the craziness of it all."

"It's cool. I just got the feeling you wanted to talk."

He coaxed some more of the Woodford Reserve out of his glass. "Maybe when it's all over?"

"Is it ever?"

He put the glass down. "No."

Angela stood and smoothed the wrinkles out of her skirt. "I'm going forward to see if the pilots need anything."

"Okay."

She smiled and headed for the cockpit. He passed the time looking down at the mountains of Mexico, rippled in shadows from passing clouds.

The sweaty immigration officer cast his beady eyes over Boysie. He took out a Kleenex, blew his nose and wiped the excess, left and right, into his already crystallized moustache. Filled with self-importance, he examined the US passport, glared at Boysie, stamped it and handed it back to him. He nodded his thanks and went outside.

Mariachi music danced quietly out of the radio as they sped past the newly constructed Spanish Villas of the burgeoning American and Canadian communities. Jesús kept the Lincoln as clean as he kept himself and smiled constantly.

"You from San Carlos, Jesús?"

"Sí, señor. I live here my whole life."

"It's expanding then?"

"Sí. Good for me. Not so good for my people."

"Who are they?"

"Gyamenas," he answered proudly. "You know what this is?"

"Indians."

"Sí. Muy machismo," he replied and turned off the main highway onto a less traveled side road, on which the occasional truck or taxi journeyed.

"And what about the people that run the orphanage?"

"They are friends of mine. Very bueno."

"But the town's growth is not so good?"

"No, not so much."

Boysie nodded. "What about the orphanage? Is that good for your people?"

"How do you mean, señor?"

"It's mostly local kids, right? You know, ones abandoned by their families?"

Clearly, this made Jesús uncomfortable. His smile took a vacation as he shifted in his seat and glanced at Boysie.

"Have you ever seen or heard of a white kid there?"

"Señor?"

"Mira, no habla Ingles?"

Boysie's perfect Spanish took him by surprise. "Sí."

"Then answer the question."

"But I do not know."

Boysie took out his billfold, slid out two, one hundred dollar bills and offered them across Jesús' right shoulder. The Benjamins waited patiently as the driver glanced from Boysie to them.

"This is why you are in San Carlos, to see if they have any white kids?"

"Yes. This is why I'm in San Carlos."

"You don't like Mexican childrens?"

"I like Mexican childrens just fine. But I'm interested in finding a young white girl, that was adopted many years ago."

"La Jura?"

"No, I'm not a cop."

"How you speak Spanish so good?" asked Jesús slyly.

"I live in Mexico, only now it's called California."

Jesús burst out laughing and when he had laughed enough, he snatched the money and glanced at Boysie in the rear view. "You pretty cool, for a Gringo."

"And you're pretty cool, for a lying Mexican."

Jesús jammed on the brakes; the tires screamed in protest, spitting out clouds of blue-black rubber smoke. The Lincoln slid off the blacktop onto a dirt side road, and Jesús accelerated at blinding speed into the Sonoran desert. Boysie waited for him to stop, which he did about a mile or so in. Angrily, Jesús jumped out and pulled his gun, glaring at him through the black tinted windows. As he yanked the door open, Boysie shouldered it as hard as he could, slamming it onto the unsuspecting driver. He flew backward, dropping his gun into the sand. Boysie scrambled out and obliged him with a swift kick to the groin. Jesús screamed, grabbed his balls and doubled over, trying desperately to force air back into his lungs.

Boysie ignored the burning pain in his side from the healing bullet wound. He picked up the nine millimeter and aimed it at the belligerent Mexican. "Where were you taking me?"

"To the orphanage, man," lied Jesús.

"Bollox. You think I can't read a map?"

"But Señor--"

"--Shut it."

Jesús looked genuinely hurt, which made Boysie laugh, but without mirth or merriment. He aimed the gun at his face. "I'm gonna ask one more time. Where were you taking me?"

Jesús saw the hardness in Boysie's, cold, blue eyes, and swallowed. "To meet my cousins."

"And why were you taking me to meet your cousins?" Jesús shrugged the answer. Boysie nodded. "Who called 'em?"

"No se." Boysie stuck the gun onto Jesús' groin. "No!"

The nine millie spoke for Boysie. The bullet chewed desert between Jesús' legs. This was too much for the limo driver, who let go of his bladder, soaking his pants. "That's your only warning. Who called 'em?"

"Señor, I am sorry, man. Please, do not kill me. I beg to you. I have a family."

"Leave it out, mate. You were taking me on a one way bender and now you expect me to show you mercy?"

"Sí señor. Please?"

Boysie had no intention of killing him, but the longer Jesús thought he might, the more information he would give up. "It had to be someone in L.A. So who the bloody hell was it?"

"My sister."

"Your sister?" he repeated, his heart beginning to race.

"Sí."

Revelation fought a brief, but pitched battle, with the fog of denial and won. The implication was now so awful that for a split second, Boysie could only swallow away the burden of it. His mouth became as dry as the desert he was standing on and echoing across the barren mountains, came the hysterical laugh of the mocking jester of betrayal.

"Carla," he said quietly.

"Sí," Jesús replied fearfully.

The pretty face of Marjorie's housekeeper flashed into Boysie's mind. He lowered the gun, turned around and took a few shaky steps away from the Lincoln. A wave of nausea swept across him and he wretched so hard, that his ears rang. Jesús cautiously backed away, turned and ran out into the shimmering heat. Boysie heard him and snarling, turned around and shot him once in the ass. Jesús screamed in pain and tumbled to the dirt.

Boysie walked up and stood over him. Glaring death and vengeance, he pulled back the hammer on the gun. The driver, bleeding into the sand, put his hands up in front of his face in a futile effort to protect himself. Somewhere in the world, people of honor and integrity, were going about their daily lives. Loving their significant other. Their families. Their friends. Just not here. Just not today.

"Your cell phone work out here?"

"Señor?" he asked, grimacing in pain.

"Does your fucking cell work out here?"

"Sí. Sí."

BANG! BANG! Boysie blasted out Jesús' knees, leaving him in screaming agony. Now in a blind rage, he stomped back over to the limo and emptied the remaining bullets into it; blowing out windows, headlights, tires and punching holes in the black bodywork.

Boysie searched the car and found what he was looking for - matches. Wiping his prints off the gun, he left it on the front seat and went around to where gas was spilling out of the tank, soaking into the thirsty sand. Jesús knew exactly what he was going to do and despite the dreadful pain in his knees and ass, choked back tears and started crawling away as fast as he was able out into the shimmering desert. Boysie watched as the heat haze devoured him, and waited until the he was at a safe distance. He lit the match pack, tossed it onto the leaking gas and headed back toward the road. The Lincoln Town Car exploded in a massive fireball.

Boysie flagged a cab that took him to the Orphanage San Carlos. An old, Spanish Mission complete with bell tower. The grounds were well kept and the huge double wooden doors created an effective barrier from the outside world, further secured by the two HD cameras above the entrance.

He got out of the cab and handed the driver a hundred dollar bill, whose eyes lit up as he snapped brown fingers around it.

"Wait here and there's another one to keep that company. Comprende?"

"Si señor."

Boysie smiled up at one of the cameras and rang the intercom. A woman's soft voice answered. "Yes?"

"I would like to see Father Sebastian, please."

The buzzer sounded and the huge wooden gates opened inward. Boysie took the neatly laid flagstone path up to the main building, noting the numerous discreet HD security cameras, and entered the cool, quiet, ornately paneled foyer. Waiting for him was a smiling priest and a not so smiling nun, Sister Magdalene. She looked as white-washed as the surrounding walls. Her face, wrinkled. Hands, strong from years of work.

Boysie looked at the priest. "Father Sebastian?"

"You must be Mr. Blake," he replied, nodding and smiling as he shook his hand.

"I am."

Boysie held out his hand toward the nun. She looked at it with all the disdain of a used condom and made no move to shake it. He grinned and retracted his digits. Locking eyes with her, he waited in a strained silence for her invitation to a more private and comfortable setting. The invitation never came.

Instead, the sour faced nun with a perfect English accent asked, "How may we help you?"

"I need information."

"We do not give out any information on adoptees and neither do we succumb to threats," she said in an irritated voice.

Boysie chortled. "I've never spoken to you."

"You're here about the Wallace girl, are you not?"

"Clairvoyant are we?"

"And you work for that detective, right?"

"Detective?"

The nun and the priest glanced at each other. She said, "Lawton."

Boysie shook his head. "No, I don't work for him and anyway, he's dead."

Shock creased their faces. The priest asked. "How?"

"I killed him."

Silence filled the foyer as the nun swallowed hard, and fearfully licked her suddenly dry lips. She asked quietly, "What do you want?"

"I'm not the enemy, nor do I intend either of you any harm. If I did, why would Father Murphy have called you?"

They said nothing.

"Her biological father is a very powerful and not so nice man, who desperately wants to find her. Lawton worked for him. I don't. He tried to kill me. Now stay with me and let me know if I'm going too fast. Okay?"

Neither responded. Fear had apparently fueled their imaginations.

Boysie continued, "Marjorie Wallace is a friend of mine that her ex-husband, the powerful and not so nice man, is trying to ruin because of all this. Do you understand?"

"I see," replied Sister Magdalene.

"Did you tell Lawton about the girl?"

"We never confirmed it, no," answered Father Sebastian.

"Then how did he know?"

A young Mexican boy came out of a side door, bowed politely and ran off.

The nun motioned to a closed, wooden door. "Please, this way."

She led them into a quiet side room, furnished in beautiful hard wood, with several comfortable leather chairs. The unmistakable scent of Frankincense hung in the air. Boysie wondered if it was responsible for the perpetual smiles on the statues of the holy ones set into recessed archways. She closed the door and they sat down.

Father Sebastian adjusted his frock coat. "The girl was not with us very long. In Mexico, a white child is not something one sees every day and we had a lot of people that wanted to adopt her."

Sister Magdalene nodded piously. "She was very beautiful; all blond curls and big blue eyes. We thought she was very special."

"Yes," agreed the priest. "She had the eyes of an angel."

"What happened to her?"

"She was adopted by an American family," answered the Sister.

"I know you can't tell me who they are, but can you at least tell me where they live?"

Sister Magdalene shook her head. "No, I'm sorry. I'm sure you understand."

"Yeah, I do, as a matter-of-fact."

She looked relieved. "Thank you."

"Her mother's not doing too good. She's very depressed and lonely."

Father Sebastian smiled his concern. "She would call all the time to see how she was, even after she had been adopted. But once the child has left us, we do not monitor them. She even offered us ten million dollars for her whereabouts, but we refused, of course."

"Of course."

The nun and the priest smiled benevolently. Boysie grinned and looked around the room. "So who's your benefactor then?"

"Sorry?" asked the nun, her piety beginning to fade.

"It takes a lotta wedge to run a place like this. How do you pay for it?"

"Wedge?" asked Sister Magdalene.

"You're English, right? And you don't know what wedge means?"

"I'm sure I don't," she snapped, her smile flapping lifelessly on the floor.

"Oh, come on now, Sister, don't be coy."

"It doesn't concern you how we support the orphanage." Indignation as hollow as her eyes.

"It's the Vatican that keeps you afloat, isn't it?"

"We are under the guidance and protection of the Catholic Church."

"If I didn't know better, Sister, I'd say that sounded an awful lot like a threat."

A smarmy expression reshaped Sister Magdalene's face. She stood up. "I believe we're done here. Have a nice day."

Boysie remained seated. "Then again, ten million dollars goes an awful long way in Mexico, doesn't it?"

"Leave or I'll be forced to call the police," she hissed.

"Go ahead. I'm sure they'd love to be involved in an international investigation of murder and bribery, that'll lead all the way back to the Holy See."

Father Sebastian motioned for her to sit back down. Meekly, she complied. He turned to Boysie. "Whatever you may think you know, you do not."

"Father, this a Catholic orphanage supported, in part, I'm sure, by contributions and whatever the Vatican gives you. I have no issue with that."

The priest took a contemplative breath. "We have never, nor will we ever, take money from anyone to reveal the location of one of our adoptees."

He said it with such conviction, that Boysie was compelled to believe him. "Understood, but her father--"

"--We know of David Gandolfo."

"I'm sure you do," he agreed with a sarcastic smile. Father Sebastian lost some of his benevolence. "Anyway, Father, then please enlighten me. I mean I can't get my head around the fact that as he's so tied in to the Vatican, that they simply wouldn't have you tell him who adopted her. Yeah? Can you explain that?"

Father Sebastian regained his composure. "The same rule of non disclosure applies to everyone. It doesn't matter who they are, or whom they're connected to."

Boysie opened the door and left.

21 ~ THE DEAD DON'T LIE

THE CHARTER JET LANDED AT Van Nuys Airport later that evening. Boysie paid Angela the bill, twenty thousand, seven hundred dollars with his black AMEX, adding a ten percent tip. After being cleared at Customs, about an hour later and deep in thought, he pulled Celeste up outside of Father Murphy's church. The doors were locked, so he went over to the rectory and rang the buzzer.

"Ah, there ya are, Boysie."

He followed the priest in, who closed and locked the door securely and led him into the living room. A bottle of Bushmills sat on the table; a half full glass of the Irish whisky next to it. The priest filled another glass and pushed it toward him.

He stared at the priest, took a sip and put it down. "San Carlos is an interesting place."

"Did ya get clarity?" he slurred.

"Wherever she is, they're not telling."

"So ya wasted your time. I knew it."

"Someone's paying them an awful lotta pesos to keep it that way."

"What makes ya think that?"

"Have you ever seen the orphanage?"

"No."

"Well they're not broke. Know what I mean?"

Father Murphy drained his glass and replied, "It has to be Marjorie's money."

"No, I don't believe so."

"Then who?" He poured another glass of whisky.

"Someone with deep pockets and enough reason for not wanting the kid found."

"Except she ain't a kid anymore."

Boysie shook his head. "No, I suppose not. How old would she be now?"

"Late twenties maybe."

"What're you talking about?"

"The Queen Mother. Who do ya think?" snapped the priest.

"Marjorie told me she had her in seventy-two. So that would make her forty-two."

"Impossible. Ya must've misheard her." The priest tried to focus, gave up on that and sipped his whisky.

Boysie rolled his bottom lip between his teeth. "Why do you say that's impossible?" Father Murphy shrugged and looked around the room. Boysie studied him intently. "I asked you a question."

"Twenty-six," he spat out and added, "there, are ya happy?"

"You knew?"

"Boysie--" sighed the priest wearily.

"--Did you, or did you not now know about the kid?"

He nodded. "Aye, I baptized her." Boysie felt numb. Father Murphy made an apologetic face. "Marjorie swore me to secrecy. I made a promise. I couldn't break it, no matter how much I wanted to."

Boysie popped a Fisherman's Friend into his mouth, locked eyes with the priest and stood up. "So Marjorie was still involved with Gandolfo sixteen years after she told me she was. I don't get it. Why?"

"You remember I came over here in 87, to suss out the parish?"

Boysie nodded. "Four years after my dad was topped."

"Aye. That's when I first met Marjorie and David. She confided in me that she was pregnant and begged me not to tell him. I agreed to baptize the baby and….and I went with her to San Carlos when she gave her up for adoption."

"You fucking knew all along."

Father Murphy, his hand shaking badly, finished the glass of Bushmills. "I uh---."

Boysie leaned down, glaring at his old friend. "Who else? Who else fucking knew?"

"Ya ma."

He felt the blood drain out of his face. "Of course she did."

"Boysie--"

"--You lot've had a right good laugh at my expense."

"No, it's not like that."

"How is it then, really?"

The priest lowered his eyes. "I wanted to tell ya, but couldn't break me word. You can understand that, right?"

"But you could hang me out to dry, chasing all over God's creation instead of giving me the info I needed."

"I'm sorry."

"I don't know who's more treacherous; you three or Gandolfo."

"That's not fair."

"Not fair?"

Father Murphy poured himself more whisky. "When your ma first asked you to help, I tried to dissuade her 'cause I knew it was going to get messy. But you know how she is. I'm sorry."

Anger flexed Boysie's jaw muscles. "I'm gonna find his kid, well, woman now, I guess, because it's the only way to make sure Gandolfo doesn't bury us all."

Father Murphy nodded and found himself unable to look him in the eye. "I understand."

"Eddie told me that Martinez admitted that he and Bergman had Michael whacked."

Father Murphy's face turned bright red as the whisky-fueled rage coursed through him. "Those bastards!"

"And I have an idea who did it."

The priest hissed venomously, "What're ya gonna do about it?"

Boysie grinned, but more from irony than humor. "It's not just me anymore, Father. You're in this too now, you know?"

"But--"

"--Don't."

"But I'm a priest."

"And now you're gonna be my inside man."

"Inside man?" he exclaimed.

"When I need to know anything, and I do mean anything that's floating around the Vatican, you're gonna get it for me."

"Jeasus. Spy on me own people?"

"Think of it as helping to put things right in the world. Very altruistic."

"You're a bastard."

"Quite possibly."

Father Murphy knew he was trapped. He shrugged his shoulders, sipped his whisky and asked hopefully, "Can't ya have 'em arrested?"

Boysie shook his head. "No proof, just hearsay obtained under duress." The father looked confused. "Eddie stuck a gun in Martinez' face."

"Pity he didn't shoot the fucker."

"How Catholic of you."

"You can be as cynical as ya like, Boysie, but the fact remains that the Catholic Church does a lotta great deeds for people all over the world. As well as providing the one true word of God the Father, the Son and the Holy Ghost."

"You forgot to say amen."

"Ah, kiss me Irish arse."

Boysie killed Celeste's headlights and turned off the motor, rolling to a gentle, gravel crunching stop on the hard shoulder. Taking out a pair of powerful night-vision binoculars, he scanned Marjorie's house for any signs of movement. Seeing none, he quietly jumped the wall, making his way around to the back. As he approached the patio, he could hear the raised, angry voices of her and Carla.

"Your brother's an idiot!"

"But Señora, Boysie is crazy. You know this!"

"Jesus Christ. I have to get out of here before he gets back."

"But he cannot prove you had anything to do with it."

"Don't you get it?" shrieked Marjorie, "he doesn't need to prove anything. Jesús damn well told him. How can I deny that? Tell me!"

"My cousins in East Los will take care of--"

"--Me?" asked Boysie as he appeared out of the darkness and ambled onto the patio, hands casually in his pockets.

Marjorie and Carla were stunned as the specter of their own demise materialized before them; or at least they believed he was. Their expressions became fixed. The blood drained from their faces and the already tense atmosphere amped itself up a thousand notches. Carla took a faltering step backward. He hardened his eyes and shook his head just once. She froze and glanced fearfully at Marjorie.

She, in turn, stared at him defiantly and placed a hand on her chest, just below her throat. "To protect her, I'd do it all again," she shrilled.

Carla's eyes filled with tears. "I am sorry, Boysie. My brother was only supposed to--"

"--What?" he snarled angrily. She fell silent and let the intent of her lies drift away into the darkness, which is exactly what she wanted to do. "Do you have a Green Card?"

"Señor?"

"A Green Card. Do you have one and by that, I mean a real one and not one that you bought downtown?"

She looked down at her feet, shook her head and said quietly, "No."

"I didn't think so."

She looked up at him as fearful realization charged through her. "No! Por favor?"

"I called La Migra and gave them your address."

The tears that had been gathering burst their banks and poured down her cheeks. "No! Please, Señor Boysie I cannot go back to Mexico!"

"Sure you can. Especially as you'll now be wet nurse to your crippled brother." Boysie glanced at his Tag Heuer. "If you leave now, you might have just enough time to grab a few things before they get to your house."

Carla looked pleadingly at Marjorie, who ignored her. The cold indifference was a testament to the vanishing ghost of their fifteen-year friendship. Stunned, Carla angrily wiped her face. She disappeared inside the house and a few moments later, her car was heard screeching away. Boysie swallowed the hurt and Marjorie continued her defiant glare. They both knew that no matter what was said, it didn't matter one iota. He rolled his bottom lip between his teeth and bit down hard. The taste of blood did nothing to calm him.

The early morning jogger discovered Marjorie's body in the cold lapping water of Stone Canyon Reservoir. The Coroner concluded that because of her high blood-alcohol level, she had taken a misstep and fallen over a thousand feet to her death.

22 ~ MAD DOGS AND ENGLISHMEN

FATHER MURPHY'S WATERY EYES WATCHED Boysie with a soft compassion not often displayed by the old priest. They sat at the back of the church and listened to the cold wind blowing in off the Pacific. Boysie shifted in his seat; the creaking wood echoed off granite and plaster. The priest's bulbous nose looked even more so and recently had taken to glowing a darker hue of crimson.

Finally, Boysie asked quietly, "She told you about us?"

"Aye, she did."

"I really liked her."

"And she you. She told me so. In fact, the day after you and her, well, you know, anyway, she confessed to me that she loved ya."

Boysie's eyes darted sorrowfully around the church desperately trying to find something, anything, other than Marjorie's coffin in front of the altar. The smell of all the fresh-cut flowers, cloyingly pungent, overwhelmed the omnipresent frankincense that usually claimed the church as its domain.

"I thought confessions were sacred?"

"They are. She told me over the phone and anyway, it wasn't in me official capacity."

"Jesus. This whole thing's such a bloody mess."

"They found something written in blood on her patio floor." Boysie looked at him and frowned his silent question. "The cops said she'd cut herself before she, ya know, fell."

Boysie looked down at his hands, wrung them despairingly and said quietly, "Fuck."

"Do you want to know what it said?"

"No."

Father Murphy took out his hip flask and took a mouthful. He handed it to Boysie who did the same. "Yeah, okay."

The priest took back the flask. "The dead don't lie."

Boysie sucked in his bottom lip and winced. "What does that mean?"

"What it says, I s'ppose."

"But lie about what?"

"The kid, maybe?"

"Yeah, maybe."

"What happened to ya mouth there, Boysie?"

"The Vatican could just tell Gandolfo where she is. So why haven't they?"

"'Cause it's against the law to violate the rules of confidentiality."

Boysie almost laughed and would have, except for the tragedy of it all. "Leave it out."

"What?"

"You don't believe that bollox anymore than I do."

The priest's caterpillar eyebrows started twitching. He had another nip from his flask. "Then why?"

"Power," he said matter-of-factly.

"Power? How do ya mean?"

"In any relationship, the one that displays the most indifference always has the upper hand."

"You're talking about insecurity."

"I'm talking about control."

Father Murphy lowered his head and was thoughtful for a moment. He looked up at Boysie and declared, "Then the only thing it can be, is that the

Holy See knows exactly where she is, but won't tell him 'cause they're pissed off with him over the Da Vinci Code."

"No, that's too petty. There's no advantage in that."

"Then what?"

"That might've been the catalyst, but I believe they've got a much bigger agenda in play now."

"I take comfort in the fact that the Holy Father knows what he's doing."

Boysie smirked. "A well deserving reward after all his years of loyalty, hey?"

"Ya reap what ya sow," replied the priest with an emphatic nod of his head.

"I doubt Gandolfo sees it that way."

"Will ya be here for the Requiem?"

"No."

Father Murphy watched as Boysie hurried out of the door, which the wind caught, held open and slammed shut. The boom echoed around the church and reminded him of an anguished cry. He crossed himself, looked up at Jesus on the cross, suffering for all eternity, and had another drink.

23 ~ DEAD IN SAN PEDRO

BERGMAN CLIMBED OUT OF HIS Mercedes, closed the door and chirped the alarm. Humming to himself, he looked admiringly at his own reflection in the black tinted windows and froze as Boysie materialized behind him. He turned around, his mouth twitching fearfully as he licked his dry lips. Hands in his pockets, Boysie continued to stare at him.

Bergman tried to smile. "Hi, Boysie."

"How's Martinez?"

"He uh, he told me that one of your associates spoke to him."

"He was very talkative."

Bergman found some courage and smirked at him. "Doesn't matter. You can't prove anything and he'll never appear in court."

Boysie put a Fisherman's Friend in his mouth. "How's Gandolfo?"

"Who?"

Boysie grinned and studied him. "I'm gonna give you one more chance and if you don't tell me, I'm gonna hand you the beatin' of your life."

"Is that right?" said the voice behind him.

Boysie turned around. Paul Windsor and Meathead were ambling toward him. "Yeah, that's right."

Bergman sneered. "The only one that's gonna get a beatin' is you, asshole!"

CRACK! Boysie back elbowed him in the face. His head snapped back and smacked onto the Mercedes roof edge, knocking him out cold. His nose popped like a blood blister, spraying claret all down his suit.

"Motherfucka!" screamed Windsor.

He leapt at Boysie, who sidestepped and brought his knee up into Windsor's gut, knocking the wind out of him. Meathead hit Boysie hard, sinking him to his knees, blood pouring out of his mouth. Windsor got slowly to his feet and began kicking him in the ribs. Meathead joined in and he tried to roll under the Mercedes, but Windsor grabbed his foot and pulled him back out. Boysie kicked as furiously as he could, but he was out of gas and out of time. The roar of unconsciousness overtook him and the last thing he remembered, was Paul Windsor's fist slamming into his face.

Normally, cracked ribs cause tremendous agony and rob the injured of breath. Add a healing bullet wound and the pain increases to unimaginable heights. Every lungful feels like a blunt knife being jabbed into your side and nothing can ease the pain, except morphine and time, of which he had neither.

Boysie could hear the anguished cry of a man and as the black void of confusion loosened its grip on him, he realized that the painful cries were his. The distant echoing footsteps of Paul Windsor emerged out of the gloom. He strolled over to him, as if he didn't have a care in the world. Dressed in his black uniform, he eyeballed Boysie with death filled eyes.

"You don't look so good," he sneered. "Don't worry, I'll put you out of your misery soon enough."

"Like you did that Muslim family?"

Windsor shrugged his indifference. "Collateral damage and anyway, who gives a crap about ragheads?"

Boysie spat blood-clotted phlegm into his face. Windsor wiped it away and smeared it back across his face. Boysie didn't flinch or protest, instead, he smiled up at him. In a side room, a toilet flushed and Meathead appeared. Seeing that Boysie was now awake, he grinned nasty, making a bee-line for him.

"Paul, does Meathead comprehend language? I need to take a leak."

Meathead balled up his fists, glee filling his face. "You gonna wish you never said that."

Boysie smirked. "It's a miracle. It speaks."

Meathead snatched him by his throat and drew back a meat club to pound him with. Windsor ordered, "Don't!"

"But--"

"--I need him awake." Meathead continued to squeeze Boysie's throat, choking off his air supply. He started to black out, his eyes rolling up into his head. Windsor snarled, "Let him go!"

Meathead backed off. Boysie, able to breathe again, started to regain consciousness. He managed to stop his eyes rolling around and fixed them on Paul Windsor. "I, I uh, I need the bathroom."

"Hold it."

"I can't. Sorry."

Paul Windsor hesitated and nodded at Meathead. He untied Boysie's feet, yanked him up and escorted him over to the Men's Room.

Inside, he stood in front of the urinal and looked at Meathead. "How am I gonna get it out?"

"What?" asked Meathead, not quite getting it.

"You know, my Willy?"

Meathead followed Boysie's head nodding down toward his zipper.

"Oh, right."

Tentatively, he moved his hand toward his fly, then stopped and retracted it. "I ain't no fag."

"Look, mate, if you don't hurry up, I'm gonna wet meself and then I'm gonna stink the place up. You don't want that, do you?"

"I better ask Paul what to do."

"This isn't rocket science. Just undo my zipper, pull out my Willy and hold it while I go."

"Hold it?"

"Yeah otherwise I'll just pee all over myself. Know what I mean?"

Meathead hesitantly flicked his eyes down at Boysie's zipper and grimaced distastefully. "Dude, I ain't holding your dick."

"Then how am I am gonna nash the slash?"

"Huh?"

"Take a leak?"

Meathead sighed, glanced one more time at Boysie's zipper and undid his handcuffs. "Hurry up."

Boysie nodded, undid his zipper and relieved himself. "Ah, man, that feels so good."

"You done?"

"Not quite." Boysie spun around and peed all over Meathead.

He involuntarily jumped back. "You mother--" was all he managed to get out.

Boysie head-butted him so hard and fast, that he was unconscious before he hit the concrete floor, the warm pee soaking into his black uniform. Grimacing with pain from his cracked ribs, he bent down and grabbed Meathead's gun and three spare clips. Flicking off the safety, he cracked the door open.

Paul Windsor was talking to a woman in her thirties, also dressed in black, gun on her hip. Boysie scanned the area for a side door. The illuminated exit sign was halfway down the building, and he would have to get past them to use it. He took a couple of shallow breaths and aiming the gun at the unsuspecting Midnight Securities operatives, walked toward them as quickly as he could. The woman's mouth dropped open. Windsor spun around and froze, staring down the barrel of Boysie's gun. He flicked it toward the woman.

"You."

"Me?" she asked, shocked.

"Cuff him. Hands behind his back, and lady, don't do anything stupid."

Unsure, she glanced at Windsor who snarled, "She's not gonna cuff me."

"I'm gonna leave and you're going with me, so for all I care, it can be feet first."

"Fuck you," replied Windsor.

The woman regained her composure. "Paul, what the hell's going on?"

"He's wanted for murder."

"He's a bloody liar! He and his opo kidnapped me."

"Arrested you!" screamed Windsor.

"What's your name?" asked Boysie.

"What?" she asked, surprised.

"Your name, what is it?"

"Marcy."

"Okay, Marcy, don't believe me? Call the cops and let them figure it out."

"Don't listen to him."

Marcy glanced at Windsor. "Maybe he's right."

"No. He's the piece'a shit that killed that cop."

Any doubt Marcy was having instantly suffered the same fate as the Dodo bird. She hardened her face and glared at Boysie. "That's him?"

"Yeah, that's him," smirked Windsor.

A wave of nausea crested over Boysie and he squeezed his eyes, trying to keep the bile down. The moment passed but the accompanying sweat soaked his face and neck. "Marcy, don't listen to him. Please, just call 'em."

Paul Windsor barked, "Why don't you just put down the gun?"

BANG! Boysie's bullet seared the air next to Windsor and blew out the windshield of one of the black SUVs behind him, setting off its alarm. "Call 'em!" he snarled. Marcy hesitated. "Do it! Now!"

Marcy looked like she didn't take crap from anyone. "Look, sir, whatever's going on, put the gun down and we can work it out."

Paul Windsor glanced past him and grinned. Boysie looked at Marcy for confirmation that Meathead was indeed coming up behind him. The fact that she remained focused on him, assured him that he wasn't. Windsor started inching his hand toward the gun on his hip.

Boysie warned, "Don't do it."

Windsor's expression changed from fear-tinged uncertainty, to suicidal determination. He put his hand on his gun and glared insanely at Boysie.

Marcy, either emboldened by his recklessness, or working off her own self-preservation instinct, did the same. Boysie shook his head but it was too late and they all knew it. This, after all, is exactly what they had been trained for. Windsor and Marcy drew their guns. Boysie shot him once in the chest. Surprise bubbled out of his mouth, red and gooey. He staggered back, blood soaking the black military ribbed sweater and slumped against the side of an SUV, sliding down to the floor. Marcy had never been in a firefight before. She sidestepped and fired too quickly. The bullets screamed past Boysie who dropped to one knee and returned fire, hitting her once in the throat. Paul Windsor, not quite dead yet, managed to squeeze off several more shots. Boysie dived behind one of the black SUVs as some of the bullets slammed into it. Others ricocheted off concrete and steel. The deafening sound of the gunfire died in a volley of echoes, replaced by the incessant blaring of car alarms. Boysie picked up a piece of broken side mirror and used it to look past the SUV. Windsor brought his gun up, but the clip was now empty, and near death, he was too exhausted to reload. Marcy was lying on her back, gasping for air as she choked on her own blood. The bullet hole in her neck was spurting out dark red liquid as she tried desperately to suck air back in. It was to no avail. He watched as her life force oozed out of her, spreading across the dirty oil-stained concrete toward the center drain; a slow moving puddle of wasted life. She looked at him with frenzied eyes, desperate for help that would never arrive. Her mouth, moving, trying to form words that clogged in her throat. He knelt down and held her hand. She locked eyes with him, took a final, gurgling breath and died. He stood up, went over to Paul Windsor and, loading in a fresh clip, stood over him.

"Help me," pleaded Windsor.

"She's dead."

"Call 911."

"Who ordered the hit on me?"

"I dunno," he replied and coughed up dark blood from deep within his lungs. "I'm fucking dying, man."

Boysie knew that he'd never tell him anything. "That Muslim girl you shot in the head? I still see her face."

Windsor let out a coughing laugh. "She was a fucking sand nigger."

Boysie aimed his gun at Windsor's head. His eyes widened in terror and he jerked from side to side, as if that would avoid the inevitable.

He screamed, "Don't man! Who cares? Who cares what she was?"

"I do."

Boysie shot him in the face, exploding gore and brain matter out the back of his head. He slumped over, made no sound, no movement, and never would again.

Detectives Chang and Rodriguez of the San Pedro police department stared at Boysie with equal parts disdain and curiosity. As he told them what had happened, paramedics cleaned up his wounds. The cops didn't believe him. However, this was something that they could now use to shut down Midnight Securities. So, they went with his story. Two uniforms were leading Meathead away, who, covered in blood, was still dazed and confused. He always would be.

Detective Chang nodded pensively, took a breath and waited for the paramedics to leave. "Lawton was a friend of mine."

Boysie touched his painful side and winced. "And?"

"And I don't buy any of your bullshit."

"And I don't care. Charge me or discharge me."

Detective Rodriguez flexed his jaw muscles. "You've got a big mouth for someone that just got away with this."

"Take a look at me, detective. What the hell did I get away with?"

Rodriguez gave a begrudging shrug. "We'll pick up Bergman."

Boysie called Eddie who arrived double quick, pulling up in his truck. "Dude, you okay?"

"Nothing two Thai chicks couldn't fix."

"I know just--"

"--No, I'm cool."

"You wanna crash at my place?"

"Just take me home, please."

"Okay."

Fu Dog, Eddie's Shih Tzu, was staring intently out of the truck. Boysie climbed in and Mr. Fu sat quietly on his lap and went to sleep, which is exactly what he wanted to do. He arrived at the Georgian an hour later and took a long, soothing bath. He washed down his cheese and Branston pickle sandwich with several shots of Beaulieu bourbon. Climbing into bed, he instantly passed out.

24 ~ PEACE, LOVE AND NO REDEMPTION

TONI, SUMMER AND AUTUMN WERE serving pints. Harry, as usual, was propping up the end of the bar, sipping a glass of white wine. Boysie entered, wearing a dark blue, shark skin suit over a tan cotton shirt. On his feet, a pair of tan, Oliver Sweeney, chisel toe Drifters. His face, still bruised and slightly swollen, was partially hidden under his Ray-Ban aviators. Toni looked at him and gasped, causing everyone in the pub to stare, although no one said a word. He ignored them and went to his usual booth in the restaurant, where Gianni was waiting for him.

"Holy crap, Boysie, you look like shite. What the hell happened?"

Amanda came out of the bar behind them and winced as she saw his face. "Oh, wow."

"Looks worse than it is."

Harry wobbled in, clutching a wine glass to his chest as if it were the last drink he would ever have. "I love girls with tattoos."

Amanda looked at him and frowned. "The answer's no."

"Fine," he slurred and wobbled off.

Boysie said, "What's he on about?"

Amanda replied, "I was telling him about how my sister has a tattoo and she just got a gig in G's next film, but the director asked her to cover it with Dermablend."

"Oh, I see."

She glanced at Gianni and they smiled at each other. He said, "Can I get a Black and Tan please, Amanda?"

"Sure." She looked at Boysie. "And for you?"

"Earl Grey and a big breakfast, please. G?"

"Aye, I'll have the same, please."

Amanda smiled at Gianni and left, casting him an over-the-shoulder glance.

"Anything I should know about, with you two, <u>G</u>?"

"We went out on a date. So what?"

"To ask you, nothing. To ask her, I'm betting a lot more than nothing, judging by the way she goo-goo eyed you."

"Let's just say I'm cautiously optimistic. She's an amazing woman."

"Nice one, my son. Makes me very happy."

Gianni grinned. "Glad we could put some joy back in your life. Anyway, I thought you were gonna get Harry in rehab?"

"Been a little busy."

"I still haven't forgotten about his banger remark to her the other day. It was bloody embarrassing."

"He's a little crass, but it was funny though."

Gianni allowed himself to smile and nodded. "Aye, I s'ppose so."

"What did you find out?"

"To all intents-and-purposes, Gandolfo's doing business as usual. But, in reality, something big's going on with his daughter, which I never knew he had."

Boysie nodded. "Who did you hear this from?"

"A DP friend of mine, Vince Toto."

"And what about Valentine?"

Anger, rarely seen in Gianni, flashed across his eyes. "Aye, the wankas now got seven films in pre-production and Vince is actually DPing two of 'em."

"Valentine's one slippery bastard."

"He and Gandolfo are gonna be at the fight on Friday night."

"This for certain?"

Gianni nodded.

Amanda placed down their breakfasts. "Here you go, lads."

"Thanks," replied Boysie.

Gianni smiled up at Amanda, who gave him a lingering stare.

Harry wobbled past them and opened his mouth again to say something, when Gianni pointed at him, gritting his teeth, "Don't."

He thought better of it and went back into the bar.

"I'll be right back with your drinks," said Amanda and left.

"Sorry, Boysie, but I've had enough'a him."

"He's over eighteen, mate. Handle your business."

Gianni nodded and took a bite of toast. "What now?"

"Now?"

"What're you gonna do about Valentine and Bruno?"

"They're the least of my worries."

"By the way, I was sorry to hear about Marjorie."

Emotion gripped Boysie's heart. He took a moment, choked it back down and replied, "Thanks."

"I thought her and your mum were best friends?"

"Yeah, they were."

"No offence, but she doesn't seem too broken up by it," he said and dipped his toast into the egg.

He snorted his disgust and nodded. "Yeah, does seem odd, doesn't it?"

Boysie left the pub by the side door, crossed Santa Monica Boulevard and entered the parking lot. He chirped off Celeste's alarm and was just about to open the door, when his iPhone buzzed.

"Yeah?"

"You okay?" asked Detective Hampton.

Boysie hesitated and considered hanging up, but for some reason that completely escaped him, he felt compelled to answer. "I'm alright. You?"

"You scored some major points with both the SMPD and the LAPD."

"And I achieved that how?"

"Midnight Securities. Turns out that one of the decedents, Paul Windsor, was suspected of having shot and killed a DC detective who was the lead on a series of rapes in and around the Virginia and DC areas, that he suspected Windsor of having committed."

"Anything else?"

"He was also a suspect in the killing of an off-duty uniform, in a San Pedro bar fight last month."

"So why the hell was he still walking around then?"

"Because although the evidence pointed to him, nothing was solid. No witnesses. He was under investigation."

"Okay. Thanks for calling."

"Wait."

Boysie waited.

She took a breath. "Can we have dinner?"

"Why?"

"I dunno, I just, you know, miss you."

Boysie climbed into Celeste. "Wouldn't have anything to do with me being back in favor now, would it?"

"That's not fair."

"No, you're right, it wasn't."

"Can't I say sorry?" He didn't respond. "Boysie?"

"Yes?"

"You didn't answer me."

"Sorry, I was waiting for the apology." He started the powerful V-12.

"You are an asshole."

"So I've been told."

"Screw you," she hissed and hung up.

He guided Celeste out of the lot and headed north on PCH. The cold wind was refreshing and helped to blow away some of the melancholy that was beginning to threaten him. The drive up to Sycamore Cove was uneventful and thirty-five minutes later, he pulled up at the booth.

"How she running?" asked Ranger Willis.

"Great."

"And you?"

Boysie shrugged. "Comme ci comme ca."

"That's French, right?"

"Yeah, but my pronunciation sucks." The Ranger smiled, but more out of empathy than humor as he sensed his melancholy. Boysie looked at the deserted beach. "It's dead."

"Yeah, there's not too much business during the week unless it's a three day weekend." Boysie nodded and the Ranger asked, "So what brings you this way?"

"Not really sure. I was just out for a drive, you know, clear out the cobwebs?"

"Yeah, I do the same thing sometimes."

"I love driving PCH."

Ranger Willis nodded at Celeste. "Especially in her, right?"

"Yeah. I always wonder what it must have been like here in the sixties."

"Hippies."

"Hot chicks in bikinis."

"Beach Boys, grass and free love."

Boysie laughed. "Simpler times, mate."

"Was it? Or does every generation think that?"

Boysie nodded. "Yeah, maybe you're right."

"Not prying, but I've been reading about you on Google," said the Ranger with a concerned frown.

"Don't believe everything you read."

He smiled. "A couple of days ago, this cop was asking questions about you and your father-in-law's death."

Boysie turned off the motor. "Did he leave a card?"

"Yeah, as a matter of fact she did," he replied and turned to look for it. "It's right here."

"It's okay, I already know who it is."

"You do?"

"Brunette, pretty, late thirties?"

"Yeah," confirmed Ranger Willis with a grin, holding up the card. "Detective Hampton. SMPD."

"What did you tell her?"

"What could I tell her? Nothing." He shrugged and added, "Where I'm from, you better know what three monkeys mean."

Boysie grinned and held out his hand. "Now I'm even more indebted to you."

"Just take care of my car," smiled the Ranger, shaking his hand firmly.

Boysie kicked the motor to life and cruised South on PCH.

Looking out of the French windows, wearing a thick, soft bathrobe, Boysie sipped his Earl Grey. He watched the punters go about their business on the boulevard below. The late afternoon sun danced mischievously on the horizon as Mozart calmed the airwaves. The house phone rang.

"Yeah?"

"Father Murphy is here," announced Jimmy.

"Really? Okay, send him up please."

"Sure."

Boysie clipped the end off his cigar, stuck the half toothpick in, bit down on it and lit up. The priest hurried out of the elevator. He reminded Boysie of a Triffid as his arms flailed excitedly.

"I think I know what's going on with ya man there."

"Who're you talking about?"

"Who am I talking about? Think, man," urged the priest.

"The possibilities are endless," he replied as languidly as the smoke curling up toward the ceiling.

"You've taken one too many shots to the head." Boysie sat down. The priest loomed over him. His watery blues, intense. "Gandolfo."

"And?"

"And you're right. That book and the subsequent movies, oh b'Jeasus, cost him an awful lotta good will with the Holy See."

"It's gonna cost him a lot more than that."

Father Murphy went over to the bar and poured himself a large glass of Bushmills. "Ya want one?"

"Please."

He poured a second, brought them over and sat down. "What're you plannin' to do there, Boysie?"

He took a sip and studied the beveled, heavy crystal glass. "It would seem that Gandolfo really is untouchable. I aim to change that."

Concern deepened the creases on the priests ruddy face. "How?"

"I'm working on it." He puffed some more on his cigar and smiled at him.

"I don't like this. It's not you, Boysie. I mean, I've not seen you like this before."

"I've not felt like this before. But mark my words, Father, that fucker's gonna pay for what he's done."

"I understand the desire for revenge, believe me, but it's not our domain."

"I don't suffer from Catholic guilt."

Father Murphy tried to wash his concern down with a gulp of whisky. "I called an old friend a'mine in Rome. He confirmed that the powers that be are really pissed off with him and that's why they won't tell him where his daughter is."

"I don't really care anymore."

"But he warned me about something, or someone, should I say."

"Yeah?"

"Did Marjorie ever mention Cardinal Christoforo?"

The name startled Boysie. "Yeah, why?"

Father Murphy crossed himself and took a nervous breath. "Aw Jeasus. He's in charge of protecting the Holy Father, in a manner of speaking."

"I don't follow."

"Gandolfo's just one of several, uh, Warriors for Christ, as it were, that they've installed in positions of power around the world. Not only in obvious things like government, but in entertainment or the private sector as well, and Cardinal Christoforo is the one who oversees it all."

"That's some very heavy intel, Father. This friend of yours must be very connected."

"Never mind that. What ya need to focus on is that Gandolfo didn't clear everything with the Cardinal. Apparently his Eminence had no idea about the Jackson Pollock and what he had planned."

Boysie smirked and sipped his whisky. "Gandolfo's gone rogue, is that it? Is that what I'm expected to believe, that the church had no idea what he was gonna do?"

"Aye. That's basically what I was told."

Contempt curled his lips. "Leave it out."

"Why do you hate the church so much?"

"Are you kidding?"

Father Murphy stood up. "Cardinal Christoforo is a power unto himself, with the full weight and authority to protect the Pontiff with all means necessary."

"I'll keep that in mind."

"You do that, Boysie. Ya can't forget that the Vatican is a legally recognized country, and they have the global power to do whatever they want to protect their national interests. Threatening ya man there is one thing. Threatening the Pope is quite something else."

"The Pope? Are you mad? Like, have you lost all your marbles?"

"The Pope is the church and you need not to forget that."

"I don't give a crap about the Pope or the church. I've no interest in either of them. It's Gandolfo I'm after."

"What's keeping ya from understanding that they're one and the same?"

"Bollox."

"It doesn't matter what he's done. He's tied to the Holy See and they're not gonna let you bring any kind'a shame to them."

"Pedophile priests notwithstanding?"

"Aye, there's that and it'll take us decades to get over it, if ever. But they've been dealt with and that's why the Vatican is particularly sensitive to any other type of scandal."

"You've delivered their message and now you can go."

"Alright, but you need to think long and hard about this, son."

"I already have."

"I made a promise to your father, God rest his soul, that I'd always do me best to look out for ya, but I don't know what else to do now." He started to tear up and continued, "I love ya like ya was me own and I can't bear the thought of anything happening to you."

He had never seen his old friend like this before, or ever heard those words from him. Boysie finished his whiskey and put the glass down. "Mad dogs and Englishmen, Patrick."

Father Patrick Murphy wiped away the tears and said, "Then you better brush up on your Italian."

"Why's that?"

"Do you know what Christoforo means?"

"No."

"Christ bearer; defender of the faith."

Boysie pondered this revelation for a moment. He looked at the priest who had, indeed, been like a surrogate father to him and stated, "I'll take my chances."

With a shaking hand, Father Murphy put down the unfinished glass of whisky, nodded and left. Boysie tugged on his cigar but had lost the taste for it and dropped it into his whisky glass; the remnants of which hissed, dousing out the smoldering ash.

25 ~ IT'S SHOW BUSINESS, NOT SHOW FRIENDS

MATT STUDIED BOYSIE EARNESTLY AS he finished telling him about the Cardinal and the supposed power he wielded. He nodded thoughtfully, came from behind his desk and looked out of the window. The rain hammered down, ricocheting off the Wilshire Boulevard, nine stories below.

He turned to Boysie. "Go and plead your case."

"Plead my case? But why?"

"Because you either do that, or forget the whole thing."

"I'm not scared of the Vatican."

Matt looked at him earnestly. "You should be."

"What about going to the cops or the FBI?"

"And do what? Tell them about suspicions and conspiracies you can't prove?"

Boysie shook his head and gently rolled his lip between his teeth. "Christ, Matt, there's gotta be something I can do?"

"As you point out, no crime was committed as the money or painting never changed hands. You can try to get him on the fraud angle, but for that you'll need someone to swear out a complaint. And corroborating witnesses and anyone that could've incriminated him are either dead, have

271

been bought off or are too scared to get involved. So how do you prove anything?"

"What about those poor bastards, the family that got whacked right in front of me?"

"The police are calling it a hate crime."

"That's nonsense. Lawton told me it was a hit on me."

"And you killed Lawton."

"Yeah and Windsor admitted being the shooter."

"And you killed him too."

"I did," said Boysie, his anger hardening his eyes.

"That doesn't exactly make you a reliable witness. Especially considering your relationship with the police." The phone rang. "Hold all my calls, please." He hung up and turned to Boysie. "Anyway, even if you had proof, I doubt any charges would ever get filed."

"Why the hell not?"

"Come on, be serious. What D.A. in their right mind is gonna take on David Gandolfo, even without the Vatican to protect him?"

"But what about the law, justice?"

"The law isn't about justice. It's about the perception of justice."

Boysie stood up and ignored the buzzing iPhone in his pocket. "So either I get on a plane and go to Rome, or he gets away with it?"

"If Father Murphy is to be believed, yeah."

"I'm so totally gob smacked, I don't even know what to say."

"You can think about that on the way there."

"You're not funny."

Matt sat back down. "Aren't you being a little hypocritical?"

"Hypocritical?"

"Didn't you just make a deal to have the rape case go away?"

"Yeah except I didn't attempt to rape anybody," protested Boysie.

"Then if you didn't--"

"--If?"

"What I mean is, in the eyes of the world, if you're innocent as you claimed, then why not trust the judicial system?" Boysie knew he was right.

"Because you couldn't be sure of the outcome, and you had enough leverage to make it disappear."

"Yes, but I was never guilty of it in the first place."

"And neither is Gandolfo, or that we can prove, anyway."

"Leave it out. No one's that untouchable."

"Really? Then I suppose that's between you and the Cardinal."

Boysie slumped back into his seat and stuck a Fisherman's Friend in his mouth.

Matt continued, "You'll never guess who called and asked me to partner with him on a three picture deal?"

"I dunno, Valentine?"

"How did you know?" asked Matt with a wry smile.

"It was a joke."

"Not in this town."

"Why? Why would he want to partner with you when he knows full well that you're my brief?"

"Because this is show business. Not, show friends."

Boysie ran a frustrated hand through his hair. "This is a bloody nightmare."

"Personally, I'd let this one go."

"That's a little hard for me, after everything that's happened."

"Boysie, over the last ten days you've been charged with attempted rape. Shot at. Had the crap kicked out of you. Killed three people, which you're not gonna get prosecuted for. Witnessed an entire family get wiped out. Lost your stepfather. Marjorie committed suicide and now, it would seem, that if you don't heed the warning, so will you be." Matt hesitated and added, "Did I leave anything out?"

"No," he sighed heavily.

"Bring me back a pizza. If you go, that is."

"You think I should?"

"No, I think you shouldn't. But what I think and what you'll actually do, are two completely different things."

"Yeah, there's that."

They shook hands and Matt opened the door. "Dinner this week?"

"I'll give you a bell."

"Okay."

Toni was sitting at her desk, nursing a vodka and Orangina, looking at a photo of her and Marjorie in happier times. Boysie walked in and she glared at him.

"Mum." Annoyed, she sipped her drink. "What's wrong?"

"You! You are what's wrong!" she yelled.

"What are you talking about?"

"You broke Marjorie's heart. That's why she committed suicide."

The shock splashed over him like ice water, robbing him of breath and numbing his face. He waited a moment to regain his composure. "That's not what happened."

"You're a liar! She told me everything!"

"I don't believe you," he replied as calmly as he could.

"She said that after you slept with her, you broke it off. She told me she begged you, but you wouldn't listen."

"That's not true."

"You disgust me."

"But--"

"--Get out!" she screamed and threw her drink at him.

The glass sailed past his head and smashed on the wall behind him. He was not so lucky with the escaping vodka laced Orangina, that splashed his shoulder. Casually, he wiped it away, all the while locking eyes with her. He flicked the residue in her face and left.

Harry, leaning against the bar, smirked. The urge to knock him out had never been stronger. "Think that's funny? Yeah?" Harry shrugged and took another mouthful of wine. Boysie snarled, "You're going into rehab."

The smirk slid off Harry's face and drowned in his glass of white. He stammered, "What?"

"And you're paying for it."

"Wait. Who said? Mum?"

"Me. Chew on that, you arrogant, shit stirring prat."

Standing nearby in the crowded bar, some of the regulars looked at each other in silent, nodding, agreement. Harry opened his mouth to respond.

Boysie jabbed a hard finger at him, "Don't say a fucking word. I mean it."

Boysie showered and changed into a black, two-piece wool suit, grey cotton, Fred Perry, black socks and Italian brogues. Grabbing his US and British passports, he packed two clean shirts, two sets of socks and underwear into a brown leather, overnight bag, added some toiletries and left.

Entering the Stanford Mills gallery, he looked at Jackie, who was once again texting. "Where is he?"

Startled, she looked at the last person in the world she wanted to see. "Uh--"

"--Go and get him."

His demeanor told her this was not up for debate. She almost tripped over her feet, hustling to the back office. He waited for them to come out and as they appeared, he turned and locked the front door. This frightened Jackie.

"What the hell're you doing?" demanded Stanford.

Boysie popped a Fisherman's Friend, waited a few seconds and said, "We have unfinished business, mate."

"Do you have any idea who I'm connected to?"

"You, my son, are up to your ears in it and you're going down, if you don't come clean."

"Is that supposed to be funny," he snarled.

"No, but it is a fact."

"Get out!"

"How much did you make on that deal?"

"Out!"

"Are you sure that's how you wanna handle it?"

"Jackie, call the police."

Jackie busied herself calling the police.

Boysie said, "I know all about the bait and switch. So ask for Detective Hampton. She works Homicide. Tell her I'm here and to come on over."

Jackie hesitated and looked at Stanford for further instruction.

"Homicide?" he stammered. Beads of panic-propelled sweat forming on his face.

"Yes, Stan, homicide, because this is no longer about fraud and deception; this is now about murder."

"Murder?"

"That's Detective Jackie Hampton. You'll like her. She's thorough."

Jackie put the phone down and looked like a very frightened schoolgirl.

Stanford sagged down into one of the over stuffed, leather chairs. "Who got killed?"

"My stepfather."

"Your stepfather? What did he have to do with all this?"

"It's complicated, but the police and the FBI will gladly explain it to you both on your way to prison."

"Prison?" screeched Jackie.

"Oh my God." Stanford buried his face in his hands.

Jackie was now frozen in place; a look of abject horror on her face.

Stanford asked, "What do you want to know?"

"How much did Gandolfo pay you to authenticate the fake?"

"Fifteen million."

The shock wave swept over Jackie and she glared incredulously at him. "Fifteen million? You gave me ten grand, you cheap asshole!"

Boysie chuckled. "Oh, my. Perhaps you should've thought that one through more clearly, mate."

Jackie spat out, "I didn't know anything about anybody getting killed. In fact, I really didn't know about the whole deal 'til it was done."

"Is that right, Stan, she didn't know?"

"She a lying bitch. She knew everything. Not the murder. I didn't either. But she did everything else."

"You fucking piece'a shit!" she screamed.

"Oy!" yelled Boysie. They looked at him and stopped their bickering. "Tell me, Stan, does your wife know you've been shagging the help?"

Stanford looked embarrassed. Jackie didn't. He stammered out, "No, that's not what, uh, that's not true."

"Shut it," advised Boysie.

He shut it.

"So here's what's gonna happen, Stan. You're gonna do a confession cam, right into my iPhone telling everything that you know and who paid you to do it."

"Then I might as well stick a gun in my mouth."

"That's not the worst idea you've had."

"But I have kids."

"You should've thought'a that as you were slippin' her the length, mate," said Boysie, glancing at Jackie. "Know what I mean?" he added with a nasty grin.

"How do I fit into all this? I'm not guilty of anything," she lied. Self-preservation kicking into overdrive.

"I've meet a lotta ruthless cunts in my life. But you, you really do take the biscuit." The disgust in Boysie's voice cut through her. Her mouth quivered, her eyes filled with tears and tumbled down her face. He ignored her and looked at Stanford. "Where's the money?"

"In the office safe."

Boysie smiled cheerfully. "Let's go raid the piggy bank, shall we?"

She sneered, "So that's why you bought that new stupid safe." Angrily, she looked at Boysie. "He had to have the floor specially reinforced."

Stanford led them into the back office. The safe was a green John Deere that went from floor to ceiling. Brand, spanking new.

"Bloody 'ell, Stan, couldn't you find a bigger one?"

Stanford, for his part, was beginning to look more and more depressed. He opened the huge safe, revealing the fifteen million dollars. They stood there in quiet admiration of the stacks and stacks of neatly wrapped bank notes.

"Whew. That's a lotta wedge, ol' son."

Stanford nodded. "Yeah."

"You do know that's ten percent of the value of the painting, right?"

He nodded again.

Jackie said, "I've never seen anything like that in all my life."

"Stan, how much is it worth to you to keep your marriage, your business, and stay outta jail?"

He looked at Boysie. "All of it."

"Good answer." For the next several minutes, Boysie counted out one million dollars, stacking it on the desk. He looked at Jackie. "What do you know about me?"

"You kill people. I mean, that's what it said on CNN."

"Here's what's gonna happen. That's a million dollars. It's yours."

Her eyes popped out of her head. "Really?"

"Yes, really."

"Hey, come on. That's my money." Stanford blurted out.

He glared at him. "Not any more."

Jackie made a grab for it and Boysie snatched her wrists, forcing her hands onto the money and holding them there. Fear flashed across her face. He wasn't sure if it was fear of not getting the money, or what she thought he might do to her.

"You will leave L.A. tonight, and forget everything that's happened. Yes?" Jackie nodded vigorously. "Just in case, I'm gonna get your social security number, your parents address and any other info that he has on you."

"I won't say anything, I mean it."

"This amount of money, in cash, it's a big temptation to spend. Buy things. Feel important. You getting my drift?"

She nodded. "My hands hurt."

He let her go and as they came up, each had a bundle of cash in it. He chuckled and shook his head at her greed. "Anyway, that attracts attention. If you get popped, that would be bad."

"I won't. I promise," she assured him and swallowed, hard.

"You have any garbage bags?"

"Yeah, in the kitchen."

"Go get some."

She scurried past Stanford, who was sitting on the edge of his desk, looking mournfully at the million dollars. Quickly, she returned and started filling one of the plastic bags with it.

Boysie said, "Start a new life somewhere, but make it far away. Another country would be great."

"Hey, I'm cool with that, Boysie."

"Mr. Blake," he said, glaring at her.

She corrected herself quickly, "Mr. Blake." She looked at Stanford. "It's been real."

Struggling to lift the black garbage bag, she turned to leave and Boysie said in a low and menacing tone, "Jackie." She stopped and looked at him. "If you ever do say anything, to anybody, or come back, try blackmail, or anything else that I don't like," he paused and dread filled her eyes, "I want you to hear me now, girl. I'll kill you and your family." She tried to swallow but her suddenly dry mouth was not cooperating. "Do you understand?"

"Yes," she replied meekly.

"Say it."

"Yes, I understand."

"One last thing." She looked as if she was about to pee herself. He added, "I'm the one that killed your boyfriend."

Jackie stared at Boysie as the words sank in.

"Boyfriend?" asked Stanford, the hurt clearly edging his voice. She looked at him and her mouth moved as if she wanted to say something, but nothing came out. "But I thought you loved me?"

"Loved you?" she smirked, and laughed tauntingly. "As if."

"You bitch."

With a shrug, she turned to Boysie and callously said, "I don't love him, and I didn't love Paul either. I don't give a shit."

Boysie nodded and said with disgust lacing his voice, "Piss off."

She left.

He turned to Stanford. "Beside all this, how much personal money do you have stashed away?"

"Around seven hundred and fifty grand."

"Property?"

He looked like he was about to cry again. "You're not gonna take my--"

"--Property?"

"Yes, yes I do. Our house on Benedict Canyon is almost paid off, and we bought a cabin in Big Bear that we still owe over half on."

"And what about this place?"

"Yeah, it's paid for."

"So you're doing alright then?" Stanford shrugged. "I want you to bring me the deeds tomorrow."

"Why?"

"They're no good to you in jail, are they?" said Boysie rhetorically.

"But I thought--"

"--Tomorrow."

"Please, man, what about my family? They'll be homeless. You can't do that to them."

"You did it to them when you agreed to help Gandolfo."

"I'm sorry. Please--"

"--Shut it."

"Okay, sure. I'm sorry," Stanford agreed tearfully, wiping them away with badly shaking hands.

Boysie considered him and said, "Grab one of those garbage bags."

Stanford grabbed one of the garbage bags.

"Put the money in it."

He started putting piles of money into the plastic bag. When he was about halfway done, Boysie said, "Stop."

Stanford stopped.

"The other half in the safe is yours."

"What?"

"It should still be around six mill."

"I don't understand."

"You're a greedy sod, Stan, but I don't believe you're a bad person. Except for cheating on your wife, that is."

Stanford lowered his eyes. "I was stupid."

"You couldn't be anymore of a stereotype, could you?"

"No, I guess not."

Boysie resisted the urge to clip him around the ear. "There's no need for your wife and kids to suffer because you're a prat." Shame filled Stanford. He couldn't look at Boysie. "And I don't want your property. So keep the deeds."

He could no longer hold back and turned on the waterworks again. "Oh, thank you. Thank you, man. Thank you so much. I don't know what to say."

"I do." Boysie held up his iPhone. "It's time for your confession-cam." Stanford's euphoria evaporated. "Tell the truth and I give you my word that no one will ever use it against you. I promise."

"Then why do you need it?"

"To nail Gandolfo to the cross."

26 ~ KEYSER SÖZE

VIRGIN ATLANTIC TOUCHED DOWN AT Heathrow Airport exactly as promised, ten and a half hours after leaving Los Angeles. Boysie took his Alitalia connecting flight to Rome, arriving there late in the afternoon. The limo whisked him to the Inn At The Spanish Steps, where he was shown to his top floor suite. After unpacking, he took a shower, ordered some food and a bottle of 2003 Sassicaia. He sat on the veranda overlooking the historical Spanish Steps, several floors below. The delicate angel hair, flavored with black truffle and prosciutto, was legendary and he washed it down with the incredible wine. He loved Rome; the history and the romantic ambiance that the locals and tourists alike helped to generate. He lit one of his Cubans and contemplated the upcoming meeting. It was about an hour later as he was getting ready for bed, when his iPhone rang. He looked at the screen, but the ID was blocked. Normally, he would not have answered a mystery call, but this was different. "'Allo?"

"Signor Blake?"

"How may I help you?"

The smooth, Italian accented voice purred across the digital airwaves. "His Eminence, Cardinale Christoforo, has generously granted you an interview."

"When?"

"The car is waiting." He went to the railing and looked down. A black Mercedes limo with two motorcycle cops up front and two in back, was, indeed, waiting. "I'll be right down."

Boysie walked into the lobby and was not surprised to find two intense looking men. One was around thirty and the other early forties. Both were dressed in black suits, white shirts and black ties that bore the official emblem of the Holy See; the crossed keys and crown. They had sharp, intelligent eyes that examined Boysie with laser beam precision. The older one stepped forward.

"Signor Blake?"

"And you are?"

"Detective Inspector Madruzzo."

No friendly handshake. Not that Boysie expected one. The Inspector stood to one side and waved Boysie toward the limo that also bore the same emblem on the doors.

The ride through Rome was interesting if uneventful, as was the complete lack of conversation. The cavalcade swept through the heavily guarded wrought iron gates of Citta del Vaticano. They crossed the cobblestones glistening with evening dew and pulled up in front of a building that looked to be centuries old. The two detectives escorted Boysie inside, where more armed security were stationed at strategic points. He drank it all in; the beautiful hand carved woods, religious icons and paintings, plush carpets and elegant lighting. He followed them down a long and quiet hallway; their footsteps eaten by the deep pile carpet.

Madruzzo stopped in front of a wooden door and tapped lightly. He waited a moment, went in and closed it quietly behind himself. Muffled voices tried to seep out, but the wood was too thick. Moments slid past, grinning at Boysie with knowing insinuation. The door reopened and the Inspector stepped out. He pointed at the wall and Boysie knew exactly what he wanted. He placed his hands on it and the second detective expertly searched him. Finding his iPhone, he handed it to Madruzzo.

"You'll get it back when you leave."

"I'll get it back now." Detective Inspector Madruzzo indicated for Boysie to go through the door. He didn't move. "It's an iPhone. Not a gun."

He held out his hand. The cop tossed it to him and he slipped it into the breast pocket of his jacket.

The room was large, beautifully furnished, subtly lit and had the air of supreme power. Portraits of all of the pontiffs, each illuminated from above by a small, brass lamp, proudly looked out from three walls. At the far end of the room, an ancient oil painting, depicting the fearsome Angel Of Death, Azrael, stared menacingly out. Sitting on a small throne under the painting, was Cardinale Christoforo. A shrewd looking man in his sixties, with hard, brown eyes, set deep into a small and finely boned face. He was so slight, that he looked as if he might snap like a dry twig with a little pressure. The Cardinale was draped in the traditional black wrap-around tunic with a line of red buttons that went from collar to toe. On his small feet, soft, black leather slippers. His left index finger looked as if it might have trouble moving under the weight of the large, jewel-encrusted ring. It bore the same cross keys brand in the middle. He looked at Boysie without malice or warmth and studied his every move.

Boysie stuck his hands into his pockets and ambled across the room without haste; his footsteps swallowed by the deep, red carpet. He stopped in front of Cardinale Christoforo, who languidly offered his ring for him to kiss in reverential supplication. Instead, Boysie placed a Fisherman's Friend in his mouth and offered the Cardinale one. He smiled, nodded thoughtfully, but didn't accept the offered lozenge and with an almost lazy loop of his ring finger, pointed to the chair that had been placed perpendicular to his elevated throne. Boysie remained where he was and casually draped an arm across the back of his indicated seat. He was the one now looking down at the Cardinale, instead of the intended power play of the other way around. Much to his surprise, instead of being annoyed, the Cardinale smiled and scratched his ear. He stood up and aided by the platform, was able to look him directly in the eyes. He held out his hand. Boysie smiled and shook it.

"Signor Blake."

"Cardinal Christoforo. Cardinale. Sorry."

The Cardinale spoke with a slight Italian accent. "You have traveled a long way. I am sorry for the short notice, but I felt time was of the essence."

"Yeah, I'd say so."

"I am informed that you have proof that Signor Gandolfo has been involved in a, how shall we say, an unsavory affair?"

"Theft, deception, bribery, oppression, fraud and let's not forget the most unsavory of all, murder," smiled Boysie.

The Cardinal nodded. "These are very serious allegations which, I assume, you can prove?"

Boysie took out his iPhone and played back the video of the Stanford Mills confession.

Cardinal Christoforo watched without expression or comment. When it was finished, he said, "What do you wish to do?"

"Make sure he pays for every rotten thing he's done."

"Perhaps I have another way."

"If it involves him skating away scot-free, I'm not interested."

The Cardinal nodded slightly and turned toward the French doors. As they ambled toward them, a black clad security officer, with a .40 cal Sig Sauer strapped to his leg, appeared. He opened them, stepped respectfully to one side and bowed curtly.

"Grazie," said Cardinale Christoforo.

They went out onto a beautiful terrace, lit with subtle colored light. The night air had a chill and wrapped itself around them. Boysie was not surprised that none of the security or police followed. He knew that hidden on the rooftop, were marksmen that locked onto him with their night scopes. Any sudden movement he made, would result in a silenced bullet to his heart.

"So what do we do?" Boysie asked.

"I will give you a present that if you use wisely, will turn him from a foe to a friend."

"Keep it. All I want is justice."

"Ah, justice."

"Antiquated concept, I know, but I'm old fashioned."

"Justice for one, is injustice for another. Such an intangible, no?"

"You must know my lawyer."

"Matt Sugarman."

It didn't surprise him that the Cardinale was well informed. "With all due respect your eminence, Gandolfo's a vile, murdering bastard that needs to be put down like a rabid dog."

"And what if I gave you the name and address of his daughter?"

"And that benefits me how?"

"He will give you almost anything to learn this secret."

Boysie felt the irritation rush through him. "I don't need his money."

Christoforo smiled and said with quiet intent, "There are greater rewards than money."

"Do you really think I would trade on her?" asked Boysie.

"What I think is of no consequence. What you do, is."

Boysie stared at him, the underlying threat, clear and unmistakable. He nodded and replied calmly, "We all have to give up something to get something."

Cardinale Christoforo said in an almost imperceptible voice, "Are you willing to give up your life?"

He watched as Christoforo's finger and thumb moved slowly toward his right ear, as if to rub it. Boysie knew instantly that his answer would decide if he lived or died. He looked into the eyes of this man that held absolute power of life and death over him. Nothing registered. They were as cold and flat as death.

"You're not gonna let me take him down, are you?"

The Cardinale let his arm drop to his side. "It does not fit in to our policy for moving forward in this time of healing, that is greatly needed for the church."

"And now we get to the reality of it."

"Which is what, Signor Blake?"

"That according to you, the Vatican, truth is where you find it."

"I can tell you this much, Michael's killer will be brought to justice."

"I already took care of that."

"I know, but not the one who gave the order."

"And now you're playing word games."

"Escusa?"

"I don't want him, the one who gave the order. I want the one who ordered it."

The Cardinale shook his head slightly, more in mild admiration than anger and replied, "David will cease to pursue his own agenda and resume the path of the Church and you, will be a hero to him and his daughter."

"What about right and wrong?"

"Either you tell him and use what that can bring you, or we will tell him and you will lose more than you already have."

Boysie rolled his bottom lip between his teeth. He knew that he was overmatched, completely out of his depth and as close to death as he had ever been. He sighed his acquiescence and said, "I see."

"I hope so, Signor Blake. Truly."

"So this knowledge brings me privilege?"

"It does," smiled Christoforo. Suddenly all love and light.

"It's been my observation that privilege is based on the sufferance of others. Know what I mean?"

"Profound."

"My grandmother was, yes."

"Agnes Creamer. Survived two world wars. She owned a Laundromat in Iserlohn, did she not?" Boysie couldn't help the shock that spread through him and registered on his face. All he could do was stare at Christoforo who added, "A devout Catholic that was, in actuality, a Jewess."

"What?"

"Creamer is derived from the Hebrew word Kohen, meaning priest. The Kohens were descendants of Aaron, and they served as religious authorities in the First and Second Temples. Kohens still have a special role in Conservative and Orthodox Judaism."

"What the hell are you talking about?"

"You're a Jew."

"Except that would've been my grandfather's surname. Doesn't your mother have to be a Jew in order to qualify?"

"Your grandmother's maiden name was Goldschmidt."

"But I was raised Catholic."

"Throughout history there have been many anti-Semitic pogroms and many Jews changed their last names in order to survive."

"I don't believe you."

"Christ was a Jew. You should be honored."

Boysie looked over at the massive painting of Azrael, the Angel of Death. He nodded for no reason and said, "Religion; a festering sore on the ass of humanity."

"Interesting opinion, Signor Blake."

"No offence, your Eminence, but I guess all roads do lead to Rome."

"None taken and yes, they do." Boysie desperately wanted to feel something, anything, but all he felt was numb. He locked eyes with the Cardinale who asked, "You have no faith in God?"

"I have no faith in humanity."

"A desperate and lonely place to be."

"It'll pass."

His Eminence smiled and held out his hand. "Do I take it that we have an agreement?"

"An agreement?"

"Yes. Do we have one?"

Boysie took a deep breath and replied, "Keyser Söze."

27 ~ ANGEL EYES

SAFELY BACK IN HIS LOFT, Boysie dropped his overnight bag and plopped himself onto the sofa. After his trip to Rome, everything now felt so temporary. He went to bed but sleep was elusive and he spent the next few hours tossing and turning. He got up, took a shower and made a cup of Earl Grey and two slices of wheat toast. Sitting on his balcony, he watched the flat and glassy Pacific, roll endlessly up and down. His ribs still hurt but the bullet hole was healing well enough. He finished his breakfast, slipped on a pair of charcoal grey dress pants, black Stanza Hush Puppies, a light grey bowling shirt and a black, faux, suede jacket. He took the last two remaining antibiotics and left.

On the steps of the Georgian, he stood and watched the seagulls hover on the breeze. Jimmy was just getting in and bounced up the steps.

"Morning, Boysie."

"How're you doing, Jimmy?"

"Good. You?"

"Enlightened."

"Is that good?"

"I'm not sure. Still trying to figure that one out."

Jimmy nodded. "I better clock in."

Boysie headed for the pub. His meeting with Cardinale Christoforo had been one of the most intense experiences of his life. He knew that absolute power corrupts absolutely, but he had never seen it until then. Comparatively, David Gandolfo was nothing more than a storm in a teacup. An annoying irritation. He knew he would be reigned in quicker than an errant schoolboy by the headmaster, the Cardinale. Boysie walked in and sat at his booth. Amanda came over, smiling from ear-to-ear.

"You look happy," he said.

"I went out with Gianni again last night," she replied.

"Oh, yeah?"

"He's really cool."

"Yeah, one of the good ones."

"Coffee?"

"Please and chicken curry and chips."

"Okay," she replied and bounced off.

Father Murphy came out of the bar, pint of untouched Guinness in hand and stood in front of Boysie. "Can I sit?"

"Why even ask?"

He sat and replied in a hushed tone, "I got a call from Rome yesterday."

"Oh, yeah?"

"I don't know what ya said, Boysie, but the Cardinal, I mean, he was the one that called me himself. I was stunned, to say the least."

"Is that a fact?"

"Aye and what's more, he gushed about ya."

"Gushed?"

"It was all very surreal."

"I can relate to that."

Amanda placed Boysie's coffee down and skipped off again.

The priest asked, "What happened?"

"We had a nice chat and uh, I'm now a reformed Catholic and might even go into the seminary."

"Blasphemy. Will ya never learn?"

"I learned a lotta things on my trip, Father, except how not to be blasphemous."

The priest shook his head, blessed the pint and took a few gulps. He wiped the residual froth and burped into his hand. "Are ya alright now?"

"I'm not sure. Part of me feels oddly euphoric and the other feels like I should be in the knacker's yard."

Amanda placed down his curry and chips, "There you go."

"Thanks."

She smiled at the priest and left, humming to herself. Father Murphy looked quizzically after her as she bounced over to another table. "What's with her?" he asked and picked up his pint.

"I believe Gianni ploughed her furrow."

The priest tried not to laugh. He turned his head away, choked on his Guinness and sprayed it over the well-stained carpet. Toni came in, stood in the entrance and waited for the priest to stop guffawing. He calmed sufficiently and she drifted over, staring at Boysie, biting her lip that quivered emotionally.

"I owe you an apology," she said, the words fighting to escape her mouth.

"And what, pray tell, is this apology for, Mum?"

"Detective Hampton came by yesterday and told me that Michael's killer is dead."

"Is that right?"

She nodded. "She said it was you who killed him. Paul Windsor, I think." Boysie didn't respond. "I am glad it was you. Thank you."

Her being glad that he had taken a human life didn't so much shock him, as disappoint him. She hesitated, kissed him on the cheek and went back into the bar. He had hoped that she might also apologize for the rotten things she had said to him about Marjorie. He knew that would never happen. Even the priest ignored the death of another human being.

"Eat ya food there, Boysie."

Harry wobbled out of the kitchen, carrying his usual glass of white wine. He smiled at the priest, gave Boysie the finger and continued his haphazard journey to the bar.

"What's the matter with ya man, there?"

"I told him he's going into rehab."

"Jeasus. Thank God I'm not an alcoholic." Boysie and Father Murphy locked eyes and grinned at each other. He finished his pint, looked longingly at the empty and stood up. "Can I get'cha one?"

"No, thanks. I'm leaving."

"Fair enough," he replied and went into the bar.

Boysie was about to take another bite of his delicious curry and chips, when he heard sudden angry voices in the bar. He got up as quickly as he could, being careful not to twist his ribs and went in.

Standing in the center, surrounded by several of the regulars, was Bruno. The leg cast was gone, but not the rage in his eyes. Glaring at Boysie, he snarled, "You ready, motherfucka?"

Boysie signaled the regulars to back away. They did. Peter, holding a well-used cricket bat, was quietly coming up behind the big Samoan. Boysie shook his head, "No." Peter stopped where he was, but held onto the bat.

"Bruno, this is not the time or the place, mate."

"I told you I'd pay you back for what you did."

"I'm not gonna fight you."

Bruno hit him in the ribs with a quick hard left. Boysie doubled over from the intense pain in his side, inadvertently managing to avoid the second blow. He staggered backward and Bruno, like any good boxer, stepped forward to press the advantage.

Mistake. His.

Boysie, screaming with pain fueled rage, hit him with a straight left to the solar plexus, knocking the wind out of him. Bruno's mouth sagged open as his hands involuntarily covered his stomach. This is exactly what Boysie knew would happen and with his left, grabbed his face. Simultaneously, he jammed his right into the big mans open mouth, gripping his jaw and snapping it down as hard as he could. The sickening crack of breaking jawbone could be heard around the entire pub, as could Bruno's horrific scream. He collapsed, writhing on the floor in agony. Toni, Amanda and two of the regulars almost passed out. No one said a word or moved a muscle as they looked at Boysie with a mixture of abject terror and reluctant admiration. With his heart pounding, amplifying the pain searing through his body, he went over to the bar.

"Large scotch, please."

Autumn, her mouth hanging open, stared at him. Her sister, Summer, poured him a glass of Dewar's Premium and slid it across the bar. He picked it up with his left, looked at the blood oozing from the teeth marks on his right, and slugged it down. Placing the glass on the bar, he went outside. No one followed. He took out his iPhone and dialed.

"Boysie?" asked a surprised Sophie Devaru.

"How are you, Sophie?"

"I'm okay. You?"

"I need to see you."

"I don't think that's such a good idea."

"It's very important."

"Important? Why?"

"I don't wanna tell you over the blower. It's got to be face-to-face."

"I dunno. I'm seeing someone," she replied reluctantly.

"It's not like that. I have something really serious to tell you, that'll change your life."

The distant wail of approaching police and paramedics grew urgently louder. "What's with the sirens? Are you okay?"

"Yeah. When can we meet?"

"Come over now."

He hung up, jumped into Celeste and pulled out of the parking lot as the paramedics arrived.

Sophie lived on Coldwater Canyon in a small, but cozy house, close to Mulholland Drive. His iPhone buzzed incessantly but he ignored it and twenty minutes later, pulled up out front of her place, parking behind her BMW. She opened the front door and greeted him with a big, beautiful smile. He kissed her on the cheek and followed her inside.

They sat down opposite each other and he took a moment to compose himself. Sinatra drifted out of the iPod stereo system, perfectly setting the mood with his classic, "Angel Eyes."

Boysie took a deep breath. "Did you ever meet my friend, Marjorie Wallace?"

28 ~ FULL CIRCLE

BOYSIE BLEW THE RICH, CIGAR smoke out of his mouth and nodded with satisfaction.

Father Murphy took a sip of Bushmills, drew on his hand rolled, Puerto Rican cigar and said, "These are really good."

"Yeah, Eddie's uncle made 'em. He's this eighty year old bloke who grows his own tobacco and even rolls 'em. Bloody marvelous."

The priest nodded appreciatively.

"So what happened to Gandolfo?" asked Toni.

"You don't know, Mum?"

"I'm sure I don't."

The faintest smile creased his mouth as he glanced at Father Murphy who, feeling the tension rise, offered, "Summoned to Rome and is now back in town, and the proud father of his long lost daughter. May they live happily ever after."

"You say he's a changed man?" she asked Boysie, probing the edge of disaster.

Fighting the growing anger that begged for release, he rolled his bottom lip between his teeth. "So the rumor goes. I believe that happened right after he closed on his take over deal, and I returned the fake Pollock."

"And you're now his new best friend?"

"Apparently so, Mum."

"He did send you the full ten percent commission, even though there was no real sale," grinned the priest.

Boysie took a sip of Irish whiskey. "He did."

Toni shifted uncomfortably in her chair, trying very hard to not let her eyes turn green. "Fifteen million dollars. Doesn't half of that legally belong to Sophie?"

"Aw, Jeasus," groaned the priest quietly.

"What happened to her?"

Boysie looked at his mother and just for a moment considered something very nasty. "As you well know, Mum, she inherited everything and is now living in Marjorie's old place on Stone Canyon."

"Have you heard from her?"

"I called the other day to see how she was, and her assistant told me not to call anymore. So I guess she's doing fine."

Father Murphy dragged a craggy hand across his craggy face and said wearily, "I'm going to see Harry today."

"I'll go with you," replied Boysie.

Toni gulped her vodka and Orangina. "I wouldn't."

"And why's that?"

"He's pissed that you made him pay for rehab."

"Only half."

"Half?"

"Yeah."

"Oh, no. Uh-uh. I refuse."

"You agreed."

"I've changed my mind."

"Either you keep you word, Mother, or repay me for your portion of the pub."

Her face twitched as she tried desperately to keep her mouth shut. She put the glass down and left the Georgian.

"I don't think ya ma's gonna be back for a while."

"You do know that's the only time she's been here in five years, yeah?"

"Aye, I do," he sighed and finished his whisky.

Boysie refilled their glasses. "I don't know why she hates me so much."

"She doesn't hate ya. It's just that, ya know, you remind her of your da."

"No peace for the wicked." A momentary sadness greyed his eyes and he turned away, gazing out to sea.

Father Murphy looked sympathetically at him. "And what about you, Son?"

"Me?"

"Aye, after everything with ya man there, Gandolfo?"

He took a moment to consider his question, shrugged and replied, "I dunno. Learning to let go, I suppose."

"Sometimes, that's all ya can do."

Boysie nodded, drank his Bushmills and tugged on his cigar.

Thirty-three miles away at Sycamore Cove State Park, Ranger Bruce Willis showed up for work. He saw the silver, nineteen sixty-eight, E-Type Roadster that Steve had meant to buy, and went over to admire it. It had been decorated with a green bow to which a business card had been pinned. On it was one handwritten word, "Enjoy" and printed right below it, "Boysie Blake. Problem Solver."

Made in the USA
San Bernardino, CA
08 May 2015